COLLARED

A NOVEL

Juliana Weber

NFB Publishing
Buffalo, New York

Printed in the United States of America
Collared/ Weber- 1st Edition

ISBN: 978-1-953610-11-9

1.Title. 2. Crime Fiction. 3. Murder Mystery. 4. Weber.
5. Fiction, Crime, Thriller.

NFB
<<<>>>
NFB Publishing/Amelia Press
119 Dorchester Road
Buffalo, New York 14213

For more information visit
Nfbpublishing.com

Acknowledgments and Dedication

I owe a great debt of gratitude to Victoria for encouraging me every step of the way. I never would have finished writing this novel, if it hadn't been for you. Thank you for always wanting to know what would happen next. You're one of my favorite people on earth.

Many other readers offered valuable feedback, criticism and encouragement including Dad, Homestar, LuEtt, Neal, Joe, Lydia and Matt. Special thanks go to Mike for the tech advice!

This novel is dedicated to my mother.

Contents

Prologue

FIRST LIGHT BROKE over the ocean waves with a sheening brightness that resembled heaven's gates parting and grace pouring forth. Molly watched her five-year-old son, Paul, negotiate the sandy shore. He raced as quickly as his twiggy legs would carry him straight towards that light. She comforted herself with the knowledge that he didn't have far to fall at his age, and sand is soft. He was already showing signs that he would become tall like a string bean, though, just like his father. Next to his friend, Nathan, Paul looked as if he wasn't getting fed, and he seemed to be at least a year or more older than Nathan on account of his height. The boy's noodly legs must be hollow, she decided.

When Paul and Nathan hit their knees and started working on the sand, Molly spread out a beach towel nearby and settled her large, pregnant body on it feeling a little like a beached whale. Nathan's mother walked a little farther to position herself closer to the children. She was a bit of a control freak. Molly tried not to be annoyed. She knew this woman didn't approve of her and thought she was too disorganized to homeschool. Both women were just beginning that massive undertaking this year, but the truth was that apart from their children, the mothers had very little in common.

Paul and Nathan were cheering one another on with fantasies of building an ark for "all" the animals. The repeatedly shouted word "all" was apparently key to comprehending the enormity of their sand ark. The boys were very excited, and Molly hoped they would attempt to make little pairs of animals all lined up for a ride in the ark.

"I think they're about to find out why you aren't supposed to build a castle on sand," Nathan's mother commented in a patronizing tone. She smiled as if proud of herself for being smarter than her toddler.

Molly realized that what the woman said was true. The boys were too close to the water, and the tide was still coming in. She didn't give it the energy that a shrug would require. The first ark would likely be a "test" ark anyway. They could make several in a few minutes with all the energy they had, and she felt more than ready for a nap. The baby inside her was always lulling her into another nap.

She decided to relax and let the boys play in peace. Lying back on the beach towel, she searched for a conversation topic. There absolutely was not a way to recline on the sand without the baby weighing down directly on her bladder. Molly sighed lightly over the probable state of the porta-potty as she adjusted her sunglasses.

Nathan's mother only had three topics that really interested her: the homeschool coop, her very practical garden, and politics. Molly would rather avoid all of those things today. And really, why was it wrong to have just a few frivolous things in one's garden? The whole world wasn't made of vegetables and useful herbs.

She expected that even her son, Paul, was aware of the power struggle, the sometimes-judgmental tones from Nathan's mother, and Molly's lack of response to it. Sometimes Paul seemed so observant, she wanted to know what he thought about things, but he didn't have the vocabulary to tell her yet. Molly couldn't wait to watch him grow up and tell her what was going on behind those beautiful blue eyes.

Left to herself, Molly was a flittering butterfly, not a deep thinker. She sacrificed a great deal to focus on one thing, homeschooling Paul. He'd be four and still in preschool when Molly finally gave birth to this nap-happy baby. Without really listening, she "uh-huhed" something the other woman said.

"Oh, Nathan!" the woman scolded, finally earning a conscious reaction from Molly. Nathan's mother was already on her feet and closing the distance to her guilt-stricken son.

Laboriously, the pregnant woman sat up and looked about. Paul's hands were clenched at his sides, and the boy was not thinking good thoughts. "You need to calm down," she warned Paul, nearly shouting to be heard over the ocean and the fifty feet separating them. He gave her eye contact until he had taken his calmness from her, it seemed. Hands unclenched now, he ran over to her, perhaps to get away from Nathan's mother.

Nathan had used his bucket to dump water on the "ark". He must have foreseen the inevitability of losing the ark to the tide, and he dumped water out of frustration or impatience to move Paul to a better location for building their serious things. Nathan's mother was talking to Nathan about playing nice and how he would feel if Paul had done something like that to him. Nathan was sure he wouldn't mind, because the ocean was coming anyway. It was stupid to keep building there. Nathan didn't think Paul should be mad.

When Paul reached his mother, she pulled him in for a kiss on the forehead. "I guess we didn't see that Nathan was getting upset. I'm sorry we missed that and didn't help him to handle it. It's really hard when you forget to stay calm and forget to think about other people. It can make even nice people act mean for a little while." Paul gazed into her eyes in the way of toddlers. He could have been asleep on his feet or solving a quantum physics problem. Molly waited. When she relaxed, she had the sense that he was drawing from her calmness again.

Paul took a deep and very serious breath—deep relative to his little body. Molly suppressed a smile, but it was incredibly cute.

Searching for words, he said, "I want to … be nice to other people. I don't want to be mean and dump water on their arks." Paul might have still been a little frustrated. His statement contained more blame than wish for self-improvement. She already had him in a pretty good habit of forgiving people quickly through prayer, which she was sure he'd remember in a moment.

"You can pray for that," Molly told him. "God will help you be a good person. Ask Him to help you know how other people feel, so that you don't treat other people that way."

Her serious little boy bowed his head and prayed silently. Molly really wanted to know what he was telling God. In her own heart, she prayed too, *Let him really feel how others feel. Let him stand right in their shoes*. Then she gave her son time to finish.

"That prayer made God really happy," Paul said in amazement. Molly would treasure those words in her heart for decades to come. Her son was excited that he had pleased God!

Nathan and his mother were ready for company again and paying attention to the conversation now. Molly didn't want to know the other woman's opinion about something so fragile, so delicate as her little boy's heart.

"I'm sure it did, sweetheart," Molly told him, hoping her little saint wouldn't say anything further. She looked to Nathan and asked, "Are we going to build another ark?"

Nathan instantly bounced back from sulking. He ran uphill to a level spot the tide would not disturb, and his knees hit the sand again as he piled it up and shaped it into something roughly boat shaped. Paul joined him and simply watched until Nathan slowed his frantic pace and asked for help making windows. "You can do that," Nathan allowed. Paul complied with peace beyond his years.

Nathan's mother watched with the air of a great painter observing her canvas. "You know, sometimes I want to tell God that if he's trying to build a church, he should pick something more solid than people to build on. We're all just sand," the woman observed. "And what possessed Jesus to pick a guy like Peter and name him 'the rock'? That apostle was turbulent like building on quicksand! It's strange that it worked."

Molly thought that was the most interesting thing she'd ever heard the woman say.

Chapter One

Thirty years later...

Storm clouds advanced to assault the chancery just as Father Paul also arrived, having been summoned by his bishop. The fronts marched in quick time, one from his right and another from directly ahead, a veritable D-Day. He watched helplessly as the fronts took up positions to surround the battleground. They resembled just the sort of ominous, black, sooty clouds a wall of hellfire might belch forth. The young priest took pleasure in the spectacle for the reminder of God's strength and righteous anger, although it looked sinister from his vulnerable position. Father Paul parked and ran for the building, buffeted by early warning bursts of wind that blew him inside and then banged the heavy wooden door shut behind him just as the first fat drops of rain landed.

That slam resonated with an echo of finality that Father Paul tried not to ponder several minutes later, while he waited alone in a fussy, florid room. He distracted himself by staring at his unpolished shoes while absently listening to the storm howl around the building and batter the roof. The frantic, wild energy of it was enough to raise his heart rate, so he tried to block it out. Even one year ago, Father Paul thought, he would have cared enough to polish his shoes, especially on the occasion of being summoned by his bishop, but not anymore. He prayed to know what this change portended. There had to be meaning to it.

Perhaps, he considered, he was becoming spiritually lax, and this was the outer sign of inner negligence. He suspected that was the case. Then again, he could be learning to prioritize things properly. A priest with unpolished shoes was looking up and setting the eyes of his congregation on heaven. It sounded nice, but he wasn't sure, and God wasn't answering. He could ask his bishop as soon as the man arrived.

Nah. Father Paul simply did not care about his shoes anymore. The bishop wasn't going to notice, and the shoes would get water spots as soon as he ventured out into the deluge. Frowning, Father Paul realized he hadn't felt the slightest stirring of the Spirit to answer this question. Experience taught that these moment of too much calm were the moments when God was working in secret on something pivotal, something that may or may not hurt at first. He stilled himself and listened intently with his heart, then sighed in resignation at the silence he found there. Since he was alone in the room, no one to see him do it, Father Paul nodded his consent to whatever was coming next. "Your will, Lord," he whispered.

Time ticked by slowly for several long minutes until Bishop Teddy rolled into the museum of shiny, fragile furniture like a bowling ball. He wore a smarmy smile intended to convey warmth and paternal concern. Father Paul tried—and failed—not to notice the bleached teeth and the falseness of the expression. With a little relief, he noticed the bishop did not so much as glance toward his shoes. Polishing definitely would have been a waste of time. Father Paul gave himself a mental pat on the back.

"Paul…." The bishop drew out the name as if it were a leash attached to a rambunctious puppy, drawing that good little tail-wagger back from a busy street. They shook hands over an uncomfortable stretch of time, Father Paul's long fingers clasping Bishop Teddy's plush yet damp paw. Father Paul separated himself awkwardly and resumed the edge of his chair, wondering how soon he could wipe his hand on his pants without being obvious. Bishop Teddy lounged back into his couch like a great big caricature of buddha.

"Your Excellency, I'm sorry for the trouble this has caused." Not that Father Paul felt particularly responsible for the trouble, but he was sorry, nonetheless. Everyone knew bishops were busy. Then again, it felt as though Bishop Teddy had not a care in the world and was only playing games at the moment. That couldn't be right, Father Paul thought, and then he shivered, suddenly cold. The storm must be causing the temperature to plummet, he realized.

"Tell me what happened," Bishop Teddy prompted, as though he hadn't been told. He wanted to hear Father Paul tell the story of his folly. Catch him out. Make him feel stupid for being intelligent. Father Paul knew this game too well for having been ordained a priest less than a year ago. He'd been playing it through eight years of seminary. His story was rehearsed this time. Still, his heart started to race, and his palms sweat. He'd never been in the principal's office as a kid. Would it have felt like this?

"Somehow, I missed being told that we had Thursday morning volunteers who did carpentry. I usually take Thursdays as my day off, and this was the first time I ran across them myself. It just caught me by surprise, that's all. I could have handled it much better, if I'd had any idea what I was walking into." Father Paul shook his head ruefully, playing along with the game.

The truth was, the pastor might have told him back in autumn when he began to assist at this parish, but these volunteers stayed home if it snowed. It had snowed the first week of October and continued right through Easter. The pastor, Father Bob, had given a homily about the fittingness of white snow falling on the holiest of holidays, rather than a homily explaining Scripture. Father Paul had waited for Father Bob to explore the differences between Lutheran and Catholic ideas of justification from there, but it was really just a homily about snow and whiteness and how much fun kids have playing in the snow. Important things didn't come up often with this pastor, and the volunteers sidelined by the weather had been among those important but forgotten points.

"It's all right, Paul. You ran across them when they were working on your office," the bishop prodded.

"Right, and I honestly thought it was a prank!" He widened his eyes in feigned disbelief at his purported stupidity. "I came in around noon, and my office door was unlocked and standing open. That's odd, since I have confidential files in my office, and the file drawers don't lock. So, I was already uneasy before I turned on the lights. Imagine when I saw everything that should have been inside and on top of my desk scattered on the floor, except for the phone and the monitor! The desk was painted blue, and the drawers alternated red and yellow. The phone and the monitor were back on the desk, though, and they are now permanently fixed to their spots by the blue paint. I guess it was still tacky when they started moving things back, but fortunately, they didn't have time to deal with the papers. The Josephites only work until noon on Thursdays, and then they go home for the week no matter where they are in their current project."

"Ah, so they *weren't* still working in your office. But when you came in around noon, I'm sure there were still a few of these volunteers in the rectory?"

"Yes—."

"I see," he interrupted. "I'm just trying to get this straight." There was a gleam in Bishop Teddy's eye, the kind a sumo wrestler might have before sitting on an opponent who is obviously too small for technique to avail him.

"Right. Well, when I shouted my surprise, the entire group of volunteers heard me and came to see what the problem was. It turned out that it wasn't a prank. They've been doing this for more than fifteen years, and they felt

I had disrespected all fifteen years of their hard work. I tried to apologize, to show appreciation for their thoughtfulness… I just really wish I'd had some warning. The whole thing could have been avoided with a little communication."

Bishop Teddy's eyes narrowed. Not a good sign. "What exactly was it that you shouted?"

The wind outside circled about with renewed interest. Father Paul wondered whether God was laughing at him. "Whoa."

"Whoa?"

"Yes, *whoa*. I remember distinctly." And he did remember it distinctly. That monosyllable had been his most intelligent response to what he was seeing. The aged desk had formerly been a stained and polished wood. Then it was primary blue and red and yellow. *Whoa* was wholly inadequate but all he could think of. He'd needed the permission forms that should have been on top of his desk so he could take middle school students on a field trip that afternoon, and his desk was blue. And red and yellow.

"The, ah, letter I received from the Josephites states that you shouted something much more colorful." The bishop paused, as though granting the opportunity for Father Paul to rethink his final answer. "They were quite scandalized," he added.

"I won't make you repeat whatever it was, Your Excellency, but I assure you, I didn't shout anything except *whoa*."

"Unfortunately, that's irrelevant now." Hands raised in

a *stop* gesture. "I need you to formally apologize in writing for your language. In that letter, please reiterate your appreciation for the Josephites' hard work, dedication for over fifteen years, thoughtfulness," and the bishop motioned a *keep-it-coming* gesture to demonstrate the length of the saccharine missive he vaguely had in mind. "Have Father Bob review a draft before you deliver it to the volunteers, and take Father Bob's advice." A sausage-sized index finger fired the command at Father Paul's forehead.

Father Paul nodded. His failure to take the pastor's advice had blown the drama way out of proportion and instigated the dreaded complaint to the bishop. Father Paul had been searching on hands and knees for the permission forms that should have been on his clownish desk, when Father Bob discovered him and asked, "How come the Josephites seemed upset in the parking lot just now?" In a fit of inspiration, Father Paul had pointed out to his pastor that *not* apologizing any further might completely alienate the group, saving the parish from future incidents! The young stripling of a priest had, in fact, refused to apologize any further.

And he had wondered at his new attitude. Where had it come from? Was he just tired? Even in hindsight, he struggled between being "pastoral" and being efficient. He'd been praised for maintaining a synonymous balance in the IT business: He had been professional and friendly enough to work well with everyone, but he'd gotten his job done, too. He could never be sure he had gotten his job done now that he was in ministry. He wasn't sure what he was doing.

Bishop Teddy instructed, "Remember, these are volunteers entrusted with keys to the entire parish. You want to be able to trust them. Build rapport with them, Paul. These are your best local support." But Father Paul hadn't heard the second half of his bishop's words at all. The words *keys to the entire parish* and *trust them* reverberated ominously and finally sparked an emotional bonfire as he realized that this humiliating experience was only the beginning of a lifetime of similar experiences, if he stayed where he was.

With dread, Father Paul grasped the notion that had been sneaking up on him for some time. What he was doing did not match God's will for him. Where had he gone wrong? Hadn't God called him to be a priest? And yet he was suffocating here and possibly losing the little sanctity he had started with. How would he ever make it to heaven surrounded by this brood of vipers? He had to leave. He knew had to. And he was terrified.

What were his options? He could go back into the IT business. He had felt unfulfilled there, as if something were missing from his life, but it wasn't as if this had been the answer. The few good things that had happened... like that field trip with the seventh and eighth graders to serve Habitat for Humanity... he could continue to do as a volunteer. He would miss celebrating Mass as a priest, hearing confessions, anointing the sick, baptizing young and old... He groaned inwardly at the ache those thoughts tore open. Could that loss feel nearly as deep as this petty betrayal? He'd been accused of using a bad word that he didn't use, even though the situation had warranted… something. He could hear his own shallowness. This last straw was, in all truth, a very insignificant one.

The quiet voice inside him that was not his own prompted him to pause and pray. And the peaceful presence that enveloped him and filled him asked how he could leave.

And yet, he felt equally convicted that he couldn't stay. The air was being crushed out of him here. He would lose his soul, if he stayed long enough. What could he do? He needed a miracle.

The wind had died outside, Father Paul realized, when all of a sudden it kicked and bucked furiously back to life.

BANG. A door slam?

Dress shoes clacking down the hall.

A man resembling a squirrel in search of nuts poked his head in the door. Father Paul was surprised the shoes weren't high heeled for all the noise they made. It was the diocesan Director of Child Protection. "Bishop Teddy, please excuse me. I need to speak with you as soon as you have a moment. It is urgent. I'm so sorry for interrupting," he apologized in Father Paul's direction. Whatever emergency he had news of was likely to be criminal, Father Paul realized grimly.

Bishop Teddy wrapped things up and left quicker than Father Paul could react. Mind whirring, Father Paul wondered whether he should wait for the bishop, so he could quit today, if he was in fact quitting. That could be a long wait, and he wasn't sure what he would decide anyway. Maybe he should sit tight and pray, or he could wander over to the cathedral and wander back when he was ready. He could go back to his pastor and quit there. Or he could just pack up his things and find an apartment, start looking for a job, and avoid the whole confrontation. Running away sounded good.

He caught himself studying his shoes again.

Congratulating himself once more on his unpolished shoes, he decided to go home and begin crafting his apology to the Josephites. He was never going to quit. He would never go back into the IT business, certainly. If he quit, he'd become a social worker or a counselor, most likely. He loved being an instrument of God's healing, though the opportunities to develop the gift had been scarce at this assignment. He just needed to give God more quality time, maybe read a book on a martyr... This delay was for the best, preventing him from making a rash decision he would regret for the rest of his life. *Thank you, Lord.* He showed himself to the front door, where the elderly receptionist sat behind her desk, quiet as a librarian.

A forty-something-year-old woman flapped in the front door, showering the floor from her umbrella and raincoat as she waddled along. She slipped dangerously on the shiny and now wet floor, but she recovered quickly, much to Father Paul's relief. He'd braced himself, intending to launch forward and catch the woman. Her slide meant she reached the reception desk before he did. "I need to see Bishop Teddy. It's urgent."

"May I inquire as to the nature of your visit, please?" The old woman whispered, intimating that she knew this was confidential, as all visits to the bishop are.

The indignant woman squawked back, "My students were victimized by that monster in a collar they just arrested. I'm the school counselor at Sacred Heart Prep in Limekiln, and I need to see the bishop right now!" The horror of the situation slapped Father Paul in the face, as it did every time he heard of his brother priests behaving so foully, but the woman had dropped the bomb without warning. Now, she was in danger of giving herself an aneurysm and perhaps the receptionist as well.

Father Paul recognized that most of his emotions in this moment were not helpful, except for the spark of protective instinct for the counselor. He observed the woman from a distance, allowing time for that spark to flame.

Since the receptionist's eyes had popped in recognition, Father Paul deduced that this counselor must be known, might have been involved in turning over the offender, presumably Father Max, to the police. "Let me just track him down. Please take a seat, ma'am," the receptionist instructed as she scurried away, leaving Father Paul alone with the furious woman in the reception area.

Flapping her arms in protest of the soaking rain and her frustration in general, the woman's eyes followed the receptionist, perhaps considering whether to chase after her, but Father Paul accidentally distracted her with his open-mouthed staring. She turned to eye him, must have seen something that mitigated her hostile reaction to him, then primly hefted herself into one of the cushioned armchairs.

"Ma'am, I am so sorry for what your students and their families are suffering. You'll all be in my prayers," Father Paul proffered, knowing it was inadequate.

Another long, this time considering look, as though she could read his soul through his serene blue eyes. People told him that his eyes were sky blue, usually with a sigh that connoted their calming effect. Self-consciously, he ran his hands through his shaggy red hair, pulling it away from his face. Her quick once over paused on his shoes, and then she lifted an eyebrow in curiosity. He knew what Mother Goose was trying to put together. His long hair, short-cropped goatee and unpolished shoes contrasted oddly with the straight-backed way he carried himself, the lean muscle that showed even through long sleeved clerics, and the muscle in his jaw that ticked when he was nervous, as presently, while he was being scrutinized.

Eyes floated back to his with a watery smile. "Thank you," she finally answered. Nodding, she repeated, "Thank you very much. Were you in the military?"

"No, ma'am. I was never in the service. My father was," he added, uncertain of where this was going.

"You have the bearing of a Marine, almost. Obviously, your hair is all wrong, but your shoes are the real give-away. Marines scrupulously polish them. My husband is downright silly about it. That's just his way." She shook her head still smiling, searching her purse now.

"My father was a soldier. Army. He never would have grown his hair this long either," Father Paul chuckled. At the beginning of seminary, he had buzzed it like he was heading off to boot camp, off to change the world. He just didn't like cutting it often, so he let his hair grow out to his collar before starting over again. "Whenever my father's hair started looking good to my mother, he went straight to the barber and buzzed it off. She learned not to tell him eventually."

The woman laughed easily with him, blotting her eyes with a wad of tissues her purse had protected from the lashing rains outside.

Father Paul reached out with his emotional radar and felt the woman's anger and raw pain. The feelings tasted wild, almost like an animal's. She was pushing that into the background for his sake, but it wrangled to fly free.

Father Paul couldn't name this odd gift of his, but he knew that not everyone had it. Just as well, since it could be exhausting, probably the reason he was attracted to computers. The thought crossed his mind that he must have learned to shield himself, because he had been shielding himself from feeling the bishop's emotions just now. Father Paul had wrapped himself in ice rather than accidentally take the bishop's emotional temperature, and he had mentally taken down some sort of barrier for this woman. He had been protecting himself. From his bishop. The realization made him sick.

Putting that aside, "If there's ever something I can do, even if it's just praying with the families, please call me. I'm Father Paul over at Ignatius of Antioch."

She nodded. Then winced. Her hands covered her face, and she cried. Driven by impulse, Father Paul took the seat next to hers, laid an arm across her back, bowed his head, and prayed silently over her. It was a prayer without words, offering this woman and her tears up to God's sight with trust that the Father would care for her. They sat like that for some time. In all that time, the receptionist did not return to her station.

When she was spent, the counselor continued to blot her eyes ineffectively with her now sodden wad of tissues. Father Paul looked around, finding none in the reception area to offer her.

"You're a very nice man," she sniffled. "Why can't all priests be like you? Why did we get this *predator*?" It was a cross between a growl and a sob. "You cannot imagine what this did to them, what they will have to go through to recover." She worked to catch her breath. "*Where* is *God*?"

Father Paul rubbed circles on her back, as she rocked herself and the tears fell freely. She was in no shape for a theological answer, so he didn't bother putting one together.

In his silence, she pressed on, "These were good girls, just young and naive. I knew something had changed in them. I tried to protect them, find out what it was. They've been savaged inside!"

Guilt. How had he missed that? The counselor blamed herself, not God. She needed someone to be at fault—someone she had control over, who could make sure this never happened again—because otherwise this situation was too out of control, too much for her to handle.

Quietly, Father Paul asked, "Where was God the Father when His Son was being crucified?" He let that sink in. "The fact that God allowed it to happen makes it no less evil. But hear this—God only allows evil, when He already knows how He's going to draw some great good out of it, something good that could not have been without that suffering."

"Oh, God..." The sound could have been exasperation, disgust, a lot of things. Only Father Paul's emotional radar rescued him. She was mostly confused and a tiny bit hopeful. She wanted this to be true.

Father Paul pushed forward just a little more. "How could we have paid the price for our own sins? Jesus' suffering brought about the possibility of salvation for all of us. I don't know why God allowed this to happen to your girls. But I trust that He has a… darn good reason, if you'll excuse my language." He rolled his eyes at himself.

She offered another watery smile. "I'm Dolores."

"Dolores, I'm so sorry for what you're all going through. Please let me know if there's anything, anything at all…" He let himself run out of steam, when he heard the unmistakable thunder of Bishop Teddy trundling down the groaning, wood floored hallway.

No one could have predicted what Dolores would do once the bishop rounded the corner. Perhaps her first words should have been no surprise at all. "I demand that this priest be assigned to replace that *animal*." She growled the word. "This is exactly what our parish needs in order to heal. He is what my girls and their families need. If you care at all," her eyes dared Bishop Teddy, "you *will* send him."

While Bishop Teddy recovered from bug-eye, Father

Paul saw it all unfold before him. The professional counselor who helped victims tell their stories could get a lot of airtime, and what a politician knows never to do is to give an enraged expert fodder for her fire. Bishop Teddy was nothing if not a consummate politician. He saved face, bluffing that he would "consider" Dolores' recommendation, but Father Paul knew that the pieces were set in motion. Bishop Teddy couldn't stand up to a stiff breeze. And Father Paul would never walk away from the priesthood when there was so much work to be done. The pain that Dolores radiated was a mere echo of the cries he would encounter at Sacred Heart in Limekiln.

Father Paul would be administrator of his own parish. There would be room to breathe in Limekiln, a forty-five-minute drive outside of the city. He could breathe freely again, and he was a priest. God be praised!

Bishop Teddy suggested a "private chat" with Dolores and led the way to the accompaniment of thunderous groans beneath him. Father Paul imagined the floor finally giving out under the bishop, nothing ever breaking his fall, bishop forever lost to a black abyss. Father Paul shook off the vision, chastising himself, and turned back to Dolores just as she collected her purse and moved to follow along behind the bishop, who appeared to have forgotten her.

"Dolores," he whispered, "I won't let you down."

That sentiment appeared to surprise Dolores. Father Paul assumed that her next words were merely an attempt to say the right thing quickly. "And I won't let you down,"

Dolores whispered back conspiratorially. "I've got your back, if you've got my girls'." She winked and departed.

She couldn't have known that he needed his back protected, Father Paul mentally asserted, even as he took her words to heart. A sense of rightness and conviction filled him. Things were going to be alright.

The following morning, Father Paul received his marching orders through Father Bob, pastor of Saint Ignatius. Stony-faced behind his wide beard, the pastor was unhappy but determined to make Father Paul unhappy, too. Beady black eyes ineffectively attempted to bore into Father Paul's as the older priest gloated. "We'll still be in touch," he explained in a smooth voice that held a distinctly patronizing note, "since Bishop Teddy asked me to mentor you through the first year of your new assignment. After that we'll see how it goes." Father Bob smiled, waiting for the meaning to dawn on Father Paul.

"Mentor? What exactly does that entail?" This was not standard operating procedure, and Father Paul had no idea what sort of training had equipped Father Bob for such an assignment.

"Bishop Teddy and I are determining what would be best. Such a young and newly ordained priest receiving such a hefty pastoral load is not the norm, so we'll be sorting out what's best for you as we go along." Making it up as they go, Father Paul translated. Father Bob was positively gleeful, though he was putting on his pitying face for Father Paul's 'hefty pastoral load' at such a young and vulnerable time in his adulthood.

Father Paul had a choice to make then. He could despair of God's help again, as though he hadn't learned a thing. Scripture was littered with people like that. Or he could trust that God would take care of this micromanagement problem. Trust would take a little more effort than mistrust, and Father Paul wasn't sure he could do it. So, he prayed. When he felt he had completely given the problem up to God, set it squarely on God's shoulders, he let himself start packing in peace.

A priest friend from seminary, Father Jeremy, called and warned Father Paul that small town living is "very different" from the city. "You keep tripping over the same people in different roles all week, so be extra careful about ruffling feathers. Anyone who volunteers, volunteers for *absolutely everything* and is irreplaceable. And anyone who isn't volunteering is friends with the ones who are." Father Paul thanked him for the warning and pressed the "end" button.

He didn't dare put calls on speakerphone, since discovering Father Bob eavesdropping outside his bedroom door one evening. (Secretly, he was amazed that a man of such proportions could move stealthily at all.) He didn't dare use the landline for the same reason. His friends and parents knew to call his cell phone, and he counted on really sitting down to listen, not attempting to multitask, which was a blessing in a way. Too many people spent their lives distracted, not really hearing the people they talked to. Father Paul thanked God again, because he'd been dealt another sweet hand. He was packed and ready to leave Father Bob's rectory almost immediately. And it *was* Father Bob's rectory. At best Father Paul had felt like a guest in this place. In fact, having no place to shelve his books, he had never unboxed them. Now, he felt like an escaping convict, almost completely convinced that the threat of a mentor was an empty one. He would be too far away from here to be supervised by Father Bob.

While he was packing up his few personal items in the kitchen, Father Bob informed him that their relationship would now entail weekly phone checkups with on-site visits as deemed appropriate by Father Bob. That probably meant surprise visits whenever the whim struck him. Of course, the whim would strike him when he was in the mood to boss someone around. Father Paul sighed inwardly and told Father Bob, "Wonderful," with what he hoped was a courageous smile.

The rotund man beamed, leading his tiny, yappy dog out the front door. When the screen door swung shut behind them, Father Paul expelled the breath he'd been holding. What was he worried about? Ministry is an ambiguous thing. It's hard to look back over your own day and list your accomplishments, but a supervisor can only listen to complaints or judge the results of a goal they told you about (or one you foolishly told them you'd set for yourself). It's very difficult to assess what goals are relevant from a distance. Father Paul was soon to be a free man. With that cheery thought in mind, he loaded his car and then hid in his bedroom until dawn.

He escaped, racing out the door without breakfast,

steering the car to face a rosy sunrise that morning. He was ready to take on whatever challenge his loving Father had chosen for his next adventure, he thought, and he mused on the goodness of God. Remembering a chant from summer camp, he fist-pumped the cushioned ceiling of the car, shouting, "God is good – ALL THE TIME! ALL the time – GOD IS *GOOD*!"

That chant had worked a lot better when he was a kid.

Chapter Two

His first Sunday morning at Sacred Heart parish was sweltering. As the eleven o'clock Mass exited, Father Paul imagined that the sweat was permanently dry-sticking his friendly smile in place. He had stepped out onto the concrete landing, shaded by the little bell tower, but since he couldn't tear his vestments off yet, the light breeze was scant relief. "Have a blessed week! Have a blessed week!" He was aware of himself impatiently pulling parishioners out the door as he shook their hands in dismissal, but he couldn't stop himself. Why were they moving so slowly?

Every inch of his skin had melted and then become sandy with grains of perspiration beneath the vestments and dress blacks. The sweat was probably steaming itself dry, he thought, completely disgusted. He was making sticky salt crystals along the surface of his skin, sharper than they were wet at this point, especially in the crooks of his elbows. Put it on the list of things they had never told him in seminary.

Actually, he realized, if he had stopped sweating, that was a very bad sign. He had to get to water. He was thirsty. And he wasn't thinking too clearly, he finally realized.

Be reverent. Pray each Mass as though it were your last, a professor had told him. No one had mentioned that his first solo assignment would be at a church too small to afford an air conditioner. This made Saint Paul's shipwrecks look like child's play. Relief, actually. Water. He needed water.

Father Charlie, the pastor at his first summer assignment, had given him advice with his health in mind. Charlie was ordained in '73, a typically weird priest from that era, so Father Paul had inspected most of his advice with automatic suspicion. But Father Charlie had years ago told him very seriously, *You can't be reverent when you're unconscious, Paul.* Father Paul was certain that the older priest's nose wart sometimes surprised him and made him look into his peripheral vision. *Get some water now but think about it. Wearing sandals, shorts and a t-shirt might be more reverent in the long run than what you're doing.* As though reverence were Charlie's goal. He had obviously mashed up his liturgical style from a game show and a rodeo. But he might have made a good point despite himself in this one, isolated instance, Father Paul grudgingly allowed. Dressing lighter next week was a must. It was supposed to get hotter.

"I'm so sorry, everyone. I have to go get water right now. I'm so sorry. If you need to see me, please follow me back to the sacristy." Father Paul pushed past a crowd of worried looks. He couldn't tell if they were genuine or not. His emotional radar was off. If he'd had a low battery light, it would have been blinking. Even his lungs felt dry, as if they were baking. He was done. Water. The candles around the altar area, coupled with the lack of windows up there, meant that he would boil every Sunday when bodies filled the pews of the rustic church. He was actually tempted to replace the wax votive candles with battery-operated ones just to bring down the heat. As he blazed by the altar, he shook his head at his crazy thoughts. What was wrong with him? The door to the sacristy flapped shut like a bar door in the dusty wild west. He made a beeline for the sink.

Father Paul scrambled, confused and unable to make sense of what he was seeing in the cupboards. It took too long to see there were not cups on any given shelf. Gradually, he discerned that there were only liturgical vessels, no simple drinking glasses. Looking back, surprised by a clinking noise, he discovered a group of four men counting the collection money on a table behind him. Possibly they would know where to find cups, or possibly they would slow him down. Thoroughly out of patience, he rinsed his hands, splashed his face a few times, and then drank right from the tap by forming a little bowl with his hands.

"Here's a glass, Father." A gentle clunk as the glass came to rest on the counter next to him.

Father Paul recovered from the shock of a voice so close to him and glanced over his shoulder to see a man almost as tall as himself in a white undershirt and clean jeans walking back to the money counting table.

"Thank you." Receiving a nod, he continued, "What's your name?"

"I'm Luke. This is Will," indicating a man of sixty or seventy years who was probably retired from the military. "This is Josh," he said, pointing out a man younger than Father Paul with a greasy ponytail. The black smudges on his waving hand gave him away as a mechanic. "And this is Don," he said, indicating a man roughly Will's age, definitely military, and less approachable than Will. "We're your entire Knights of Columbus Council," Luke introduced soberly. That was a little sad, Father Paul decided.

Before the priest could pull together his muddled thoughts and respond, the doors from the altar area flapped again applauding the arrival of a man in an expensive business suit. "Father Paul!" the newcomer greeted warmly, "Brad Coppini." Father Paul set down his water glass and they shook hands. "I think I can help you restore those statues."

Father Paul had mentioned the possibility of fundraising to hire an artist to repaint and revitalize the Sacred Heart statue, the Immaculate Heart of Mary statue, and every Station of the Cross in the sanctuary. They had been whitewashed back when that sort of thing was in style, and it had the effect of making even Jesus and Mary look like ghosts, more dead than alive. Fundraising—or attempting to—would allow Father Paul time to see whether he was the only person who thought the work needed to be done. Pulling hundreds or more out of parish savings on arrival for a personal pet project was not the best way to build rapport with the people. Apparently, he hadn't been clear about how much it would cost. He named the starting estimate that the artist had quickly emailed back after evaluating the pictures and dimensions Father Paul had sent.

Brad pulled out a checkbook without batting an eye.

"Are you sure?" Father Paul asked. "The artist needs to see the statue in person before naming a full price for the work," he hedged.

"Just let me know if it ends up costing more, and I'll take care of it," Brad replied smoothly.

"Wow. I really appreciate this," he took a breath to let his brain adjust to the new plan. "I really believe in the power of prayer, and I think this will help people who get distracted to focus on God. This is a tremendous gift." He was probably rambling, still suffering the effects of dehydration, so he stopped himself there. Noticing Brad's wedding band as he watched the man write a check, Father Paul nervously joked, "I hope you asked your wife about this!" He started laughing before Brad reacted.

"She doesn't mind." He said it so dismissively, Father Paul was not only certain that Brad hadn't asked his wife but that he didn't care what his wife thought. Were they in the middle of a divorce? There wasn't a polite way to get to the bottom of that obvious problem today in front of an audience. He would have to wait for a better moment. He read Brad's name, upside down, on the check he was writing and tried to commit it to memory despite his clumsy mental state.

"Here, I should at least show you pictures of the artist's work," Father Paul realized. The web browser on his phone was still open to the right page. "Here are some before-and-after pictures," Father Paul turned his phone toward Brad.

"That will be beautiful, just beautiful." But Brad didn't actually seem interested. He turned a charming smile to Father Paul as he handed him the check. "Churches should be filled with beautiful things, Father. Good eye," and he winked at Father Paul. "See you, gentlemen!" He waved indifferently to the money counters over his shoulder on his way back to the sanctuary. The money counters mumbled something vague in response.

Father Paul took quick stock of himself. Why was he so nervous? Was shaking part of the recovery from dehydration? He peeled off his vestments, which were certainly heavier than when he'd donned them. Was he nervous as a reaction to something Brad was feeling? He thought back. He actually hadn't felt anything from Brad, no emotions at all. Well, that should have been restful, if anything. Brad would be a handy guy to have around next time Father Paul started feeling overwhelmed with the emotional burdens some people carry with them. He just had to remember to follow up about Brad's marriage. And he hadn't gotten the wife's name.

Father Paul got back to drinking water again. He noticed that the mood was a little dim in the room, so he tried to stir up some conversation.

Luke answered Father Paul's questions about the process of counting money, a process considerably tighter than what Father Paul was used to. In standard parish protocol, as far as Father Paul knew, there were almost always moments when individuals were left alone with the money bag before and after counting. In common practice, the money was only counted once, and when money went missing, it was assumed to be a mistake during counting. If the amount was small, everyone moved on without quibbles. Here, money was never left alone with one individual, and they took turns checking one another's totals. He was impressed. "Don came up with it," Luke gestured with his eyes, in case Father had already forgotten which guy that was. Don nodded once without taking his eyes off his counting.

"You didn't get all of that from the diocesan guide," Father Paul observed.

"Nope." Don was a man of few words, and he was on a mission to count money, not to be disturbed. Definitely cranky.

"Well, I thank you for your care of the parish's resources. Good work." Father Paul had finished his third glass of water, he realized, and things were obviously well in hand here. "I should let you all count in peace," he decided aloud.

Luke's eyes were intense as he looked Father Paul over. He seemed to let go of whatever he'd been about to say. He turned back to the task on the table. It was plain that Luke was bothered by something, but Father Paul would let him keep it a secret.

Father Paul's stomach sloshed with the water in it, as

he shuffled back out to the sanctuary, knelt in the first pew and began to pray about the victims and their families. The rosary felt hot and damp from his pocket. The rest of him was gritty, and he wasn't sure which he hated more, the slime or the grit. He scrunched his nose in disgust and carried on, kissed the crucifix hanging from the pendant, made the Sign of the Cross and got to work. He interceded for healing in the hearts of the girls, for faith in the hearts and minds of their parents, for compassion and empathy to take root in their classmates, for his own mission in all of this, and for law enforcement officers to bring to justice those who had victimized the teenage girls. He got stuck on that last petition, certain that God was trying to speak to him. There was something wrong. It was a big something...

Luke and the other money counters had the bank deposit sealed in one of the plastic envelopes every parish seemed to use. They were done, but instead of heading out the door, they filed into his pew and knelt with him. He paused to wonder at them.

"You could have told us you'd be praying. We would have joined you," Luke noted, handing Father Paul a cold bottle of water. It must have come from a refrigerator. Yes, now that he thought about it, Father Paul remembered bottles of water in addition to the single opened bottle of sacramental wine kept in the sacristy mini fridge.

He took a grateful swig. "Thank you."

The other man nodded. All of them were fishing out rosaries, except for Don, who got Will's extra. Father Paul showed them which bead he was on in the fifth decade, The Coronation of Mary, and began to lead the prayers, the others joining in reciting the second half of each Hail Mary. The repetitive prayers coaxed Father Paul to quiet himself and to meditate so deeply and vividly on heaven, he was surprised to awaken and find his fingers at the end of the fifth decade. The time had flown, but his soul felt rested. He hadn't prayed like this since seminary, when he had others praying alongside him just like this.

The consolation of finding brothers here was tender, too new to dwell on. Father Paul focused instead on the image behind the altar. Chubby little cherubs formed a creepy cabbage patch of heads around Jesus, but Father Paul did a fair job of blocking them out. His eyes were drawn to Jesus' heart on fire with love and surrounded by a crown of thorns. The heart was pierced and dripping one copious splotch of blood. Jesus stoically gazed forward, using two fingers to direct Father Paul's attention back to His Heart. Father Paul floated on that assurance of love, while the words of the rosary flowed under him like a river.

There was no voice speaking in his mind, nor had he heard something audible. There was only a movement in his heart, and he knew a truth as if it had been placed there by someone else. It was as though a voice said to him, *You will burn with love for these girls, just as I burn with love for you. You will lay down your very life for them, and you will unbind many who are bound.*

And he didn't mind. It was as though his death had

already happened, and he was satisfied at how he'd spent his life. Prophetic words like that were almost never literal anyway. He filed away the exact words for future reference, not needing to understand them today, and he was utterly at peace when they finished off the rosary with a prayer to Saint Michael the Archangel.

"Well Father," Luke offered, "would you like a tour of Limekiln's one and only watering hole, The Brew Ha-ha? There's a pool table, and it's a quiet place where families come to eat. The food is pretty good, too."

"Sure, it sounds like a barrel of laughs," Father Paul grinned.

Luke, Will, and Don all chuckled, and Josh joined in belatedly, eyes shifting in search of the punch line.

Luke gave Josh a backslap and enthused, "Let's do it!"

The Brew Ha-ha turned out to have a bar area for bachelors, booth seating for families, and a pool table tucked into a side room you could only see from the bar, not from the family area. The pool table furnished the warmest—that is, the least air-conditioned—room in the place, but Father Paul was determined to get to know the local area and spend time with some of his volunteers, so he wiped back his sweat-dampened hair. There would be air conditioning in the car on the way home, he consoled himself. After that, a cold shower. He'd be right as rain.

Don and Josh dropped off the deposit at the bank, meeting the others at The Brew Ha-ha some minutes later. A skeletal middle-aged waitress brought a round of beers and some appetizers to get them started, but Luke's piercing eyes bore down on Father Paul with the quiet command, "You should keep drinking water, Father." Realizing the man was right, Father Paul did order some water, and the waitress kept the glass filled, while the priest battled Josh on the pool table. Don and Will pleaded off with complaints about their aged, worn-out backs and knees and other ailments. Luke waited his turn to challenge the victor of this first match. Father Paul beat Josh handily—to the roaring appreciation of the peanut gallery, Don and Will—and then faced off with Luke.

"So, what do you think of Dolores?" Luke was taking aim to break the balls, and Father Paul could tell he was trying to make the query seem as offhand as possible.

"What do you mean?" Father Paul asked.

"Just that. What's your impression of her?" Luke took his shot. Balls pinged every which way.

Father Paul took the question seriously. If he was going to fail an unknown test, he wanted to do his best on it anyway. "She loves the girls at her school and protects them fiercely. I trust her completely to do what is right."

Luke's calculating blue eyes met Father Paul's softer ones. Luke nodded. "Your turn."

Father Paul decided he had passed, so he focused on the pool table. Meanwhile, he couldn't help but overhear as Don and Will harassed Josh with dating advice, watching the game and occasionally commenting on it from the bar. When they got around to things like showering more frequently, combing his ponytail, and generally not smelling or looking like the mechanic's shop after work,

Father Paul kept his agreement silent, deciding it was best not to gang up on the young man. Then an attractive lady, whom Josh appreciated with his eyes, walked in alone. With back slaps and encouragement, the men sent Josh to go talk to her, but he refused, blushing fiercely red. He refused to answer any questions about why he wouldn't approach her. "I just don't want to," he said. Eventually, the men stopped pushing him, though the guffaws were never-ending.

"Can I ask you a question?" Father Paul intended the question for Luke alone, but the rest of the group was suddenly listening.

A shrug. "Sure, let's do it." Whatever 'it' referred to, it wasn't in Luke's playbook, but he was cool like Paul Newman.

"What do you think of Brad?" Father Paul asked.

A carefully blank look. "You're worried about him?" Luke asked.

Father Paul couldn't find a way to resist giving away more information and getting none back. "He just didn't seem too interested in the artist or the sacred artwork he was paying to restore. I wondered if he's like that all the time."

Another pause. "*You* don't need to worry about him." But Luke said it in a way that insinuated someone was worrying about him, and they had reason to be worried. "Your big meeting with the victims' families will be Tuesday night. You feeling good about that?"

Small towns. "Yeah, I've got a chocolate cake in mind

for it. That should break the ice." He figured the Betty Crocker talk would foil Luke's attempt to redirect the conversation. Maybe Father Paul would still get some information about Brad.

He'd been mistaken. After an oddly domestic conversation about boxed mixes versus from-scratch baking, Father Paul found out that Luke owned the local grocery store, and the man knew his food. Father Paul was beginning to like this group of guys, even though he felt they were hiding things from him. He couldn't trust them yet, but he couldn't help liking them just the same.

WHEN FATHER Paul walked into Savory Foods early Monday morning, the food he needed was set aside and prebagged. The solitary cashier called out to him and told him it was on the house.

Mental Note 1: It does you no good to take off your collar for a grocery trip in a small town.

"How did you know me? Were you just looking for an unfamiliar face?" Father Paul asked the girl.

She looked uncomfortable. "I was at Mass yesterday. You were meeting a lot of new people, it's no big deal."

Mental Note 2: Must improve at remembering faces. She did not look vaguely familiar.

"Of course, Mandy," he read from her name tag. She did not warm to him. "Thank you very much for holding these for me. Please tell Luke I said thank you."

He made a hasty retreat, melting in the heat as soon as he stepped out of the store. A lady in an SUV stopped and waved him through the crosswalk to the loud, honking displeasure of whoever was driving the pickup truck behind her.

Mental Note 3: He was going to have to preach about car horns. Walmart, which he had visited just prior to the grocery store, had master-minded the worst parking lot Father Paul had ever seen, and the accompanying soundtrack beat a flock of geese. But these people all knew each other. It was madness that they could be so aggressively impatient.

He wondered hazily whether he had met either of those drivers, carrying with him a lingering notion that he was being watched. Maybe repeated dehydration could lead to paranoia. He labored under the heat to get the groceries to the rectory, and from there, he rushed to Hill of Beans Cafe for his morning meeting with Dolores, his Mother Goose of a school counselor, and Bonnie, the school principal, in preparation for meeting the families the following night.

"BYE!" SHE called after her friend, watching with just a little envy as her friend's long legs jauntily cut the way to her campus dorm. Long-Legs dressed like she was going on a date every day of the week, and guys appreciated it, if the jeep jumping the curb on the opposite side of the street was any indication. Long-Legs kept walking as if nothing had happened. She really didn't know she was the center of so much attention. She dressed and carried herself with a carefree attitude. It was her lack of self-consciousness that was most enviable.

Looking down at herself, Best Friend could obviously use a dose of what Long-Legs had. Best Friend wore clothes that, if they were cut just a little different, would be men's clothing. Jeans and a polo shirt and not a trace of jewelry, perfume, or makeup. Long-Legs always wore all three, as if they were a part of her. Then again, with the way she carried herself, it didn't really matter how Long-Legs dressed.

Left to walk the rest of the way to her apartment solo, Best Friend shifted her enormous textbooks to rest on the other arm. Why did all college textbooks have to be huge?

Suddenly, there was a handsome older man walking beside her. "Hi there," he greeted with a charming smile. She couldn't place how old he was, but he wasn't in his early twenties.

"Hi," shyly, she tried smiling back. Then she decided he must be looking for information on Long-Legs. His arm around her shoulders was a bit too friendly. She shrugged at it, hinting that he could let her go.

He held on a little firmer. "I was hoping that you don't have a boyfriend," he said, and the friendly, hopeful expression on his face made Best Friend doubt she was reading the situation right. She didn't understand what was happening.

"Who cares if I do?" she scowled at him. She had decided he was playing with her and insults were imminent.

"Just a guy who wants your number," he drawled with that charming smile again, as if the smile alone were convincing. He was handsome and wore an expensive

suit with a jacket despite the heat. It was a lot nicer than anything the professors on campus wore. He obviously thought a lot of himself. Suddenly, he didn't look so certain, and she wanted to fix whatever had caused his face to fall. She felt guilty.

"Don't you know you're beautiful?" he asked. It was a genuine question, as if he couldn't believe she didn't know.

She decided she was angry. "No, I'm not beautiful. If you want her contact info," she said, gesturing in Long-Legs' direction, "why don't you follow her home?" For a fraction of a second, she wondered whether it had been a mistake, sending this man to follow her friend.

"I'm not interested in her." He actually looked offended, and his hand halfway retreating from her back.

She searched his face, certain she would find him fighting a smile. She found nothing suspicious there.

He planted his hand back on her shoulder, leaned until his face was at her neck, and inhaled deeply. "Mmmmm," he sighed out with obvious pleasure. "You smell the way a woman should smell. You are so beautiful."

Realizing her mouth had popped open slightly, she shut it. She must have stopped moving, she realized. Gathering herself, she studied him a moment before resuming her walk. He kept pace. If he was joking with her, he was a winning poker player. She wasn't even sure she cared whether he was being honest. If he could fool her like this, she'd trade a lot to feel this way for a while. In fact, he'd better be careful, because she might even chase after him.

Chapter Three

Everything within the village of Limekiln was a maximum ten minutes' drive from any other place in town. Or it should have been. Traffic circles and Father Paul's white-knuckled certainty that few other drivers knew the laws about circumnavigating them added a few minutes. Since he had the time, Father Paul studied faces, especially around the traffic circles, and he discovered quickly that he wasn't the only people-watcher that morning. Frequently there were waves and smiles of recognition from behind a steering wheel. How on earth could a priest carry on scandalously in a village like this? Father Max was over sixty and had been assigned to this parish for more than ten years. These girls couldn't have been his first victims.

Getting lost and having to pull up a GPS app on his phone added another few minutes. And the search for a hidden parking lot behind Hill of Beans Cafe necessitated a final U-turn prior to his second arrival, as announced by the mobile app. Hands damp, Father Paul parked in the gravel lot behind Hill of Beans, which was, to Father Paul's disappointment, located on a level stretch of road.

People say a lot of things to ministers. It's not just the

seal of confession that attracts them. Father Paul thought he discerned a cultural assumption that ministers have no set agenda. Talk to a policeman, the officer wants to open an investigation. Talk to a counselor, and you end up with a treatment plan and concrete goals. The job of a minister is to be present to people. Ministers hear everything.

Father Paul hadn't been surprised when, prior to his shopping trip, an elderly man had stopped after daily Mass to tell him that Father Max was innocent, and this whole story was just a conspiracy to bring a good man down. "They can do these things to videos and photographs and digital records these days. I don't believe any of the so-called *evidence* they claim to have had. Journalists are all just looking to sell papers anyway." Derision dripped from his tone. There was always one naysayer, Father Paul reminded himself, and nothing would convince the old man of what he didn't want to know. However, Father Paul did stop the man, when he began saying something unkind about the girls. "But they started this!" the man protested. "They're trouble-makers. You should be worried about who they'll accuse next!"

"Don't say anything about them to me. They are daughters of this parish, and I'll be the one to decide what their spiritual needs are. Believe what you will about Father Max – I don't know any more about it than you do. But the girls are minors, and they deserve more discretion than you're showing right now. Don't say another word about them to anyone." Never did Father Paul imagine he would find himself glaring at someone in the course of his priestly duties, yet there he was with a ticking jaw muscle to boot. The petty, attention-seeking man had wilted and retreated under Father Paul's stare.

Where had that come from? Father Paul hadn't even met the girls yet. He had met Dolores, though, and he had felt her pain at the chancery office. She was the one whom he had defended this morning, he realized, the counselor with a heart full for the girls in her care. He wondered how much farther he'd be willing to go once he'd met the girls for himself.

The families involved had released confidentiality so that Dolores could get Father Paul straight on the sordid story before he met the survivors. Then, Dolores had asked him for a coffee meeting away from the school. That she habitually called the girls "sweethearts" reminded Father Paul of his mother, even though the two women looked very different. Dolores had the skills for counseling, but she thought the girls needed a new spiritual father, since the last one had betrayed them so badly. Father Paul was happy to be needed.

He wasn't sure what part of this had him nervous. Father Paul was more than willing to learn better counseling techniques from Dolores. He also needed to meet Bonnie, the school principal, sooner or later, and since Bonnie wanted to be kept in the loop, she would also attend the coffee meeting. Perhaps it was the gravity of this new assignment. Father Paul had the sense that this was the beginning of the story that would prove his mettle. He could only do his best.

The pastor ordered black coffee and a bran muffin, making a breakfast out of it. The ladies had already gotten their frothy lattes with whipped topping. Those tooth-achingly sweet drinks, combined with the aromas and grinding noises of expert coffee-making, seemed to have infused the ladies with a double-shot of living large. Bonnie and Dolores practically bounced in their seats. Father Paul decided that at least a little of that excitement was caused by his arrival, too, and he found himself smiling at them.

Seeing Dolores like this was a revelation after their first meeting. Her relaxed face revealed easy laugh lines, which to Father Paul made her plump face look more distinguished. There was a joyful light in her eyes, and she could only be described as solicitous and nurturing. She hardly resembled a furious Mother Goose today.

Bonnie appeared to be in her late twenties, maybe early thirties from a distance, her dark, sleek ponytail swishing behind her. Father Paul had to look closely to see the crow's feet framing her eyes. She was at least in her forties, now that he was close enough to tell. Nonetheless, the lithe woman looked tough enough to take down a quarterback if she were to put her mind to it. Today, she was all polite business with a little spunky attitude mixed in.

Bonnie jauntily left the table clacking her high heels and returned bearing a small pile of napkins, apparently in response to Father Paul's muffin.

"I shouldn't be worried about this since I'm drinking my weight in sugar," Bonnie said in a surprisingly heavy alto voice, "but did you find everything you need for chocolate cake tomorrow night?"

Dolores squealed her anticipation.

Father Paul nearly dropped his coffee. He was absolutely being spied on! He hadn't even mentioned the cake to Dolores yet.

The look on his face must have given away his astonishment. "Luke is my husband, he told me," Bonnie explained. "I asked him to include a bar of chocolate so you could sprinkle chocolate shavings on top."

Dolores bubbled with laughter. "It's not fair that you stay so thin!" Dolores gave Bonnie an exaggerated once-over, only playing at being envious. Bonnie barely glanced back in response, looking like a clothes hanger under her pantsuit.

Father Paul shook his head to clear it, assuring himself that indeed, Luke and Bonnie had different last names. He let go of that detail for the moment. "I only glanced in the bag, but it looked like Luke thought of everything. Your husband knows his food."

Dolores nodded emphatically. "Keep him in mind when there's a parish picnic. He tends to donate things for funeral receptions, too."

"He always will," Bonnie confirmed. "Call on him anytime. Oh, and whatever you do, don't add nuts to the cake. One of the girls is allergic."

"Roger that," Father Paul answered, filing the information away.

Bonnie's promise and her warning lingered with

weighty seriousness very briefly before she attacked her dollop of whipped cream. Dolores enjoyed hers with a gentler but no less focused approach. Father Paul blew on his coffee and watched the ladies sigh out their relish. He knew better than to get down to business until the whipped cream was gone. He waited, sipping gingerly at his own strong brew.

As Dolores told it and Bonnie filled in details, the story took shape for Father Paul. How had Father Max kept his behaviors hidden in a town this small? The answer, it turned out, was hidden in Father Paul's question. Even Father Max's local victims were trafficked in the city, and these girls didn't go missing from their families as in stereotypical trafficking cases either. The coercion, threats, and intimidation came via texts all week from men whose faces they never saw. The girls served as one another's cover stories, claiming to be studying at each other's houses, when they all headed to the city to "work" at the same hotel. Father Max frequented that hotel for his sick, criminal activities, and, Father Paul guessed, he couldn't have been expecting to visit one of his own schoolgirls there. Apparently, he hadn't even recognized Renee, the young woman from Sacred Heart Prep, who first publicly named him a criminal with the support of Dolores and Bonnie.

Chatting beneath the din of two hard-working baristas, a radio playing, and the hum of refrigerators and ovens and fans, the counselor and the principal animatedly explained the steps that police had taken. Police had traced text messages back to burner phones purchased on cash. Bonnie helpfully gestured to her own cell phone at the appropriate moment, and Dolores pulled out the edge of a dollar bill to indicate the concept of cash. (Really, Father Paul didn't believe the shop to be noisy enough to require visual aids, but he was aware that his hearing was keener than that of the ladies.) They went on to explain that a store had lost critical security camera footage, and police had managed to lose the few pieces of evidence they had collected. The rest of the tale followed this frustrating pattern. Two officers had been fired from their jobs, and another had been demoted in the course of it all.

In Father Paul's mind, it all added up to a lucrative and intimidating criminal organization that wasn't going to be easy to forget. The girls would have to heal in the midst of an ongoing, possibly never-ending investigation. They might never know the faces or names of their blackmailers, who forced them to "work". The faces they knew were the "customers", including Father Max's face, and his was the only name they knew. That would be the most vivid and horrifying of all, because of the trust he had broken with them.

Had the girls visited their pastor for confession and said something to him about their situation? Father Paul could never ask, but he hoped they would tell him eventually, if that was one of their many injuries, one of the many ways Father Max had betrayed them. He hoped that he could help them find healing for every single injury they had suffered in this ordeal.

Father Paul absorbed all the details, bookmarking the places in the story that were likely to be deeper injuries and things that were most urgent to heal. It was both a relief and a horror to hear that the evidence against Father Max had been definitive DNA left on Renee's clothes. That record had since gone missing in bagged, paper, and electronic forms. However, Father Max had already confessed by that time, so he would have stayed behind bars. Considering the way evidence kept disappearing, the possibility occurred to Father Paul that Max hadn't really committed suicide in his cell, either. But Father Paul couldn't let that possibility distract him from healing the girls. He was only grateful that Renee wouldn't have to face the disgraced priest in court.

"The most important information is in the way each girl describes her story. If you go in thinking you know the story just because we told you the facts, you could do more harm than good," Dolores instructed him.

He thought about it. "Some people say I have a gift for knowing when someone is speaking from pain. When they actually open up and show me a wound, I'll know," he assured her. He waited for her smile before plopping the next pinch of muffin in his mouth.

"He does have a gift," Dolores told Bonnie.

"We're counting on it." Bonnie's eye contact was inspiring and nearly made Father Paul feel sorry for whoever wasn't on her team.

Father Paul liked her. "I won't let you down. You can trust me. If I don't know what I'm doing, I'll ask Dolores for help." And they did trust one another. It was nice having one or two people back him up, trust him. People he trusted in return. There was a herculean amount of work to do, too, but he was in a good position to accomplish it.

The meeting wrapped up on a positive note, everyone clear about their roles in the meeting at the rectory. Bonnie was moral support. Dolores was the trusted counselor who would lend her own credibility to Father Paul and help him gain the girls' trust more quickly. The girls would receive individual counseling during school, and Father Paul would meet with families in back-to-back meetings Tuesday nights for the foreseeable future, after this initial group meeting. Bonnie, he had no doubt, would keep a sharp eye out for signs that the plan was failing. She would work with him on a solution, but she would find a solution with or without him, as necessary. She was intense.

Father Paul left this meeting feeling enervated despite the caffeine, a feeling he realized as soon as he was alone, driving again. If he were being honest, he would admit to feeling mildly ashamed of his Roman collar. "Lord, have mercy," he prayed over and over on the way home.

On Tuesday afternoon, Father Paul was forced to turn on the oven and make it even hotter inside. Father Paul searched on his phone for a way to keep cool without air conditioning and settled on pouring water over his head. He could perform that trick repeatedly and cheaply, two huge pluses in his book so long as he didn't fall on the wet floor.

He accepted a call from his sister, Grace. She had phoned to complain that she'd found out from their *mom* that he'd taken a new assignment and moved to a new town. "I get that you're busy, but it was days ago. Why wouldn't you want to call and share good news with me?" she whined. All he could do was apologize. It would probably never occur to him to call her when he was moving and busy taking on a new assignment.

"I should thank you for the cake decorating things. I'm planning to use the icing squeezer to make a border. Never made anything this chocolatey in seminary, but the icing squeezer thingy has always added that extra touch a cake needs. Do you think I should use a veggie peeler to put chocolate shavings on the top?"

Grace was back to feeling appreciated as she filled him in on details she must have thought he'd forgotten. They had been homeschooled and had decorated many a cake together, but this flow of information meant that he was forgiven. He let it pass with gratitude. The last thing he wanted was to hurt her.

While the cake was in the oven, he checked over the accounting books and made sure he knew what monthly bills to look for, the recently completed maintenance, and so on. There were several lines he didn't understand and would have to research. It was hard to tell whether those lines were sinister or simple. He wasn't an accountant. When the cake had cooled, he decided the frosting would only hold up if it was refrigerated, in consideration of the heat and lack of air conditioning. He frosted it, decorated it with icing, and topped it with shavings of the high-end chocolate bar. Then he slid the whole cake carrier onto the one shelf he had cleared in the fridge.

There was a casserole on the bottom shelf, and there were several more in the freezer from elderly ladies looking out for him. He had gotten his standard ketchup, BBQ sauce, pickles, salad dressing, milk, and other door shelf items for himself. At some point, he'd have to remember bread and peanut butter, but he felt quite at home.

Father Max had established a weird custom of hearing confessions on a random weekday after school until 5 o'clock. Father Paul found himself lonely as he tried it out this particular afternoon, so he would likely phase it out in the first month. He cringed to think of why Father Max wouldn't want his Saturday afternoon clogged up with confessions before the Saturday vigil Mass like every other parish in the diocese scheduled it. Really, he tried not to think about it. And he tried not to think about the accounting ledger while he was sitting in his little confessional box either. He tried to pray for his new parish.

He wiped his slightly sweaty fingers on his pants before turning a page in his breviary. The pages were delicate. They would stain and decay with skin oils.

Just as he reminded himself of that fact, a huge bead of sweat ran to the tip of his nose and jumped, splatting right in the middle of the page. Greedily, the thin paper guzzled it as if determined to self-destruct. He had no handkerchief, and the box of tissues was on the other side of the screen.

Someone padded into the confessional box opposite his, closed the flimsy door, and knelt down. He slipped the ribbon over his current page and shut the breviary on his lap.

"Bless me, Father, for I have sinned. My last confession was a few months ago—I can't remember when. Maybe it was last year." It was a woman's voice, somewhere on the high end of middle-aged, he guessed.

"Okay, and what would you like to confess today?" Father Paul blessed her, making the Sign of the Cross in her direction as he prompted her.

"It's hard to say exactly without just telling you the whole story."

Father Paul hated whole stories. They were long. But since he had no way of helping her shorten it, he was stuck. "Okay."

In sum, her husband was in a bad habit of leaving his shoes where she would "fall all over them." At least Father Paul thought that was the issue. In desperation, she had resorted to leaving a pile of cosmetics—she was a dealer—in a place where her husband would "fall all over them," and he had actually injured himself. Those little glass bottles of foundation must be strong, because he stepped on a few, and they rolled him like he was wearing skates. The husband managed to dial 9-1-1 despite his head injury, and she had cried the whole time she had cleaned up his blood from the coffee table, two carpets, and the phone. He was resting now and would likely still be in bed rather than at work tomorrow. This hadn't been her best idea.

He asked, and she confessed that she was sorry for all the sins of her life.

"Okay, say one Our Father and now make a good Act of Contrition," Father Paul told her.

"That's it?" She sounded annoyed with him.

"What do you think you should do?" he asked.

"Something!"

He felt for it and found what he thought would be there. "I'm not going to make this your penance, but have you confessed to your husband that you did this on purpose?"

Silence.

"The reason I'm asking," Father Paul continued, "is that it might help you feel like you've really faced the issue and come clean. I'm not making it your penance, though. Just think about what it might be like to tell your husband and risk his anger or his forgiveness. Pray about whether that might be a good thing to do for yourself and for your marriage."

Sniffles from the other side of the screen. "I'll think about it."

They wrapped things up quickly. Father Paul finished with his breviary and prayed a rosary besides. Just as he was about to close up shop and get some more water, one last penitent rustled in.

She hadn't been to confession since childhood and had forgotten the dialog. She wasn't using the "How to Go to Confession" sheet in front of her, either. "I'm… thinking about suicide."

Well, you can't confess it before you do it and get

pre-approved forgiveness, Father Paul thought. "Do you want to talk about what's going on?" he asked. He prepared himself for more of a counseling session than a confession.

"My husband is not a kind man. He … I feel used and cheap with him. And there's another man, who seems really decent and good. Oh God, he's a good man, and I don't want him to get hurt! I can't ever leave my husband. I just can't go on like this either. I'm trapped."

Father Paul thought she was finished for the moment, so he encouraged her. "Well, I commend you for wanting to stay with your husband—."

She laughed without mirth. "Oh, I don't *want* to stay with him!"

"I see. Well, it's still good that you're staying loyal to your wedding vows. You know, a lot of wives think their husbands are being neglectful and deliberately hurtful. Really, guys are just very different from women. Sometimes they express love in a different way. But for you to become suicidal over it seems like a strong reaction," he understated. "Now there's no shame in seeking out professional help. Sometimes there are medical reasons why people feel lonely or depressed. Your doctor might be a good first step to sorting this out." Father Paul sensed that she felt misunderstood, unheard, and frustrated by him. She had wanted a very different answer. Maybe she wanted permission to commit suicide or to leave her husband. As he took in her pain and frustration, he regretted his pat answers. "Would you like to talk to me outside of the confessional sometime?"

"No," she answered quickly. "I can't slip away very often. Are you going to forgive me?" she asked.

"Are you Catholic?" he asked.

"Yes, I'm a member of this parish," she defended herself unnecessarily.

Father Paul walked her through the final steps of the sacrament and forgave her for all the sins of her life. She said that she was firmly resolved to avoid temptation, and who was he to judge?

"Go ahead and take that piece of paper that explains *How to Go to Confession*. I'll put another in there later. Take a look at it and bring it to your next confession. I hope it will be soon. This is a great habit you're starting today. Everyone should come frequently." He hoped he hadn't insinuated that she was a worse sinner than most people. She did need to talk, though, and he wanted to help.

"Thank you, Father."

One of the awesome things about hearing confessions for Father Paul was that he got to witness moments of luminous transformation in the lives of his people, and then somehow, he would promptly forget them. Part of it was a natural forgetfulness of things he knew he wasn't supposed to remember, but Father Paul believed part of it to be supernatural. He believed that God helped him to forget confessions. Most of the time.

For whatever reason, this last confession stuck with him. It troubled him, and he was out of sorts.

While Father Paul stood at the sink drinking a glass

of water immediately after leaving the confessional, he stupidly looked out the window and saw exactly one person outside. She projected a powerful, clamorous wave of fear, doubt, and worry that attracted his gaze. People didn't ordinarily broadcast their emotions like this. Father Paul's theory was that emotions were "louder" for him when they were experienced by individuals emotionally isolated from others, as though emotions themselves desire to be shared, and those emotions seek out empaths by shouting.

The woman walked briskly home... to Brad's house, just a few doors down the street, and Father Paul knew without really wanting to that it had been Brad's wife in the confessional. He shouldn't have looked out the window and accidentally watched to see where she was going, but now that he had, the damage was done. Now he knew who had confessed to him. And her confession was lodged in his brain. What to do?

Conveniently, Father Paul had a ready excuse to invite Brad over for dinner as a thank-you for the donation to repair the statues and Stations of the Cross. Inconveniently, he couldn't reason a way to bring up Brad's marriage over dinner. He absolutely couldn't mention the woman's confession. The seal of confession was sacred. He didn't actually know enough to help the couple either. Based on the little contact he'd had with Brad, it made sense that Brad's wife would feel small. The man didn't talk to her before making a large donation. How else did he take her for granted?

Father Paul made a mental note to set up a dinner date with the Coppinis soon. He just couldn't call right after the woman's confession. He needed time, and so did she.

As the woman who had just confessed reached her porch, a very large man in a crisp black suit met her at the front door. It was not Brad. Father Paul was stunned. Was this the other man? Had she simply walked home to him as soon as her confession was over? Had the other man known she was at confession and humored her? Well, it wasn't the plumber. And he didn't look "good" in the moral sense. Oddly, his presence did nothing to change the woman's singular fear. Father Paul felt no surge of affinity between the pair.

The priest looked again, just to be sure: The man was not Brad, but the woman walked past him at Brad's front door without wavering. If Father Paul wasn't mistaken, the man loomed over her in an attempt to inspire more fear. Something was very wrong about this picture, he decided.

Yes, Father Paul was going to have to set up that dinner date soon, but he would not be making the phone call at this precise moment.

Chapter Four

The cake would have to remain in the refrigerator until the very moment they served it, so Dolores helped Father Paul set out the serving things and tea. Bonnie arrived with ten minutes to spare, appraised the kitchen and living room, and then praised Father Paul and Dolores, "Well done, you two. You make quite a team."

Renee's parents knocked at Father Paul's door dressed as if they had walked off a clothing commercial in casual yet eye-catching ensembles. Father Paul only just managed to mask his startle at the pink men's shorts Renee's father wore with an untucked button up shirt and boat shoes, but he appreciated the white tennis dress Renee's mother wore to contrast with her tanned skin. It appeared that after taking such time to dress, however, the couple had thought better of the gesture and put on their angriest scowls. Father Paul had the urge to apologize for something as soon as he opened the door to them. The other two families were not yet in sight.

The couple exchanged stiff hellos with their pastor, then parted so that Renee came into view, despite her best efforts to disappear behind them. Shoulders hunched, face down, she risked a glance through her black curls to offer a quick hello. Father Paul winked, and she smiled back tentatively. Her parents were soon engaged with Dolores and Bonnie.

"May I take your jacket, Renee, or are you comfortable?" Father Paul asked. She was the only one wearing a jacket. It was still a little sticky outside, though the sun was long gone.

"I'm fine." She stood as far away as possible, and he realized she was watching him, trying to decide whether she trusted him.

"I hope you like chocolate cake," he offered.

"Sure."

It was an affirmative if not enthusiastic response, and holding cake would get her hands out of the pockets of her tan leather jacket. Why that would help, he didn't know, but he always trusted his intuition.

Bonnie and Dolores helped to serve the tea and cake. Then, in a living room furnished by donations from someone's very sweet grandmother, it was time for Father Paul to dip a toe in the water. "How's your summer starting off, Renee?" The room went silent. Everyone watched her as if she were an animal in a zoo. Renee had her eyes on Father Paul, still feeling him out. He shrugged almost imperceptibly, aware of Bonnie scrutinizing his work with Renee.

The girl took pity on him. "It sucks. I don't even feel like a teenager anymore. I feel like a used up forty-something-year-old."

Her parents, somewhere in their mid-forties, only protested, "You're still a child!" and "There's nothing wrong with you!" The "used up" jab probably wouldn't dawn on them until tomorrow, Father Paul guessed.

Dolores calmed the pair down, while Father Paul kept Renee's eyes on him. Bonnie unobtrusively observed. The priest nodded in understanding until it was quiet enough for him to talk again, and then he ran with blind intuition. Something about the feel of her pain, the shape of her reaction, told him that he was right. "Let me ask you this. When you learn something at school, is it easy or hard to learn it from a lecture?"

She was not expecting that question. "Hard."

"What about watching a video?"

"Easier, but still not as easy as just doing it myself." She thought about it. "Actually, when we watched Mr. Lowery do part of the dissection on the cat muscles, I was doing it myself in my head. That's why I could do it, and the rest of my group couldn't. They were just watching."

"And he wasn't lecturing while he modeled, right?"

She nodded and shrugged, clearly indicating that he needed to go somewhere with this now.

"A lot of people are visual, or they learn from lectures. You're not either of those types. You learn by doing. If you want to feel like a teenager again… can you guess how to do that?"

Her parents gasped. Apparently, this answer was easy for them.

"Act like it?" Renee guessed with skepticism and not a little dread. In all fairness, this would mean a lot of work for her, Father Paul reminded himself.

"It's not the answer for everyone, but I think it will help you. Want to do an experiment and find out whether I'm right? We'll call it *Stump the Priest*."

She rolled her eyes, but she was interested anyway. "Fine. What do you want me to do?"

"Go to the movies," her dad ordered.

"Hang out with your friends and get out of your room some," her mother coaxed.

Bonnie and Dolores each sucked in a breath, almost in unison, bracing themselves against the interfering parents.

"Is there anything you wish you felt good enough to do?" Father Paul asked Renee, ignoring the audience.

"No." It was a challenge. *Make me care*, she was saying.

"Renee," her father chastised.

Father Paul cut him off. "I suggest you pick something either creative or service-oriented. Do you play any instruments? Do you like photography? Maybe you feel like trying out for community theatre."

Her father jumped in again, "She dropped out of school choir!"

Father Paul was completely focused on Renee. There was a knock at the door, and Dolores went to welcome the next family to join the group. Bonnie stayed to observe. "Or maybe you want to volunteer somewhere. Become a tutor for someone in summer school, check out the SPCA, whatever you want. It's up to you, but make sure you have something by next week," Father Paul warned her.

She sized him up for the duration of one long breath. Then nodded. It was a huge win. Father Paul felt like taking a victory lap. Renee's mind opened to the many things she was good for, things that were needed. Her pain wasn't the center of everything. Her world shifted.

Renee's father erupted like a volcano. "Is anything I say right?!" His face was red, and shame poured out of him. Obviously, Father Paul had overlooked something here.

"Why don't the two of us talk out on the porch?" Father Paul suggested. Renee's mother needed this talk too, but that could wait. Renee needed at least one parent with her right now, and her mother wasn't having a meltdown. Dolores glanced worriedly at Father Paul and Renee's father as they went back out the way she had just come with a family. He gestured a "one" with his index finger to let her know that they'd be one minute. She would take over in here. And Father Paul would start addressing the needs of Renee's father. They were already proving themselves to be a good team in front of Bonnie, who would trust them going forward. All in a day's work.

Hours later, all three families had long since arrived and taken the opportunity to share some of their experience with the group. It had been a fruitful and tiring evening. Father Paul had just led intercessory prayers affirming specifics of what had been shared in the group, and Dolores was wrapping up the meeting with the plans for future meetings when the phone rang. Father Paul gave Dolores a head shake indicating that he didn't need to get it. If it were important, he'd get a message on the machine, and if it were an emergency, he could make out the subject by listening from here. Before the machine kicked on, one family was offering to help with the dishes, but Father Paul declined, needing that time to wind down alone. It had been a draining night.

The answering machine beeped, and Father Bob's voice boomed far louder than the average message on the machine. "Hi Paul! It's your pastoral mentor, Father Bob, eager to hear how this first week on your own is going. I know you're probably overwhelmed already, and it's okay if you're feeling like a failure at this point. I just want to encourage you—I'm here to help!" There was a long pause, and unfortunately, it was all silence and confused looks in the living room. Everyone was staring at Father Paul. He turned red with embarrassment. "Well," Father Bob's voice kicked in again, "I guess you must be out right now. I hope you're not hitting a bar already! Call me when you get this. We need to talk soon. God bless!"

Bonnie was first to recover. "Well, I don't know who that was, but he has seriously underestimated you, Father Paul. I'm very impressed with you and Dolores both. What a great start we had tonight. And this cake? You deserve a round of applause for the cake alone, Father."

The little group did applaud. And Father Paul's face returned to its natural color. "Thank you, Bonnie. Yes, I think Dolores and I make a good team. We've done all we can do for one evening, and I'm looking forward to getting to know all of you better as we talk and pray and heal together." He looked around the group to see whether anyone else needed to say anything.

After an appropriate pause, just when Father Paul was wondering how to gently get everyone moving, Bonnie leaped to her feet, and the rest of the group followed suit. Was she even aware of how charismatic she was?

"Are you sure you're alright with the dishes?" Bonnie asked Father Paul.

Yes, she knew she was setting an example for the others to follow, and she knew Father Paul needed them to leave. Father Paul was sure of it. "I insist on taking care of them, but thank you," he answered with a smile.

Dolores stayed behind and helped him with washing and drying the dishes. She was so jubilant about how the night had gone, she offered him a high five before she left. The plump little woman was so adorable, he couldn't help but smile as he lightly clapped the hand she raised above her head, which was shoulder level to him.

"I don't know how you do it, but you are exactly what we needed. God is very good!" Dolores said as he helped her don her jacket.

"All the time," he affirmed.

THE FOLLOWING morning was cool and breezy. All the windows were open as Father Paul rummaged through the sacristy cabinets. He was still sorting through everything he had learned from Renee and the other girls, each of whom had her own story. Last night, they had been downright courageous about opening up. Things were going well. He gave one last look through the rectory bookshelves before deciding he had all the sacred pottery vessels collected in a clean white trash bag. He picked up a hammer from a drawer in the kitchen and then headed for the back door.

When he moved in a week ago, he had walked almost unseeingly past the ugly clay decorations protruding from the wall, only worried about smashing them as he carried boxes full of books down the narrow hallway. Reality struck him Tuesday afternoon, as he was scrubbing the guest bathroom. Someone had retired the now unlawful-to-use pottery sacred vessels onto wall sconces. Chalices and patens that had once held the precious Body and Blood of the Lord were decorating a man cave. Unacceptable. They deserved a burial, according to tradition, because they were sacred, no matter how ugly they were.

Almost at the back door, he had a thought for safety and added a paper grocery bag around a plastic double-bagging job. The last thing he needed was to get hit in the eye with holy shards of clay. Besides, the paper would be a nice, biodegradable way to contain the pile in burial. He planned to slip the plastic bags out to recycle them.

Father Paul had dug a hole in the backyard already, but he'd need to dig it a bit deeper than originally planned. The paper bag barely fit around his load. Grateful for the exercise and the glorious day, he dug and dug, perhaps a little deeper than absolutely necessary. It felt as though the sun were trying to infuse back into him all the energy Renee's ashamed voice had sucked out of him. Her parents had treated her like some kind of psychotic patient, who could only briefly feign normality. She had no strength of her own, none that her parents would recognize. She felt empty inside. Empty and hardened. He held the memory close, sifting it, separating the nuanced grains of her emotions, placing them as coordinates on his own emotional map.

The shovel hit a rock with a solid *thunk*. There were bushels of rock to be harvested in this yard, if only anyone were buying. Stuck long enough at this parish, he would probably build a wall just for the exercise.

What Renee and the other girls needed was to see themselves as survivors, their scars as hard-won trophies that showed what they could endure. Their strength was obvious. They needed to be given credit for that and the kind of encouragement that parents ordinarily give.

A nervous grumble, "Are you sure you don't want to finish your cake? No one's judging your weight or anything... crazy like that," from her father, yet from out of nowhere, humiliating her. Father Paul felt it like a lightning strike. Renee hadn't been thinking about her weight either—like a crazy person would, thanks a lot, Dad. She was just done eating. Her father fussed aloud on one side, while her mother wrung her hands on the other end of the couch.

The scene crashed against memories of his own father cheering him, "Climb higher! Don't look down!" while his mother stood back trusting her husband to catch little Paul if he fell. Dolores' tight smile at the time was an acknowledgement that she saw the problem, too. Father Paul had never been quick on his feet when emotions fell so heavily.

Dolores jumped in with, "Renee knows that. This cake is so rich, Father Paul. Very well done. Thank you."

Since Renee had been somewhat relieved, Father Paul said, "Thank *you*," with a knowing nod to Dolores. The conversation was like a volleyball game, and Dolores dug out every spike before it hit the floor. It was unfortunate that Renee's parents didn't appear to be on their team. But Dolores had been relentless. And Bonnie had sat back to make sure they could handle it on their own. She was a great leader, Father Paul decided. She trusted her people and supervised them subtly enough that she never undermined their confidence or authority.

Now that he had this big rock in his hands, he found that it would work better than the hammer would at breaking up the pottery. After a few good shots, a fragment jumped out of the bags at him. Those little things were sharp! He shifted the bags, checking to be sure he wouldn't get hit with debris on the next strike. Aiming the longest flat end of the rock overhead at what was left of the pottery, he realized he was being watched. Through the picket fence, his next-door-neighbor Barbara paused, weed in hand, to stare at him.

"Hi, Barbara!" He tried to look as non-violent as possible. "Just smashing up some holy vessels so I can bury them." Yeah, because that was normal and made sense to everyone. "It's a Catholic thing." There, now she'd be more sensitive and stop staring. She was Presbyterian.

"Oh, is there something wrong with them?" she called back over the fence.

What was it with small towns? Father Paul longed for the city. "Any use outside of the liturgy is beneath them now, but they're clay, which is no longer allowed at Mass," he hollered. "The only respectful option left to me is smashing them up and burying them."

A wave of anxiety and curiosity rolled over Barbara. He was exotic to her like a witch doctor or a sasquatch. "Well, have fun!" she shouted and almost went back to weeding. "Wait, why is pottery … no longer allowed?"

"Porous," he croaked. Father Paul cleared his throat. "They're porous and hard to clean."

She nodded, still mouth-breathing. Father Paul watched her focus on the weeds this time. She was done asking questions, but she kept him in her peripherals just in case of… anything.

His shoulders slumped with relief. All the vessels were smashed more or less, and he was scaring the neighbor. It was time to bury this project. He slipped the plastic bags out, shaking the dust into the paper bag full of debris. This really had been the most fun he'd had in a while. It felt good. He was breathing deeper and easier than he had been. Maybe last night had traumatized him a little or exhausted his brain. Building a wall, smashing things… He would need something like this on a regular basis. This was good.

The girls would find their own strength and perhaps stand up for it without prompting if only Father Paul could cut through the shame and guilt weighing down everything else. Shame and guilt filled the overwhelming majority of their emotional "grid". Obviously, forgiveness would be key to healing those feelings. The girls could start by forgiving themselves.

The best lesson in forgiveness that Father Paul had ever experienced was watching the sign language interpreter for a deaf lay woman in his seminary classes. Every time the word "forgive" came up, the interpreter had brushed the fingers of one hand over the palm of her other hand twice, as if scrupulously sweeping away the entire debt in question. The meaning of forgiveness had settled into his heart watching that over and over while they covered Reconciliation in the *Sacraments and Liturgy 501* course. Forgiveness is putting a debt behind you, agreeing never to exact a payment owed.

It was buried.

Father Paul replaced the sod over the pile of pottery and tapped it gently down. There was a noticeable bulge in the ground here. At least he'd know where to put any lingering vessels, should there be any hideaways lurking in the church or rectory.

He set his rock against the mailbox post. It was as good a place as any for his wall to start. The phone ringing brought him inside too soon. He couldn't help how dirty his hands were when he picked up the receiver. It was Father Bob.

"How have things been going? How are you finding Limekiln so far?"

"It's been easy," he lied. Advice from this clown was the last thing he wanted. "The people are very friendly, eager to meet me and get me settled. I feel very welcome here." That much was true.

"What have you been up to?" The tone was joking, but it was no joke. Father Bob wanted a play-by-play to critique.

"Oh, nothing too out of the ordinary. Outside of Mass, I've been meeting with all the volunteers, and going through the office files. I had just boxed up what I presumed to be Father Max's personal belongings, when I heard the news that he'd … already passed away in jail." He hoped that last statement would redirect the conversation, even though he'd so far studiously avoided learning the details.

"Have you been working your full forty hours per week?" Father Bob had the audacity to sound suspicious.

"I'm sure I've been working more than that, but I feel like I still have plenty of energy. I'm not worried about burnout." Ha! He'd covered all his bases on that one!

"Hmm. You know, it might be better for me to get a work journal from you, so I have some idea what's going on. I'm supposed to be advising you, while you earn your wings, young saint, and it's tough to do without a good picture. I'll make up a form for you to fill out, and after I read it each week, I'll give you a call. How about that?"

This wasn't really a question. "Sure, that sounds good," Father Paul lied easily. It sounded like a monumental waste of time, but he was certain Father Bob already knew that. If at all possible, Father Paul wanted to live at peace with everyone, not stir up discontentment, including within himself.

"All right, I'll fax it right over to you, and you can fill

it out retroactively for this past week. I'll call back after I get it. Thanks, Paul!"

It took an hour before the fax chirped in anticipation of the trick-or-treat. In that time, Father Paul prayed Evening Prayer and a rosary, then gave up waiting and checked email, thinking Father Bob might have discovered how to attach a file. No luck, but he had plenty of emails to respond to. He wrote to his parents with false excitement, but he couldn't cover up what he was feeling from his priest friends. He paused before responding to them. The deep discussions late at night in the common rooms of seminary had bonded him with several of his brothers in Christ too closely for half-truths and hiding. He had to figure out what to do about Father Bob's micromanaging.

Lord, tell me what to do.

His fear centered on the girls and their healing. He did *not* want to give Father Bob a platform for interfering in that. Renee already felt defeated, uncertain that she was worth fighting for. That thought convicted Father Paul deeply. With that, he knew the way forward.

Renee was worth fighting for. If he couldn't tell Father Bob the truth without Renee getting further abused by a meddling priest, then Father Paul was going to have to lie. Was that okay? That needed to be okay. Father Paul was a grown man wearing his big boy pants, and when he wanted advice, he would *choose* who to ask for advice. He wasn't short on trusted people to ask. His gift, whatever it was, belonged to these girls and their families. He would protect them, even if that meant lying. He had loved the people of Sacred Heart before he had even met them, and he would never let them down. Mentally citing the argument of Saint John Chrysostom's book *On the priesthood*, Father Paul let go of any scrupulosity he held about deceit that was necessary for the common good.

If he were to mention to Father Bob that he was meeting with these girls and their families, Father Bob would invite himself to attend. He would refuse to understand that he wasn't invited to the meetings, be destructively insensitive, and cause the girls to mistrust Father Paul. Consequently, Father Paul could never mention the most important thing he was doing here. If Father Bob somehow found out and pressed the issue, Father Paul realized that he would protect the girls by warning the families about Father Bob. He would help them avoid the man.

He waited for his conscience to cringe, but he felt nothing close to guilt. If anything, his conscience felt more mature, stronger. It was growing, so he praised God.

Menial tasks were all Father Paul could manage today. Maybe he hadn't actually slept last night, and maybe he would find out later that his conscience wasn't growing but snoring at the moment. This morning, he hadn't remembered dreaming anything when he had awakened. It had felt like he had just closed his eyes. He would have to go to sleep early tonight, which meant praying early. He set his cell phone to alarm when it was time to start winding down. He was no good to his people if he didn't take care of himself.

This much, they had told him in seminary.

Chapter Five

Father Paul did go to sleep early that night, but he was troubled by overdue bad dreams that strangely hadn't affected him the same night he'd heard the girls' stories. Perhaps he had needed a day to process the trauma first. The mind knows how to stitch itself back together. And sometimes a person discovers what he already knows through dreams. Father Paul's sensitive mind drowned him in sleep despite his tossing body and waves of vocal complaints.

In his sleep, he saw the three girls link arms and wobble down the street on platform and high-heeled boots, weaving about in skirts too short and pants too tight for sixteen-year-olds, giggling about something they'd never remember the next day. Father Paul, already horrified, knew where the girls were headed. He was reliving the story he had been told by Dolores and Renee, especially the trauma that sank into Renee's heart and the hearts of her friends.

Father Paul's nightmare suddenly plunged him into Renee's perspective, holding him captive behind those loose black curls. Although aware he was not Renee, he felt her unsuspecting giddiness almost as if it were his own. She expected to have a good time playing at being an adult tonight. As if he could change something, Father Paul searched for a way to get her attention or turn her feet in the other direction, but this dream didn't work that way. He was powerless to do anything except to live her experience as if it were his own.

Four men trawled the girls toward the hotel that wasn't far enough away. They had just left an out-of-season Halloween party. All four men were wearing Teenage Mutant Ninja Turtle masks, jeans and combat boots. It was so easy to imagine them handsome underneath, so hard to tell how old they really were. The girls were young and optimistic in the way customary to their age, costumed as if completely confident of their own strength and beauty: Mrs. Incredible, Black Widow, Catwoman, and Renee as Wonder Woman. They had taken liberties with the costumes, because high heels were more fun, just like Halloween twice a year was twice the fun! They passed a Dumpster and took the back entrance.

Renee noticed something was wrong after the first swallow of the drink they'd pushed towards her. Was it just a rum and coke? The men watched through their masks, expressions impossible to see, hands free of any drinks. As dizziness glazed her vision, Father Paul tried to get her to fight, to stay awake!

Why were there cameras set up?

When it was over, the girls regained a disoriented consciousness and found themselves abandoned next to the Dumpster. Their phones all had the same sick message.

A video. Themselves. Just now. Cash thrown on their bodies before the camera cut. The lighting from the night table had been positioned expertly so that the girls' faces were clear like freshly cleaned windows. A digital fuzz concealed the men's faces. The message read, "Everyone will see this, if you tell one person. You know what your parents and friends will call you." Horror paralyzed them. They didn't even cry, just stared at each other.

Father Paul felt the fear weigh heavily in his own gut, but the fear was not his own. He felt only compassion directly. He wanted to hug Renee, the others. At least the girls had each other, he thought.

The girls promised each other not to tell anyone. They staggered back to their SUV and drove home feeling adrift. Reality slammed them anew as they faced their parents and daily concerns with new eyes. They were not the same people anymore, never would be again.

More texts. Instructions. To keep it hushed quiet, the girls followed the instructions, and suddenly the video became reality. The girls were being "paid" and told by text message to keep some of the money. Unmasked clients visited now, men who didn't seem to understand what was happening to the girls—didn't ask, didn't care, were buying time with them. More videos. The girls walking away with their take of the money and leaving the rest in the hotel rooms. Them becoming the lie. It was no lie anymore. They always went out the back exit, the one by the Dumpster.

Renee watched every single video texted to her, cried

each time. In the way that dreams allow for nonsense shifts in perspective, Father Paul found himself watching Renee from outside now. Big fat tears rolled down her swollen face from reddened eyes as she lay on her bed, door closed, parents talking on their cell phones in other rooms of the house. She was struggling to catch her breath between quiet sobs. Father Paul read her thoughts as they played across her face. This was her, she thought, the new Renee, and she grieved for her former self. She was going to have to live with it, she reasoned coldly. She learned to let the clients' faces blur in her memory, just as they did in the videos. She didn't want to remember anything about them, and she couldn't let anyone else know either. It would kill her parents. She had promised her friends she'd stay quiet for them.

Father Paul's dream shifted perspective again, watching through the eyes of Renee's mother, who questioned her daughter over the dinner table, perplexed and worried. Renee was too quiet, silent, even when cajoled, "A penny for your thoughts, Renee." Again, her mother tried, "Are you sick?"

Just a head shake.

At school, Renee and the others tried to disappear. Father Paul could only watch, helplessly gripped by the nightmare. The girls wanted to wear baggy clothes and be invisible, but no one would let them. Everyone asked invasive questions instead of just letting them be. Their eyes met no one else's. They felt too tired to move. Even walking took effort for the girls. They shuffled down the hallways from class to class. Dolores saw the change. She tried to talk to Renee one day. Renee must have been a convincing actress, because Dolores really was relieved. "I guess it's just hormones. Hits some harder than others. Don't worry about it, sweetheart," she remarked as though Renee were the one worried.

The girls' grades slipped. It was easy to convince their parents that they needed to meet with a study group. They filled their backpacks with books, a sexy outfit, and a box of condoms each, in case there weren't any in the hotel room this time. They never, ever wanted to be without those. Renee's parents warned her sternly to get those grades back up. How could they not feel her sense of being hunted, Father Paul mentally accused. Realizing that his nightmare had plunged him back inside Renee's perspective at some point, that sense of being hunted was overwhelming him. He couldn't scream from inside her. Remembering how she had felt telling this part of her story, he knew she was screaming inside, too. At least she wasn't screaming alone anymore. He watched through Renee's eyes as her parents let her walk out the door again.

It became normal, lasted a year.

One man asked for a souvenir, a lock of her hair, as though he were complimenting her or this had been a lover's encounter. He was disgustingly old to Renee and could have heaved his last breath at any moment, she judged by his labored breathing.

Renee had long ago surrendered everything. Had he asked for her shoe, she would have tossed it to him. Whatever. A lock of hair? Sure. The old man seemed sick and might have lost a bit of his mind, Renee thought. Maybe he really wanted to believe she was his old sweetheart.

He got dressed, used a pocketknife to cut the hair, and tucked the strands into his breast pocket. The man was dressed the same as any teacher from school with his button-up shirt and khaki pants. The association made her feel even closer to being seen by everyone at school. She didn't move to dress until he was gone. In this world, her clothes exposed something more intimate about her, something more identifying than her nakedness did.

Finally, the dream skipped forward to Renee facing Father Max as he entered the hotel room. He said nothing, just pointed at his belt. Did he recognize her? At first, Renee was grateful that he didn't, confused at why he was there. His gaze was steady. Would he stop if he did recognize her? Renee didn't know what would happen. So, she undressed him coolly, while blood thundered in her ears. Somehow, Renee knew this was the end of the charade, and she was terrified. She thought Father Max would give away the secret, and in some vague way, maybe she considered beating him to the punch. She didn't want him to have the satisfaction of betraying her reputation on top of this betrayal of trust.

Father Paul couldn't relive this. He tried desperately to wake up, aware that his gorge was rising in his own sleeping body. His mind wrenched at Renee, attempting to pull her free from that room by his sheer will alone. Once, twice, he struggled with the dream playing before him.

With a final effort that forced a grunt from his slumbering lips, he yanked Renee out of that room. Pulled free with him, Renee ran out the door and down an empty hall. She shrank to her ten-year-old self, now wearing tennis shoes instead of high heels, now returned to energy and purpose and innocence. The Running Renee vaguely turned into adult Father Paul just as she burst through the door and blew past the Dumpster. Running was easier, faster now, because of his long limbs pumping like a greyhound's, carrying them both away from the gut-roiling horror. The dream allowed him to watch from outside himself, as if he didn't care to be in his own head just now. He'd hit the limit of what his mind could process tonight. His mind was letting him run. For now.

Dead stop. Father Bob appeared before him from nowhere. He was waving Father Paul's work journal form like a cape before a bull. He wanted Father Paul to see red, to paw the ground, to charge. He wanted a reason to fault Father Paul. He wanted to get rid of him without too much fuss. He had back-up plans, this nightmare Father Bob, but he really didn't want to have to use them. There was such an appetite for power in his heart. Father Paul sifted and sorted, trying to make sense of the jumble of his own emotions, reconnecting with his dream self. Defending. Protecting. He had to stay, no matter the cost. It had nothing to do with power and everything to do with love.

The ring of the landline phone made Father Paul bolt up in bed, jarred from his dream finally. He took a calming breath, tasted bile in his throat, and got oriented to the reality of his new bedroom. He wiped at his forehead, drawing away a palm slick with sweat as he picked up the landline with the other hand and mumbled something. He realized belatedly that he had asked, “Hail Mary?” instead of “Hello?” The woman on the line didn’t seem to notice.

He really needed to think about that dream, which meant remembering it despite this phone call, and the dream was already beginning to fade.

The agitated woman on the phone explained that her husband was at home in hospice care, and it looked like he needed the Anointing of the Sick. He would probably pass away tonight—or this morning, depending on your perspective. She gave their address located in a hamlet Father Paul had never heard of. The priest programmed it into his phone and was in his car less than five minutes later. Time was of the essence.

He passed three Catholic churches on his way to the house. Those were the three he saw from the car window. There were other nearby churches close to his route, too. It was hard to believe that those priests were out at their own sick calls, but Father Paul didn’t want to know whether the woman had tried calling those churches. Her house was actually closer to the city of the infamous hotel than it was to Limekiln.

Eyes glowed from within the tree line, too close to the road, and Father Paul saw them step out with no time to spare. He braked, and the anti-locks *clunk-clunk-clunked* rapidly under his foot. He prayed—no words, just a hope. The first deer stood on the white line, while her three doe friends bounded across the road. Deciding things were safe once the car had stopped, the transfixed doe came to her senses and bounded forward… headfirst into Father Paul's unmoving vehicle. She shook her head as Father Paul watched in disbelief, and then she found her way around the hood of his car in pursuit of her friends. The priest put on his flashers and took a quick look with the flashlight function on his phone. There was barely a dent, as far as he could tell. It would have been difficult to explain, so that was good. He asked God to watch over that crazy deer with the dented skull, belted himself in, and took off for the sick call again.

He was not annoyed, he told himself, and to some degree, he was convinced. Father Paul reminded himself that this kind of duty was a privilege.

At her front door, he took off his shoes in observance of the several pairs in the hallway and the woman's socked feet. He told the resigned, exhausted woman, who appeared to be only in her sixties, that he was glad she'd called. Considering the dream she had rescued him from, he was a little grateful, although he worried that he would forget something important. The dream seemed to contain more details than the interviews had, but he was convinced that what he'd seen was true. She led him to a room that stank heavily of sickness, and the dream flew from his mind.

The dying man was named Frank. He appeared to wax and wane through levels of consciousness, so after the anointing was complete, Father Paul asked the wife to step out of the room, granting him the privacy to coax her husband into Confession. Her practical jeans and navy sweatshirt made little sound as she retreated. The door pulled shut noiselessly, proclaiming by its hushed silence the sacredness of this space.

"You don't know what I've done," the man rasped. "My wife doesn't know. I'm only letting her do this for her peace of mind," he protested. It sounded like his lungs might heave shut and refuse to open again. The sound tugged at a memory Father Paul couldn't place in his foggy mental state.

The young cleric placed a crucifix between the old man's hands. Clumsy and weak fingers readjusted several times before Frank's feeble grip on the light object was secure. Father Paul used that time to slow himself down. The sight of Jesus naked, shamed, abandoned, and utterly fixed to that little cross called to mind Renee and the nightmare, but Father Paul pushed that aside for a moment. Jesus had suffered for this man, too. The young priest had to force himself to be patient about whatever sin this man was being so dramatic. These were Frank's last moments on earth, and he deserved Father Paul's very best. When Father Paul's hands were free at last, he quickly flipped his stole over his head and smoothed it over his shoulders.

"Everything can be forgiven," he prompted. "God is greater than anything we can do, so He is greater than your sins. Are you sorry for your sins?" After all, true contrition was the most essential part of this sacrament.

Frank narrowed his eyes at Father Paul. He might have

been trying to focus his sight or get a deeper reading on the man seated before him. Father Paul waited and studied Frank in turn. The dying man's complexion was gray, and he looked so frail, it was moving.

"I can handle whatever you have to say," Father Paul challenged. "Lay it on me."

Frank's eyes shifted to a Bible on the nightstand. Was he indicating that he wanted it? Father Paul reached for the beaten-up black book with a particular passage in mind, and Frank breathed a sigh that Father Paul interpreted as relief. He was about to ask Frank whether there was a passage he wanted read to him, but the priest froze when it seemed Frank had suddenly stopped breathing.

The man's eyes were closed, not in the final close of death, but in the wish for it, Father Paul realized. It seemed he was holding his breath on purpose.

"Oh, God!" So explosive, it could have been the Lord's name taken in vain. With that, a monstrous terror shot out of some secret corner in Frank's soul. "I'm so sorry!" the broken man sobbed in an audible whisper. To Father Paul's senses, the sincerity of it was luminous, and he felt a heavy weight lift from the man's soul. It was so heavy that if Father Paul hadn't known better, he would have thought that weight alone was the cause of the man's sickness. With Frank's final breath, he had reached for and found God's forgiveness. Father Paul had no doubt that the man was now at peace, completely free of his sins.

What breathtaking beauty in the midst of such ugliness and death! Once again, the crucifix caught Father Paul's gaze.

The Lord's presence was usually apparent at the moment of a soul's passing, Father Paul thought, and it was a blessed consolation to witness it. Truly everything can be forgiven, he mused. Father Paul put away the crucifix before he bothered feeling for a pulse. He already knew the old man was indeed gone.

About to get up, Father Paul remembered with a little surprise the Bible in his lap which had fallen open on its own. There was a loose curl of black hair tucked into the pages and a hotel swipe card, the kind you're supposed to turn in when you check out of the hotel. And it was a swipe card for *the* hotel of his nightmares, the hotel called Gilded Swan.

He tried not to believe what he was seeing, tried to un-see it. But he knew. He just knew. This was the man Father Paul had just dreamed about. He had breathed so heavily, Renee had been worried the man might die on top of her, and he had taken a lock of her hair. The hair Father Paul held in his hand was … at least very similar to her hair. And it had been stored next to the hotel swipe card.

Father Paul's stomach dropped and time stopped. He wasn't sure he could hear properly. There was a disorienting ringing in his ears, and he had to shut his eyes. This could not be. It could not be that this man had just been forgiven. And Father Paul had been an instrument of that forgiveness. It could not be.

He curbed an impulse to hurl the Bible through a window. Thought about storming into the living room, where the old woman waited in the hope that her husband would reach heaven and be free of pain. Little did she know the character of the man whom she had comforted!

He thought about the fact that he could strike back at the man by divulging his sins, breaking the seal of confession. Actually, the man hadn't even said anything particular in confession, but … Well, he had been sorry, and he had indicated that he wanted Father Paul to reach for the Bible. Had he been planning to show Father Paul these pieces of evidence as part of his confession? Was it part of his confession?

Blame it on lack of sleep, but Father Paul really couldn't figure out whether this lock of hair and swipe card were covered by the seal of confession or demanded of him by laws requiring that evidence of child abuse be reported without delay!

And he wasn't sure he cared about either of those things. He cared about the girls who were being victimized, and, if he were honest, he wanted to strike back at Frank for his part in their suffering. It just wasn't fair that this man had gotten away with so much! He would never be punished! Not ever! Frank had died with his reputation intact, while Renee worried every day whether pornographic videos of her would circulate in her hometown. Whether her father might see them! Father Paul wanted this man to suffer for the part he had played in Renee's indignity.

It hurt the priest to know how far his will was from God's will in this moment. It is never allowed for a priest to divulge a confession. He should care about the sacredness of the space he'd been in with Frank. Father Paul squeezed his eyes shut again, grasping with his soul for that sense of God's presence that had been here just a moment before! He prayed, *What about Renee?*

Renee.

She would not be helped by pointing out this man's guilt, Father Paul realized. She wouldn't be helped by remembering his face. She needed this face hidden from her forever. The only face that hurt her now was the one she couldn't forget. She had blurred the others on purpose, the smart girl. Father Paul couldn't protect her with this rage. In fact, he knew well that the first step to healing the girls would be helping them to forgive. How could he possibly lead them to do that? He could not forgive this on his own power.

Lord, if I... let you help me forgive this man, will you also give me the power to help the girls forgive, too? Will you grant the girls the healing they need?

A sense of peace cooled him, and a weightier notion settled that peace on his shoulders like a mantle. Father Paul knew that a way would open for him to end the injustice. There would be no new victims from this trafficking ring, and Father Paul would be granted the privilege of healing the girls through the power of God. He had no idea what that first part meant, but he believed it. And anyway, just the thought of the girls healed gave him more than enough strength to push through this trial.

Decision made, Father Paul clutched the lock of hair in his hand, tucked the key card into his shirt pocket, collected his things, and made sure to jiggle the knob a bit before leaving the sacred space of this confessional.

The widow was composing herself, as he'd suspected, when he finally let his gaze meet hers. She was the type to care how she appeared, even in her grief and the plain but clean sweatshirt she wore while caring for her dying husband. Father Paul was sorry to tell her that her husband was gone. Somehow, she had loved Frank, and even though she didn't make a sound, Father Paul felt the pain rip through her at his words.

That was when he realized how unfair it would have been to make her the proxy of her husband's punishment, and he thanked God for the grace to restrain himself.

"I'm going to call the hospice nurse on-call." She was quiet, not trusting her voice he guessed.

"I'll stay with you," Father Paul replied.

She met his eyes and sniffled. Nodded. "Thank you, Father. You got here just in time."

"I'm glad I did," he said, even though he was too numb and raw to be sure what he felt. He managed a reassuring smile. Forgiveness was going to take some time and would have to wait until he was at home. He needed space for God to work.

"You're so young for this," she said apologetically. "I'm sorry none of the closer priests picked up my call. I wish it didn't have to be you."

That was annoying information for later. "I'm glad I was here." And he meant it this time. No one was ever going to link Frank to Renee and make her relive that nightmare, because Father Paul had been here to prevent it. Some survivors benefit from speaking and remembering their stories, but Renee had made another choice. Renee wanted the faces in her memory to be blurry, and Father Paul was obligated, thank God, to dispose of this lock of her hair. No one else would gain possession of it. Ever. And this man's face would not be splashed on the front page of the paper some surprising day, so that she would be forced to remember it. For Renee's sake, thank God for the seal of confession. God would bring justice and healing, both, some other way.

The woman collected herself by studying a business card next to the phone, then dialing.

Father Paul went to the stove and checked the kettle. There was plenty of water inside and a generous tea box on the counter. He switched on the burner. The pinch of hair was still concealed in his other hand. When he was sure the widow was completely engrossed in the details of her phone conversation, he pushed his hand deep into the kitchen trash, underneath some soiled refuse from the sick bed and released his burden with care. Since the bag was nearly full anyway, he washed his hands and took the trash out while waiting for the kettle to boil.

For you, Renee. Through Jesus, for you. God help us!

For the rest of his life, Father Paul would remember this as the lowest, most confusing point in his priestly ministry. He had probably preserved the seal of a dying man's confession, and he had probably been kind towards both the dying man and his widow. Then again, was Father Paul so over-involved in one particular victim that he had acted solely for her benefit without regard for the common good, law, and justice? Sometimes he doubted himself, but most of the time, he thought he'd made the right decision.

It took until he changed out of his clerics early that morning to realize that he still had the key card in his shirt pocket. He was so exhausted, physically and mentally, he didn't consider what he was doing or why. He put it with his other cards in his wallet. Would it help the police somehow? He wasn't sure why, but it was probably better not to throw it away. It would be safe in his wallet. He could sleep on it and decide things later.

Unable to sleep right away, he began praying a Divine Mercy Chaplet for Frank, worrying the rosary beads as he kept count of the prayers. He prayed that God would help him forgive the man, heal the girls, and complete this huge mission. He woke up with the rosary not far from his hand in the too early morning, lights still blazing. It didn't matter how far he'd gotten in the chaplet. He, indeed, had forgiven the man, and it still hurt. Forgiveness cost him some tears as he shut off the lights and tried to go back to sleep.

After Mass later, he was supposed to have a day off. What on earth was he going to do with a day off?

He wanted to take over for the police and end the corruption. It was discouraging to be tasked with healing victims, knowing that more victims were still being made. The police weren't handling the case very well—that was true. They'd arrested Father Max, but they'd also let him die in jail. And meanwhile, the most powerful criminals, the ones with collaborators in the police force, were still attending parties and picking up fresh casualties just like Renee.

He was fairly sure that Frank had indicated his Bible with his eyes so that he could confess that sin. So, he was fairly sure that there was nothing he was allowed to show to the police, including the key card. But he just couldn't sit by and do nothing either. Sleep mostly eluded him.

SHE'D NEVER worn anything as low-cut as this flesh-toned dress before. It surprised her that she loved the color. Her dark eyes contrasted vividly giving her a sweet, innocent look.

She'd never been shopping with a guy before either. He was secretive about his age, but that was okay. If he was a little self-conscious, so was she. It wasn't a big deal. She could tell that he was old enough to be a professor, of course, but it didn't bother her.

He was texting, and then she stepped out of the dressing room and had his full attention. He studied her and the dress, rather than whistling or complimenting her as she'd expected. She felt a little like a lab rat. "Try the maroon one instead." His attention slid back to his phone again, dismissing her.

Uncertain, she turned back to the dressing room area. The attendant gave her a pitying look. She straightened her back and held her chin up. She had things this grandma had probably never had, and that's why the old lady didn't understand what a real relationship was like. Maybe this was an old maid. Ignorant people are everywhere, she reminded herself.

Real people in real relationships can't gush with love all the time. It would be exhausting, and at some point, mature people understand that they are loved without being told. Today, they were finding the right dress. Together! What more could she want? As soon as the task was done, a task she was lucky he cared to help her with, since she couldn't afford any of these clothes, they would leave and do something else. Together. That was love.

Seemingly as a reward for her faith in him, she happily overheard his phone conversation while she changed around the corner in the dressing room. "Yes, this one is different," he agreed with someone and then added, "I'm keeping this one for myself." There was a pause, and then he added, "No, she's mine. No one else touches her."

It was surprising, but she found that she didn't mind his possessiveness. It meant that he belonged to her as well, and she had every intention of acting possessive in return. She was smiling broadly as she returned in yet another dress.

The maroon dress was to his taste, but it was even lower cut on top. The slit up the side was a little flashy, too. She tugged at the top and tried to shuffle walk, so as not to flap open the slit.

"Don't pull at it." It was a flat command from someone who knew what he was doing. He commandeered the attendant's scissors to cut off the tag. "I'll text you the appointment for this afternoon, so you can get your hair done. What's your shoe size?" She told him her shoe size, didn't tell him that she disliked the way he had eyed her

hair. She figured this whole experience was probably a lot different once you'd already done it a few times. As usual, everything was new for her. She was determined to grow up and be his equal.

The dress was already paid for by the time she emerged from the fitting room, and immediately he was herding her out the door. A saleswoman efficiently folded the dress into a box with tissue paper, then slid that into the bag he carried with a shoe box already in it. She didn't even have to try on the shoes. He opened doors for her, he drove everywhere, and he bought her really nice clothes. She couldn't even remember what fancy party they were attending tonight.

So, this was what princesses felt like, she thought. Two parts spoiled, one-part lab rat under scrutiny. That's how they were portrayed in movies and books, and now she knew that was in fact reality. She stifled a giggle.

It occurred to her later that he must have left his credit card information when he made the hair appointment. She had wanted to know how much it would cost and whether they could take a check. The cashier told her that her boyfriend had an "account" there. Interesting. A girl could get used to being treated like this. She made a mental note to thank him later and, with embarrassment, realized she might have forgotten to thank him after the clothes shopping trip. He had dropped her off at her apartment so suddenly and then sent a cab to take her to the hair appointment.

The hairdresser must have been used to ignoramuses,

because he suggested she put the dress on before he did her hair. "You'll only have to pull the dress on over the hair later," he pointed out with a warning tone that said he would not have pity, would not do her hair again if she tested him on this point. The dress had no zipper up the back, and despite the low cut, there were complicated straps that formed a chokehold. They had to slip over her head like a noose, no buckles or fastenings, and they would not go gently over her hair, she calculated. She changed clothes first.

The drape he threw over her was far longer than the hem or the dress's nearly obscene slit. It was especially cold where the plastic drape touched bare skin. But he was a master with hair. She sat watching in awe until he was done. Then, after showing her the back of her hair with unnecessarily large mirrors, she realized that he wasn't done. He used a makeup remover cloth to get rid of all her earlier attempts at being glamorous, and he started over again. His efforts yielded far better results—subtler and more grown up—, so, she was grateful in the end. Still, she wondered whether she'd had any choice. It didn't seem as if she had.

Chapter Six

Father Paul groaned at his beeping cell phone alarm that morning, but he obeyed it. He needed to say Morning Prayer before daily Mass, and an extra twenty minutes of sleep wasn't going to do him much good anyway. As he prayed and his mind cleared, the needs of his people surfaced, which he took as a sign to offer up his prayer for them. He even remembered to pray for the widow from the night before, ashamed that he'd ever been tempted to expose her husband's infidelity and sins to her. For her sake, he hoped she never suspected.

It was a further comfort that he was not allowed to report anything, including the lock of hair he'd already thrown away, since it was the matter of a man's confession. In the light of day, that seemed clearer to him, and he was relieved for it. Father Paul did not want Renee to have to face the questions that would follow, because he did not want her to remember that man's face. Just the thought of causing her more pain made his gut clench.

Concern for his people drew him deeper into the Psalms, so that by the time he reached the Our Father, he was ready to say Mass devoutly.

Actually, Mass was a little off.

One elderly lady bowed too closely to Father Paul before receiving Communion. He really should have remembered her name by now, he admonished himself. It wasn't just her proximity, though. It was as if she were doing a workout video and the exuberant trainer shouted, "And DOWN! And UP!"

Somehow—he wasn't sure who moved—the paten got in the way of her head as she snapped back up. Hosts rained everywhere as Father Paul fumbled to keep a grip on the too thin, golden dish designed with nothing of ergonomics in mind.

The small congregation stood immobile, sharing the horror. Then the eyes of all targeted the little old lady who had bowed too deeply. She turned a bright shade of red and struggled to avoid the many eyes. When her own eyes found the floor and the hosts sprinkled upon it, they darted about, filling with tears.

A wave of pity flowed from the assembly, but she didn't know that. On behalf of everyone, Father Paul touched her shoulder and said, "I'm so sorry. I wasn't paying attention. This is my fault. Just wait right here and please pray for me."

Father Paul was sure everyone stared at his backside as he crawled about and gathered the somewhat soiled hosts onto the paten. The poor woman was recovering emotionally, though, and that was what mattered. Then with his own cheeks red, he distributed Communion under something like the Sixty-Second Rule beginning with the nameless but devout matron. No one complained about the hosts being dirty. Eating God off the floor is still eating God, Father Paul reflected. It's still a wonderful start to the day for any believer.

He retreated to the rectory, brewed a half pot of coffee for himself and stared unseeingly at the scarred wooden table and chairs as he downed the black stuff. When the pot was empty and he was still ready for a nap, he gave in and slept soundly for hours. He woke up disoriented and hungry and ready to pray. So, he made pancakes and prayed by the stove, at the table, and for some time after eating.

He made spaghetti around sunset that evening, but he still didn't have any answers. He'd been praying for peace in the community, for love to triumph, and for families to flourish. Taking a break to watch the sky change glorious colors, he had his answer. Pinks and oranges, a riot of hues lounging lazily over the horizon proved once again that God loved beautiful things. He didn't leave things half-finished, under-cooked, or immature. He wouldn't leave this situation in Limekiln hanging forever either. Love would triumph, Father Paul told himself.

He thought briefly of the Coppinis down the street and decided to call them this evening to set up that dinner date. His mother taught him not to call during the dinner hour, though, so he was calculating what he could accomplish before a more respectful time to call, when his cell phone took up a ring unique to one particular friend from seminary, Jeremy. It was the theme song for "Mash," a show that epitomized the personality of Jeremy, the class clown.

"Jeremy! How are you, man?" This was exactly the person Father Paul should have called to wake himself up. He silently thanked God for the gift and looked forward to the usual banter that constituted every conversation with Jeremy.

"Jeremy, are you there?" Father Paul looked at his phone to see if the call had dropped.

"Yeah, I just thought maybe I should step outside before saying anything," Jeremy whispered.

"Where are you?"

"You know I got moved to Saint Agnes," Father Jeremy said. Taking on a normal tone of voice, probably because he was outside, he resumed, "I was here to help Tom toward the end of his ministry. He was getting some kind of dementia and might not have been here much longer anyway when he died of a heart attack. He was pretty weird at the end there, so, God rest his soul, it was kind of a relief not to have to deal with all that anymore. He was so confused, I was basically running the place and then babysitting him whenever I could get back to the rectory. I never had headaches before I came here. You know what I mean?"

"And now?" Father Paul prompted.

"You're not going to believe me Paul, but I need you to believe me. Someone really was after Tom. And now they're after me, too." He waited a beat before continuing. "I feel it the most when the ladies come to cook for a funeral luncheon. The feeling lingers all the time, but when they're here I know I'm being watched. I hear weird things they claim not to hear. Everyone's looking at me like I'm another crazy Father Tom. I'm thirty-two. I'm too young to have dementia, Paul. You know?"

"Are you pulling my leg?" Father Paul asked.

"I am not." The deadly seriousness in his voice confirmed what Father Paul already knew. His friend was a joker, but this time, he was in trouble.

"You're standing outside your rectory, because you feel safer out there?"

"A little, yeah."

"Tell me you're wearing a jacket. You know it's starting to get chilly outside again," Father Paul coaxed as gently as possible, not really knowing how far gone his friend was.

"Of course, I know it's getting cold. Believe it or not, I feel better with the windows open!" He laughed a little maniacally. "Maybe I'm planning escape routes or something. I've got nothing to hide! I don't care if people overhear most of my conversations, but I feel trapped in there with the windows shut. I need the cold breeze in order to sleep, you know? This place is crazy." He was a little breathless now.

There was a knock at Father Paul's front door.

"Okay, Jeremy. I believe you, and I'm coming to visit you soon. Unfortunately, today was my day off, so it's going to have to wait a week—".

"I forgot to tell you why I called! When you get a chance to come out here, bring whatever you need to figure out my security cameras. I looked through our accounting records. I can't figure out who set them up or where the feed is going. We don't seem to be paying anyone to keep them running either. I just don't know who else to ask about them. But I swear they used to be turned on back when Tom was alive. There was a green light sometimes, not all the time. Now they haven't been on for weeks," Father Jeremy said, sounding befuddled and helpless, as if this whole situation were so unfair. Father Paul had never heard him like this before.

Jeremy continued, "Maybe Tom set up the system for himself, he was so paranoid, you know? But to cover it up in the accounting?" There was a hint of the old jokester's voice in that question. It reassured Father Paul that he could get his friend back to normal once he found a solution.

Father Paul's feet moved of their own volition to answer the knock at the door. "Maybe he put it on his personal credit card, and if it's a closed system, there wouldn't be any outside company waiting for monthly payments. I'll research what I might need. Someone's at my door right now, so I have to go. If you see anything on the cameras themselves, that would be good to know before next week. A company name would help, an IP address, a 1-800 number," Father Paul said. He was already at the front door, so whoever was on the other side probably realized he was on the phone.

Jeremy heatedly barked back, "Don't you think I would've called a 1-800 number already?"

Father Paul didn't know what to say.

Father Jeremy took a calming breath. "I'll look. Thanks, Paul. It means a lot. You promise you're coming?" Father Paul promised, and Father Jeremy ended the call as usual without goodbyes.

The organist and the entire church choir, all little old ladies, stood on Father Paul's front step. "Hello, ladies. Is something the matter?"

No one wanted to be the bearer of bad news, but the organist became the delegated spokesperson for the group, when all eyes fell on her. "Well, Father, there's a bat in the church."

Father Paul stared.

"They carry rabies, you know," she helpfully added.

"Has this ever happened before?" Father Paul asked.

Every grey head shook in the negative. "I had one in my house once, but my husband was alive then," supplied one singer. "He took care of it."

Of course, Father Paul thought. Aren't all men born knowing what to do about bats? "Let me make a quick call." Who was he going to call? He scrolled through his list of contacts. He was halfway through when he found a likely prospect. Yes, Luke would absolutely know what to do.

"Luke, it's Father Paul. Yes, this is my cell number. Listen, what do you do about a bat stuck in the church near the choir loft? … Oh! Okay, thanks! You think he'll be able to handle it? How long will it take him to get here? Okay, great!" He hung up. "Well, ladies, Josh is on his way over, and he's supposedly not far away. Let's head back over, so you can show me where you saw it."

He shepherded the ladies toward the church. Taking stock of how slowly they were moving, he looked around just before they stepped into the street together to confirm that there was no traffic in either direction. There was actually no one in sight. They waddled like a gaggle of geese, each one in turn slowing her step to tell her part of the horrifying ordeal, and they made it no farther than halfway across the street when Josh loped up behind them.

"Hey, Father. Ladies." He nodded by way of greeting.

"Where did you come from?" Father Paul asked.

Josh looked embarrassed. "Oh, I was close by. Luke told me you needed help. There's a bat in the church?"

That was enough to get the ladies started all over again from the beginning of their encounter with the supposed monster. Father Paul remained mystified. He couldn't think of a single reason why Josh would have been on this street at this time of night, much less why Luke would have known Josh was here. He couldn't shake that looming sense of paranoia.

Inside the church, the ladies led the way back up the stairs to the choir loft, no longer afraid, evidently, because they had not one but two young men with them. They actually seemed excited, as if this were the most fun they'd had in a while, and they were right in the middle of it! The choir loft was rather crowded now, so Josh carefully pulled down the ladder to the belfry. It folded down from the ceiling by a ball chain, bisecting the space. Everyone watched him, and no one spoke. With five little old ladies, it was hard for Father Paul to find room to stand,

and with Josh ascending the ladder, the priest didn't feel very useful.

"I'm going to turn on some more lights and get a better view from the altar," Father Paul announced.

Several women encouraged him with murmurs like, "Good idea," but he really didn't care. He'd been asleep all day and wanted to go back to sleep as soon as possible. After switching on some lights from the sacristy, he took a post near the presider's chair. Josh had inspected the door and ceiling near the belfry and wasn't finding any bats.

"Doesn't he smell nice?" a soprano cooed about Josh. She batted what appeared to be glued-on eyelashes at him under a frizz of hair dyed just one shade too deep of red to belong under the golden arches of a certain burger joint. It was still clown's hair, but that clown belonged in a slasher film, Father Paul determined. She finger-waved at Josh, who hesitated and then nodded a quick chin-jerk back at her.

"Ladies, why don't you go on with your practice? This could take a while," Father Paul said in his preacher voice. Josh visibly relaxed when the flirtatious matrons stopped watching him and squeezed by his ladder to take their singing positions. The organist announced the hymn number for the processional hymn. There were several requests to repeat that, please, as they gradually pulled themselves together.

The ceiling beams cast long, bowed shadows, making it impossible to see a resting bat. Josh squinted and peered about, but he obviously wasn't having any luck either. Father Paul was about to fetch one of the emergency flashlights when it happened. The organ blasted to life, and there was a flutter and a flurry somewhere. No one could see where. Shadows stirred hither and yon, but which was the bat and which the shadows? The organist noticed nothing amiss and continued to pipe on.

That poor little bat couldn't stand the noise. It took off willy-nilly, flying in every direction at once and nowhere in particular. Two of the ladies saw it and cried out, and the organist finally stopped playing. The bat appeared to faint mid-flight, continuing to glide in its last willful direction, winging toward the altar. Its landing was a slap and a flopping roll to halt just before it would have tumbled over the edge of the altar.

Father Paul's heart thumped so hard, he was afraid it would close off his throat. This was the moment! In order to keep his people safe, he grabbed the nearest heavy object at hand and slammed the bat over and over until he was very sure it would not move again. That heavy object was the sacramentary, an enormous red book with gold ornamentations on the cover and a rainbow of ribbons tucked between gilded pages. And there the bat lay dead on the altar.

He hadn't realized he was holding his breath until it was over. The music had stopped. The bat wasn't moving, he waited and saw. Father Paul looked to the choir loft to see everyone staring at him open-mouthed. Josh recovered the quickest and offered, "I'll get a collection basket."

The organist chirped, "Well done, Father!" The choir offered up a pattering little applause.

The music eventually sputtered to life again. Father Paul tried to flip the bat into Josh's collection basket by grasping two corners of the destroyed altar linen, but the little guy was stuck somehow. Father Paul ended up handling the bloody body through the far end of the cloth, unsticking the body from the formerly white linen, and pitching the grim beastie into the basket.

Josh busied himself with burying the body, while Father Paul sanitized the sacramentary and wadded up the altar linen into one of the shopping bags kept under the sink to line the small trash can. He washed his hands carefully and headed back towards the rectory, offering the choir a wave on his way out. He was going to use the rectory washing machine and give bleach the old college try.

All the while, Father Paul was thinking, and he became more and more determined as he deliberated. His priest-friend, Jeremy, might be paranoid, but Father Paul was equally suspicious that he too was being watched. It was a stupid idea, but he intended to prove to himself that Jeremy was upset about nothing real. At least in his own mind that diminished the likelihood that there was anything outlandish happening in Limekiln. As he descended the few steps from the main doors of the church, he texted Jeremy, "Don't forget to send me any info written on the cameras."

Jeremy immediately texted back that he was checking them all and hadn't found any writing so far. "Sorry about earlier. I don't know what's wrong with me. I'll be really glad when this is over," he wrote.

"Glad to help," Father Paul texted back. He hit 'send' to Jeremy in the middle of thanking Josh for coming right over. "Where were you when Luke called you?" he tried again.

"Oh, I was visiting a friend nearby," Josh said. He was burying the bat under a bush with a little help from the spotlight that illuminated the life-sized outdoor Sacred Heart of Jesus statue.

"And Luke knew you would be there? Who were you visiting?" He knew he was prying, but he wanted to see Josh's reaction. He was right to wonder. Josh flushed pink or red, it was hard to tell which in the darkness. Josh's eyes looked hard to the sides, as if he might find a good excuse hidden in the grass.

"Yeah, Luke and I talked before. Anyway…this is all set for you! I'd better get going!" He hadn't even used any tools that Father Paul could see. Maybe he had used a pocketknife to dig, but it was already put away. Josh brushed the dirt off his hands, deposited the collection basket just inside the entryway to the church, and, after a perfunctory little wave, strode the length of the street, no car parked in sight. When he got as far as the Coppinis' house, he peeked over his shoulder, so Father Paul waved at him again. Josh returned the gesture uncertainly and turned the corner.

Father Paul debated chasing after him to see how far away he was parked, but he decided not to act like a lunatic. There were limits to how crazy he would let himself behave. What a relief.

There was something distracting him, too, like a fly buzzing close to his face. He realized he was blocking something out. What was that?

As he tuned in, he became aware of someone or some animal on the porch of the Coppinis' house. It was watching him. He searched but could discern nothing lurking in the shadows. He headed for his rectory instead, when the porch light switched on at the Coppinis'. Brad's wife, Lisa, had been sitting there the whole time, right where he'd been searching. Now Brad stepped out onto the porch.

Father Paul racked his brains for a reason to stop over and talk to them. Brad was saying something to Lisa, and it didn't seem welcome. Their marriage, or maybe just Lisa, was in some kind of trouble. Father Paul remembered his intention to invite them over for dinner. He called over, "Hello, there!" The couple paused their conversation as he strolled over, attempting to look casual.

Choosing the menu as he drew nearer, Father Paul invited them to lasagna and ice cream.

Brad responded, "Why thank you, Father. We won't be able to come this week, but can I take a rain check? We'll find a time soon. Lisa and I would enjoy that." Lisa hadn't spoken or reacted in any way that Father Paul could discern.

Father Paul pressed for Brad to choose a day next week.

"I'm not sure yet, but I'll get back to you," Brad said, squelching all hope.

Father Paul had no choice but to relent and promise to follow up later.

Was Lisa the whole reason he had felt watched lately? It made sense. Apparently, she *was* watching him. She did not appear to be mentally stable, he decided, which might explain why Brad didn't want to bring her over for dinner. It would also explain why Brad didn't bother consulting her about his financial decisions. Father Paul wondered whether Brad was aware that Lisa had some man in a suit with her during the day. He sighed, realizing that he did actually need to point that out, and called Brad back outside for a private word.

After several false starts, he gave up. "I don't know how to tell you except to just come out and say it. Brad, I saw Lisa with another man here in your home. He was wearing a suit. It was Monday afternoon," he gently supplied, bracing himself for the predictable emotional outburst.

Brad only assessed Father Paul for a few moments. Then he calmly replied, "My wife … can't be left alone during the day. She has professional help to keep her safe when I'm not here to watch over her."

"For her mental health," Father Paul guessed.

"Yes," Brad smiled as though they were sharing a joke about Lisa. It wasn't a smile of relief at being understood. It was a smile of self-congratulations for being clever. Father Paul knew this, even though Brad's emotions were still locked down, revealing nothing to the priest's emotional radar.

Brad continued, "We tell her that she's a princess, and that she needs guards to keep her from the mobs." His smile broadened.

Father Paul tried to return the smile, certain that he had produced a half-grimace instead.

Perhaps Brad had something to do with Lisa's lack of mental health, Father Paul thought. However, Father Paul had seen similar callousness in combat veterans who joked about gruesome things in order to ensure that they would not break down into hysterics at the next macabre sight. Brad's ability to compartmentalize made some sense in that context. As he bid farewell to Brad, Father Paul decided that Lisa's illness probably led to a certain amount of callousness on Brad's part, and that was a coping mechanism for Brad. It was healthy enough for a man in his circumstances.

Satisfied, Father Paul hoped for equally simple explanations to Jeremy's situation and Josh's secrecy, as well. He still had some mysteries to solve. Father Paul prayed Night Prayer and fell into bed no more than twenty minutes later. Tomorrow, he promised himself, he would catch up on everything.

Chapter Seven

Dreams of bats morphing into vampires who preyed on Renee and the other girls haunted Father Paul's early morning hours. Virgin sacrifices on an altar starred on his mental stage just when the alarm on his cell phone woke him for Morning Prayer and Mass. Still groggy even after saying the seven-thirty Mass, he felt awake enough to fry some scrambled eggs, but he descended to bone weariness again when the landline rang at thirteen past eight. Still stirring the eggs in the frying pan, he picked up the call, resigned to whatever this was going to be.

"Hello?"

"Hi, Paul!" His mother sounded happy and wide awake.

Genuinely glad to hear from her, he answered, "Hi, Mom. How are you?" Father Paul's parents had been retired for the last year or two each, so this was pretty early for her to be calling. He imagined her sitting at the kitchen table still wearing a flannel nightgown and fleece slippers. She was a plump woman with a cheerful face and a generous heart who expressed her love primarily through hugs and baked goods.

"I'm very proud of my son. What's new with your very

own parish!?" Of course, she was over the moon that he had an independent assignment already. So that was why she had called on the landline rather than his cell phone, he realized. Calling him at his 'very own' parish was fresh and exciting. He grinned. She had sacrificed the hope of biological grandchildren from him as part of accepting his vocation, and she had grieved that cherished hope. Father Paul could only marvel at her generous heart. Of course, all the pressure was on his sister now, he feared. There was nothing he could do about it, though.

The priest quipped, "Well, we got a bat in the belfry last night during choir practice. Guess where it died."

"Where?" His mother giggled like a schoolgirl.

"On the altar, bashed to death by the sacramentary. I killed it myself," he reported.

He turned off the burner, slid the eggs neatly onto his plate next to the toast he'd already buttered, and grabbed a fork from the drying rack. There was a long pause, and Father Paul was afraid his mother might not see the humor in the situation. Just as he thought he was in for a lecture, he heard a snort. "Did that really happen?" Father Paul interpreted it as an expression of disbelief.

He sat at his own kitchen table. "Yes, that happened. The whole choir can testify to the story, along with one of the Knights of Columbus." Father Paul stuffed a forkful of eggs into his mouth and noisily bit off some toast, while his mother rolled out her chortles.

"I never imagined that would be part of the priesthood," his mother said, still recovering, "but we make plans and God laughs, right?"

"Him and everyone else, Mother," he responded dryly. "How's Dad?"

"He's fine, still in bed right now, and maybe a little annoyed with me…" she began.

"Why would Dad be annoyed with you?" Before he even asked, Father Paul knew that his mother would have an answer, and she would be completely unrepentant about it.

She hesitated, but then the words tumbled out like a waterfall. "I've been researching the story about the girls in your parish, not to mention Jeremy's—."

"What?" Father Paul cut off.

"You know he's dealing with female victims of sex trafficking. It's the same pattern of crime, just a different city and a different hotel. I'm telling you they're connected!"

That hadn't been his initial source of disbelief, but he was more interested than disbelieving now. Father Paul had known some details, because Jeremy had called for advice about how to counsel those girls weeks ago, well before Father Paul was assigned to Sacred Heart. He knew the details of the trauma, the symptoms the girls suffered afterwards, and the things Jeremy asked for help with.

He hadn't known that there was a hotel involved in Jeremy's case, much less the name of it or what city it was in. Jeremy wasn't trying to solve the case... like Father Paul's mom was. Father Paul had only thought it a sad coincidence that his new assignment would probably give him more clues to help Jeremy's healing ministry. Of course, now Jeremy was calling about something else entirely. Father Paul realized his mother was still talking and tuned back in.

"Everyone knows more than they're saying. There have been similar reports in recent years coming out of three hotels in the state, and guess what? They're all owned by the same man." She paused for effect.

Father Paul rolled his eyes good naturedly. "I'm sure the police know that, Mom. If there was a way to charge the owner with the crimes going on in his hotels, they would have beaten you to it." He sighed, then decided he would have to be hard on her for his father's sake. "You might not have thought of this yet, Nancy Drew, but what if the owner of these three hotels is particularly observant and quick to call the police? Perhaps other hotels are actually involved, and he's the one innocent guy reporting the problem, heroically unafraid of the bad publicity. Did you think of that?" Father Paul thought his dad was right to be annoyed. The man was being ignored by his wife over a problem too big for her to get involved in.

Not to be outdone in the creativity department, his mother responded, "Well, it's not like anyone has broken his knees yet, so I doubt that. Besides, the police need more than a little help from a Good Samaritan. There are hints that the police mishandled the cases. One detective was removed from the case involving your girls—a Detective…" the background sound of papers shuffling conveyed to Father Paul the mental image of the kitchen table piled with this mess. His dad had an office, but his mom tended to bomb the family space with projects like this one. Sometimes it was art, sometimes coupons, and apparently, sometimes a real-life crime solver. "Detective Dzielski. He was removed from the case just one day after the girls in your parish came forward. I'd love to know what he did!" she effused.

"Oh yeah, Mom. With that information, you could crack this case wide open." He said around a mouthful of eggs, hoping she would be able to hear herself.

"I know!" she exclaimed.

She wasn't getting it. "What police department does that detective work for? City, county, state?"

She named the city police force. "The state police have worked on the case, too, obviously, but they don't seem to get the leads the city cops do. These three hotels are in different cities, so it would be interesting to have them all exchange case notes."

"I want to pause you right there, Mom. You mentioned notes. You realize that they have notes that aren't going into the newspapers. Each police force working on the case has information it isn't putting in the papers. You belong to no police force, have no resources besides the newspapers, and have no expertise in crime investigating. Now, I don't mean to be tough on you, but have you paid any attention to Dad since you started this?"

"Oh, Paul," she resisted dejectedly.

"I'm serious. Have you been ignoring him for weeks? Has he been doing all the cooking and cleaning and house chores all that time? You do have a job, Mom, and investigating crimes isn't it. Your job is to stay married." He couldn't believe he was using his preacher voice on his own mother. When had he become a card-carrying adult?

He let his mother have some space.

"I'll think about it," she mumbled.

For the rest of their phone call, his mother proved once again to be a worthy collector of the latest news on his high school classmates, neighbors, and his former girlfriend, who was finally engaged to a "wonderful" man, according to the cleric's mother. He mentally checked that petition off his list. *Thank you, Father!* he prayed.

"Well, I guess that's about it from this neck of the woods. Your father and I are so proud of you, Paul," she finished.

"It's true," his dad shouted in the background.

Father Paul's mom conveyed mutual "hellos" between the men and hung up soon thereafter to cook an apology breakfast for her husband. She'd be cleaning up that mess in the kitchen today. After that, maybe Father Paul could talk her into a hobby that was outside the house and came with its own time constraints—for her sake and everyone else's. Maybe she could volunteer to visit the sick and homebound or to decorate the church. He would think about what to suggest.

He needed to think about how he was going to get his mental fitness back first. All he did was work and sleep. He needed some down time… And he couldn't do it introvert style. In seminary, it was kickball league that kept him moving. Fresh air, a little activity and healthy competition. Yes, he was going to start an adult kickball league, if that's what it took to stay strong for his people. He could not get this job done without staying fit, physically and mentally.

He made a flyer, printed a copy with little tear-offs at the bottom, and decided he'd be pinning it up at Luke's grocery store as soon as possible. There was a bulletin board hanging above the rows of shopping carts, and it featured all kinds of local interest things like pet adoptions, babysitters, and bingo at the firehouse. The kickball flyer advertised Saturday mornings games, which would fit in right after daily Mass but before his afternoon in the office, hearing confessions, and celebrating the Vigil Mass. It would be perfect for normal adult work schedules, too. He mentally patted himself on the back and headed out the front door.

He needed to replenish a few church kitchen supplies at the grocery store today, so this trip had more than one purpose. The Sunday Donut & Coffee crew was out of coffee, low on sugar, and always in need of creamer. They were also too old to carry groceries easily, so he had offered to run the errand more or less permanently. As he headed for the car, he felt something pull at him like a hook in a fish's mouth. Turning, his gaze caught on the scene through the huge window in the Coppinis' front door. He saw Lisa was cornered by two men in suits.

The trouble with empathy is that you feel the world according to someone else, not according to objective reality. Father Paul had to force himself to remember why these men were in her home. Lisa's interior felt to him like a cornered animal weighing the costs and benefits of biting someone. In fact, her average emotional state appeared to be a very stressful one, well outside of the normal range. Meanwhile, the men in suits had the same feel as Brad, emotionally locked down. Father Paul didn't have much experience working with serious mental illness, so for all he knew, emotional lockdown was a regular part of the training. And Brad must be paying these men well to take care of his wife. Their suits were evidence of a fine salary.

He made it all the way into his car before that now too familiar sensation like a fly buzzing in his face got his attention. The signal was coming from an apparently unoccupied car parked down the street a hundred feet. He was getting seriously tired of this. Just before releasing his car door handle to check it out, it occurred to him he ought to be afraid. Palms sweating, he made a furtive Sign of the Cross over himself and prayed "Protect me, Jesus," as he strolled over to investigate.

Don. He was sitting in the driver's seat with his torso contorted over the center console and his face pressed against the passenger seat. Father Paul knocked worriedly at the window, and Don's gaze snapped to meet his. His eyes bugged for a moment, but Don recovered quickly and pretended to be searching under his seat for a few nonsense seconds before obediently popping the door open to talk.

"What's going on?" Father Paul asked, trying to stay calm.

"Oh, just looking for a pen that went under the seat," he snarled, jowls quaking as if he were angry.

Father Paul knew the man actually felt embarrassed, so he raised one eyebrow and rested one arm atop the open car door.

"My wife will be able to find it later," he assured Father Paul. "I'd better get going, though." He gave a warning tug on the car door, daring the priest to stay smugly in place.

Not knowing what to ask or how to react, Father Paul lamely backed off with an, "All right. See you later." The door snapped shut, the engine turned, and Don drove off. What could Don possibly have been doing hiding in his car on this street? Was everyone in this town insane? Too bad there were only two guys in suits to deal with the whole circus, and they were occupied with Lisa.

Father Paul actively resisted the urge to panic, forcing his body to relax. He tried to reason with himself. He really didn't want to be scared. But what in the name of all that was holy could be going on? He needed at least one huge problem to be solved. Today.

He would never tell his mother about it, he decided, but he was going to pay a visit to the police force in the city. If police corruption was the problem with the trafficking cases, entire town corruption was the problem here in Limekiln. Father Paul thought he had a better chance of solving police corruption. That was the problem he could face today.

As he pulled onto the main road, he saw Don's car

rounding the block, presumably either to resume his sentinel position or to follow Father Paul. Paused at a stop sign and forced to watch Father Paul drive by right in front of him, Don's face comically turned with the passage of Father Paul's car. So, Father Paul waved at him, a friendly I-see-you kind of wave. He hoped that would be enough to dissuade Don from following—if Don had been planning to follow, which, of course, Father Paul hoped wasn't the case. Then again, maybe it was better than the alternatives. What were the alternatives?

How had he played pool in front of this man but not noticed anything odd about him? This man was a money counter at church and a Knight of Columbus. What on earth?

Father Paul rethought what Josh might have been up to the night before and why Luke would have known Josh was there. Could that have something to do with Don's presence this morning? Willie was probably in on the plot, too, since the other three Knights appeared to be. What could the four Knights of Columbus be doing? Running a patrol? A neighborhood watch? Father Paul really wanted a simple explanation, but nothing fit the behavior of a group of men who had joined the same service group at church. He shook his head to clear it, glanced nervously in the rearview mirror and probably exceeded the speed limit. It was hard to keep an eye on the speedometer and the rearview at the same time.

Once he made it to the city without sighting a familiar car behind him, he felt more secure. At a red light, he pulled up the address of the city police headquarters on his phone and let the voice navigate him to a three-story brick building. A call had gone to voicemail while he was driving. He checked it with dread. It was probably Luke trying to find out where Father Paul had gone so he could send another man to follow him. Father Paul snorted at the paranoid thought. The whole conspiracy theory was nuts.

And he was wrong again anyway! It was Father Bob checking up on him. He wanted to know how Father Paul had been keeping himself busy, and he said it in a tone that suggested Father Paul hadn't been busy at all but perhaps had been playing golf.

The familiar feeling of being hunted by the whole world reminded him of Jeremy, whose rectory was indeed far from the city in a direction that would add an hour of road time, and Father Paul made a mental note to visit him next. Father Paul decided that today was what his mother would call 'a mental health day', so he would take sick time. Father Paul needed an epiphany before things got any deeper or more horrible. He needed to make progress on at least one problem today, and he would make more than one attempt at progress just to be sure. First, the police.

The interior of the police station looked very much like a military building with its obligatory beige walls and tan floors. The atmosphere was less disciplined and less formal, and the uniforms weren't as crisp as at a military base. Still, the effort to be pseudo-military was a comforting one for Father Paul, as though they were trying to make him feel like a kid again. To some degree, it worked. It took him back to the security of his childhood surrounded by generally trustworthy, capable men and women in uniform, who were ready to offer their lives in service to their country. Maybe he could trust these people with his problems and get some help, he thought.

Now he had to answer questions. No, he did not have the case number, and he didn't know who was working on the case now. He knew the name of the detective who had been taken off the case, and no, he didn't want to talk to that detective. The uniformed officer tapped her hot pink pressed-on nails irritably on the massive wooden reception desk and huffed at him. Each nail featured exactly one sparkling stone in the center, Father Paul noticed with bemused interest.

"Take a seat over there, and I'll try to find somebody," she told him. As though she didn't know what he was talking about. This seemed like a high-profile case, since it had been in the newspapers just a few weeks ago. She should be able to figure it out. But what else could he do?

Father Paul did as instructed. He thought about calling back his mother to get more current information, but he really hoped that all her papers were in the garbage by now. There was guest Wi-Fi in the station, and he got distracted with researching apps to control the cameras at Jeremy's rectory. Once those were downloaded, he texted Jeremy about seeing him sometime later this afternoon. Eagerly, Jeremy texted back excessive details about his schedule. Alarmed at the uncharacteristic behavior, Father Paul reassured Jeremy that he would be working for hours on cracking the security system and making it usable for Jeremy. He'd be on site for most of the afternoon, he imagined. He and Jeremy would definitely have time to meet up in the course of all that, no matter how packed Jeremy's schedule was. Jeremy didn't care or forgot to ask why Father Paul was available so many days earlier than expected.

Father Paul checked in with the front desk to find out whether he'd have to call his mother after all. Before he got a word out, the officer said, "I don't have anything for you yet, please return to your seat," without looking up from her computer screen. He took a deep breath and complied.

Quite some time later, feeling desperate to make progress before leaving, he decided to go for it. This time when he approached the front desk, he cut off the officer with, "I'd like to speak with Detective Dzielski, if the current detective on the case is not available." That got him eye contact. And he felt cold fear creep through her.

"I'm expecting personnel assigned to the case to be available any minute. You need to wait," she commanded in a tone that brooked no disagreement.

Weakly hoping that he had her attention, he resumed his seat, and it was only a minute or two later that a detective greeted him wearing a coat and tie not unlike what you'd expect to find on a used car salesman, but maybe it was the detective's flashy smile that put Father Paul on edge.

"Detective Knaveson," he introduced himself.

Father Paul took the proffered beefy hand for a shake. "Father Paul Green. How do you do?"

"Fine, fine. Can I get you some coffee, Father?" the detective asked with a smirk.

"Sure," Father Paul answered just to hint at how long he'd be staying. "I'd appreciate it. Let's pick someplace private to talk."

The pair ended up in an interrogation room with just one cup of stereotypical police-brewed coffee that Father Paul felt he should have been warned about. Perhaps the smirk had been his warning. It took five packets of sugar to make the black stuff palatable.

Detective Knaveson had made a show of checking that the audio feed was off before ushering Father Paul into the room. Unbreakable metal table, uncomfortable chairs, a two-way mirror, and more military beige walls awaited them. They would have had more privacy and comfort out in the open office space. And on the second and third sips, the coffee seemed less and less palatable. Father Paul resisted the urge to dump in more sugar.

"Angela told me which case you're interested in. How did you get into it? The newspapers?" Detective Knaveson sprawled out in his uncomfortable chair, awkwardly attempting to look comfortable in a situation designed to torture his unsuspecting prey.

Father Paul assumed Angela was the officer at the front desk. "No, it's a little more personal than that. I took over Sacred Heart in Limekiln after Father Max was arrested.

The victims are my parishioners, and of course, I'm interested in making sure they're safe." Father Paul thought that any serious investigation should have included interviewing some parishioners or searching the rectory. He didn't think the rectory had been searched before he moved in, and the fact that Knaveson didn't know the new pastor's name didn't make future follow-ups seem likely.

Detective Knaveson's eyebrows stretched up and then stuck stupidly in place. "Did the girls bring forward new information?" he asked. His eyes squinted in imitation of a piercing gaze, but there wasn't quite enough of something—energy or intelligence, perhaps—to make it effective.

"No, nothing. I wondered if your investigation had turned up anything, I mean, anything you're able to share." Father Paul tried and failed to hit a nerve of pride with his tone.

"The case is cold. No leads," the detective shot back.

Father Paul had boxed up Father Max's personal things, but he hadn't gone through them, and the police had never asked for them. There was a potential for leads, but Father Paul decided he would follow up on anything found in those boxes personally.

The detective broke through Father Paul's thoughts, "Unless you have something new to offer the investigation, I'm afraid I have to show you the way out. I have cases that *can* be solved. This isn't one of them."

There was one lead that Father Paul didn't think he could investigate by himself. He offered it up. "You do realize that all three hotels in our state that are associated with human trafficking crimes matching the same pattern are owned by the same man." And then he mentally kicked himself for not having that name handy.

It appeared that Knaveson didn't care. "Do you know what *probable cause* is? Or that you need to know what you're searching for in order to get a search warrant and find actual evidence?"

"Aren't enormous coincidences the same thing as probable cause? Am I missing something?" Father Paul asked. "At least tell me you're keeping an eye on him, trying to find probable cause and actual evidence. I might not know everything there is to know about police work, but there must be something you can do to investigate at this point."

"We're done," Knaveson announced. His face reddened, and Father Paul's radar picked up shame as the cause. Knaveson was made to feel stupid often.

Father Paul hadn't done that on purpose, and now he was dumbstruck. No matter how stupid this detective was, he had a supervisor who must be asking for updates. What did they talk about? How could it be that no one was working—really working—on this case?

As the priest and detective made their way back down a flight of chipping, painted stairs surrounded by walls the same *meh*-shade of tan, Father Paul grasped for some way to prop up his sinking spirits.

He could search through Father Max's personal belongings. They were more or less in the possession of the parish, since the rectory stored those boxes for free, and possession is nine-tenths of the law. He didn't expect to find anything that way.

He was going to Jeremy's rectory after this, he reminded himself, and he might find out something from the cameras. Maybe they recorded or Father Tom left some other clues. That was a mollifying thought.

Lost in his own plans, Father Paul followed Knaveson around a corner to pass the front desk. Just then, someone stealthy caught up to them from behind, pushed into Father Paul and then veered for the men's room. Father Paul fought for balance and missed getting even a glimpse at the man. The stranger's presence felt brave. Calculating, focused, and brave indeed. The presence did not have to use the bathroom. Of that, Father Paul was certain, and he was a little disturbed that he knew it with such certainty. Instinctively, Father Paul pulled his eyes forward and got his feet moving again, covering the tracks of that brave presence. The priest had acted just in time before Knaveson turned to glare at him.

The detective slowed as they approached the front entrance. At the doors, he scolded Father Paul about wasting the public's time. The priest reached into his pocket and felt a piece of paper. Well, paper doesn't explode, he reasoned, so he took a deep breath and let it out. He could wait, Father Paul told himself. He needed to play it cool. He barely listened to Knaveson, his hand itching to pull that paper out and read it. Father Paul hoped he was walking to his car with a comportment of frustration, as if he had been utterly defeated by Knaveson. Inside, he was elated! This was certain to be a lead!

When he finally read the paper, he was in the driver's seat, and the paper was shielded from view of the station by his phone and the steering wheel.

"Mad Hatter 6:30," was all it said. At least that's what he thought it said. The penmanship left something to be desired.

Stunned at first, he decided to Google that. According to his phone, there was a bar called Mad Hatter just a few blocks from the station. Deciding among his search results that this was the most likely meaning of the note, his answer was easy. Why not go?

And he still had time to help Jeremy first. *God is good!* He texted Jeremy that he was on his way and asked what his friend wanted for lunch. He didn't need to wait for the reply, though. Fathers Paul and Jeremy would be eating barbeque chicken finger subs with provolone until they lost all their teeth. Father Paul grinned.

Feeling cavalier, he let Father Bob's next call roll to voicemail, too. Most people took voicemail as an indication that the recipient was busy, and it was Father Bob's fault if he thought Father Paul was at the beach. Father Paul simply did not have time to worry about his job right now. He was busy fulfilling his vocation. And taking a sick day to do it.

Chapter Eight

As Father Paul pulled up to Saint Agnes Church and Father Jeremy's rectory, sheltered by trees just beginning to change colors with the recent nip of cold, he marveled at his friend's newly sealed parking lot, the well-maintained grounds, and the fresh paint on the colossal building exteriors. Over the past several years, the parish council at Sacred Heart in Limekiln had been putting off replacing the roof. It seemed Father Paul was going to have to fund a new roof soon, probably from parish savings. Resigned to that, he saw the other side of the coin just as easily. The girls at this parish were even more privileged than those in Limekiln, and so they were even more likely to do anything to save their reputations on social media. It was a sad reality about wealth, Father Paul acknowledged. He could even more easily imagine girls from this parish ending up at the wrong party and paying for it just as his own girls had.

Father Jeremy was contending with a spindly man who appeared to be grieving, and oddly, they were on the back porch, not far from where Father Paul had parked. The main entrance was the front door, where a sign read "Parish Offices." People would normally make funeral arrangements there or over the phone. The back porch was a strange place for… oh, not just crying but finger-pointing. Father Paul debated whether to leave the food in the car and help his friend or give the man space to work without interference. The balding, wiry man turned heel and clipped a path of emotional turmoil toward his own car before Father Paul could make up his mind. Small gusts of air swirled the same little tuft of the angry man's limited hair up behind him like a rude gesture pointed at Father Jeremy, who passively watched the man retreat. Food in hand, Father Paul locked his car with the fob and gave a sympathetic nod to his bedraggled friend.

"Let's eat before these get cold," he said, holding up the bag with the sandwiches when the other man was in his own car across the parking lot.

Father Jeremy smiled vaguely, then dragged his feet as he lumbered inside leading Father Paul to the kitchen. "I've got some beer in the fridge," he mumbled.

"Perfect," Father Paul enthused. "You want to talk about what just happened?" he asked unsure.

Father Jeremy hesitated. "I didn't realize that guy made the pottery liturgical vessels."

Father Paul sucked in a breath. "You smashed and buried them just like I would have. No doubt." His friend nodded assent. "That's all you could have done. It's not like you could've given them back or done anything else with them," Father Paul pointed out. Internally, he was trying to sort out who among his own congregants might have made the pottery vessels he had smashed the day before yesterday. Oh well, he decided. If someone got angry, he'd deal with it later. *Sufficient to the day is the evil in it*, he paraphrased to himself.

Bottle opener in hand, Father Jeremy admitted, "You're right. But that guy, Ron, he counted on seeing his vessels on the altar. It's a major part of his prayer life. He knew that Tom died in the spring—someone told him over Facebook. But he was in Haiti until this week. He just came back to daily Mass this morning and realized that the pottery vessels were no longer in service. He asked me where they were—without telling me he had made them—, and you know how I am lately, not exactly on my A-game."

It occurred to Father Paul to wonder at how similar he was to his friend, each of them preoccupied with protecting and providing for their entire flock, even the members they didn't completely understand, like Ron. This was why the priests were friends.

Seated at the kitchen table, beer and sandwiches set out, Father Jeremy rubbed his hands over his buzzed hair, as if he were trying to shake some dirt loose or rid himself of that tough situation. "Let's just eat, have a beer, and see then if you can solve all my problems," he joked.

They said grace quickly but reverently. Then, just like that, the two men in black became two regular guys hashing over current events and solving all the world's problems aloud, feeling smarter than everyone else on the planet. No one else, not in politics, in sports, or on the news, was using the good sense God gave them. Everything was so easy. And yet, after some time Father Paul found his heart rate speeding up inexplicably.

Was he eating too fast? That was a disgusting thought. He slowed down and paid attention to his breathing. Father Jeremy noticed and shook his head. "It's easier to breathe with the windows open. I know it's getting cold, but humor me."

Father Paul didn't stop his friend, nor did he mind the cold. In minutes, he was starting to feel better, less anxious too. It was so weird, as if someone had been watching them. He didn't really want the rest of his sandwich, so he took his beer with him and went out to inspect the cameras that looked out over the grounds. Father Jeremy followed.

The priests circled the buildings, searching for cameras, finally counting nine exterior cameras. Agreeing that they had the same number, Father Paul followed his friend inside and repeated the procedure. None of these cameras were meant to be seen, and so could not have been intended as a deterrent. In fact, they were so sneakily hidden that the men weren't sure they had found all of them.

"What do you think Tom was doing with so many?" Father Paul asked. A camera hidden in the china hutch allowed easy access to the cords behind it, which Father Paul was inspecting.

"He got weird. No one knows what he was doing at the end there," and it went unspoken that Father Jeremy was getting weird, too, not to mention scared.

"Well, guess what, buddy. There's only a power cord

back here. The data is being transmitted wirelessly," Father Paul encouraged.

"That's good news?" prompted Father Jeremy.

"Yes, the cameras can't be transmitting far. Where is Tom's computer?" Father Paul asked. He closed up the china hutch with the camera stowed exactly as it had been inside.

"He was actually pretty tech savvy, so he used an iPad," Father Jeremy said thoughtfully.

"And an iPhone?" Father Paul asked and got a nod in return. "Any other devices that could play videos?"

By way of answer, Father Jeremy led the way up to Father Tom's old bedroom, which hadn't been cleaned out yet. Father Tom didn't have any living family, and his friends hadn't asked for gadgets as mementos. It seemed obvious that Father Tom had been turning on the cameras via one of the devices here, and he'd been streaming the video to it. That should be pretty easy to find. From there, it would be like falling off a log to make the system accessible to the new pastor, Father Jeremy. Father Paul could taste success already!

It didn't take a full hour to feel the misery of defeat. The deceased had used Skype, FaceTime, and Netflix, but not surveillance video, not on these devices. His browser history showed an unhealthy obsession with the victims in his own parish. He searched for them every way you could think of, and he read every news story about human trafficking in the state. Clearly, he had the same idea Father Paul's mother did about the connection between similar crimes. The only document of interest was a summary of Tom's research, but it had last been edited some months before the man's death. Why had he stopped? Father Paul emailed it to himself, just for fun. If he had any more questions, he'd be looking through this file rather than asking his newly reformed mother.

"Don't worry, Paul, I'm still impressed. I wouldn't have made it this far without you," Father Jeremy mockingly consoled. There was nothing but respect for his friend in the gentle ribbing. Father Jeremy was sitting on the floor propped up against Father Tom's bed, which was topped by the comforter Father Tom had used in life. It was vaguely creepy. Father Paul swiveled to face his friend from the desk chair and stretched out his back. They both ignored Father Paul's phone as it rang again. Father Bob was proving to be relentless.

"What other computers are around? It has to be here somewhere. The cameras were plugged in, and you said they were on sometimes. They can't transmit far unless they communicate directly to a router and then someplace more remote from there. We have to be looking for a nearby computer," Father Paul reasoned.

Father Jeremy thought about it a beat and offered, "There's one other good place to check," tossing one of Father Tom's replaced but stockpiled phones on the bed. "The secretary's computer. She and Tom were tight. She totally would have kept something like this a secret for him, if he had asked her to."

"Really?" Father Paul snickered with his friend.

"Yes. Sometimes, when I called the rectory because his voicemail was full, she wouldn't give him my messages. She thought he was overworked that day, so she didn't give him more work to do—my messages. I told him about it, and he explained to her that he could decide what phone calls to return all by himself. He just *wanted his messages*." Father Jeremy imitated Father Tom's tone of irritation rising at the end. "She went ahead and kept doing it anyway. I started emailing him instead, and I think everyone learned that eventually. But you have to say she was loyal to him. He could definitely count on her to protect him, and he knew it. That's why he never fired her." Father Jeremy got up and stretched, too. "She'll be punching out at four o'clock," he said, so both men checked their watches. Ten minutes to go. Where had the day gone?

Perched in her high-backed desk chair, surrounded by intimidating, unlabeled organizer trays, a five-drawer lateral file cabinet, and assorted electronics such as the copier, the fax machine, and an electric stapler, the parish secretary looked armed for battle in the next Paper Rebellion. The space heater was blowing to beat the band, and of course she had a chunky sweater on to help with the open window situation. Her hair was permed, the curled locks fabricating an easy extra inch of height. Her pink glasses were thick, magnifying her owl-like eyes. On her desk, there was the obligatory crucifix next to a photo of her family, and a useful church calendar hung next to the standard-issued saccharine portrait of Jesus on the wall.

What jumped out at Father Paul, though, was her sense of territorialism. She was braced to find out that this was going to be an inconvenience. Nine minutes.

"Priscilla, allow me to introduce the *reverend* Father Paul," Father Jeremy joked. "In our seminary class, he was the one we all gravitated towards for advice. He was a spiritual father before he was ordained!" Father Jeremy said lightly as if he were still joking, but Father Paul knew the praise was more genuine than embellished.

"Father Paul, how are you?" She began primly. "I'm Priscilla, the parish secretary. How can I help you?"

"Hi, Priscilla. We've been checking out the security cameras, and it really should have occurred to us earlier to ask for your help. Do you know where the computer is that runs the security system?"

In a flat tone, Priscilla answered, "I don't know what you're talking about." Her arched eyebrow seemed to imply that if she didn't know about it, it wasn't real. She had just placed this visit firmly in the category of an annoyance.

Father Paul watched his old classmate probe the matter, but he stood back and used his sixth sense to feel her out. At the mention of real cameras, one of which she presently realized Father Paul held in his hands, she was well and truly frightened. Father Jeremy went on to explain that the cameras were being turned on and off remotely, that they must be transmitting footage somewhere, and that it couldn't be a computer too far away. At this, Priscilla reached an internal state of panic she did not outwardly betray.

Appearing perfectly poised, she told Father Jeremy that it was impossible. "Father Tom never would have installed something like that and not told me. In fact, I think you *have* to put up signs telling people about cameras like that." She was soothing herself, but it wasn't working for Father Paul.

"As you can see," Father Jeremy gestured as a reminder to the camera in Father Paul's hands, "there *are* cameras in here and several outside. Who put them up if it wasn't Father Tom?" Father Jeremy wasn't getting calmer either.

"I don't know, but it's just about time for me to be going. I wish I could help. It was nice to meet you, Father Paul." She was rummaging in a drawer, retrieving her purse, and she shut off the space heater. Her early departure was no loss to the men in black. She didn't know anything, and they'd need to be at her desk anyway, the sooner the better. When she appeared reluctant to leave the men hovering at her desk, the men feigned interest in the kitchen and said their goodbyes.

"Finally," Father Jeremy said when the door shut behind her a minute later. The men lightly jogged back over to the computer, woke it from sleep mode with a mouse wiggle, and observed a login screen. Father Paul found her password cleverly hidden on a sticky note in plain view. It was her dog's name, according to Father Jeremy. Her pug was also the computer desktop picture. Cute, Father Paul decided after some effort.

He searched the woman's hard drive thoroughly and found nothing related to the cameras. She had an embarrassing history of searching unrelated medical illnesses in her temporary internet files. Father Jeremy watched with increasing frustration over Father Paul's shoulder.

"She's been feeling sick lately, too, huh?" Father Paul asked, trying to distract his friend.

No response, except the heat system kicking on again, something it was doing often due to the chilly cross-breeze the men had engineered.

Abandoning that topic, Father Paul tried again. "I'm trying to think about where else to look." Father Paul put the secretary's computer back into sleep mode and rearranged things so she wouldn't know anyone had been there, he hoped.

Another call came in. Father Paul checked it and let it roll to voicemail again. The phone pinged with another voicemail received. He was going to save up voicemails from Father Bob to listen to all at once, he decided.

"Yeah, it still has to be here somewhere, right?" Father Jeremy was so hopeful. Unfortunately, it had just occurred to Father Paul that this whole difficulty could be explained by someone with an iPad parked in the lot working the cameras. He had a horrible feeling… a truly horrible feeling that there were cameras in Limekiln he needed to find, and he might know who'd been controlling them. And watching. But what were they watching for?

When his friend didn't answer quickly enough, Father Jeremy knew Father Paul was holding back something. "What."

"It's probably nothing, Jeremy. Let me try one more

thing before I go." Father Paul launched the app he had downloaded while waiting at the police station. It took some finagling, but the computer guru got a camera turned on and sending him footage over the guest Wi-Fi, since that network was mercifully free of a password. He discovered along the way that the camera had been reset to its factory default settings, so it had no history of the IP address it had been sending to. He set the camera password and wrote it on a sticky note for his friend. By the time all that was settled, Father Jeremy was sleeping on the couch with his mouth hanging open five feet from the china hutch. Seeing that the man was dead to the world, Father Paul took some time to think.

Why would Father Tom have bothered re-flashing the cameras, setting them to default factory settings, for any reason after they had been in use? It's not as if Tom knew he was going to die that night and thought to cover up his slightly illegal surveillance system without taking down the cameras. What if Father Tom hadn't seen these cameras at all? What if he hadn't even known they were here? Who could set up cameras without the pastor knowing?

Volunteers. Volunteers with keys to everything. Their activities go unquestioned, even if they are ridiculous. Father Paul smiled despite himself at the memory of his former desk artistically reinterpreted in the primary colors without his permission. Anything could happen on a priest's day away from the office.

Father Paul reluctantly woke up his friend and summarized his thoughts.

"The usual people have keys… All of them are people I trust. I haven't changed the locks, and Tom didn't change them recently either, which is saying something, considering how paranoid he was. It's all been the same for years, as far as I know. And the same people have had keys for all those years. Everyone here tells me they've been doing their volunteer gigs for more than a decade. You know how it is. It doesn't make sense for them to set up cameras now. These are pretty new. Who wants to know what's going on in a rectory anyway?" The million-dollar question.

The men locked eyes as they both finally accepted the obvious. "It's about the girls. Tom knew too much."

"Maybe," Father Paul answered, but they both knew it was connected. And they both wondered without asking aloud how Father Tom had really died.

Frustrated, Father Jeremy ran over the facts. "Tom was paranoid, acting crazy, and then one night when I was away celebrating my sister's wedding, he got so agitated, he died of a heart attack, while he was trying to sleep. We're not sure why we feel better with the windows open, and we're not sure whether Tom knew about or installed the surveillance cameras himself." Both men reflected silently. Nothing seemed to fit, though. Eventually, Father Jeremy added, "People blamed me for his death, you know? Like I wasn't allowed to have a life outside of babysitting him. I should have known how unstable he was and supported him twenty-four/seven at the expense of my family."

There didn't seem to be anything to say to that. Father Paul had experienced the same kind of superhuman expectations from his own parishes. "Did anyone weird show up when he died?" Father Paul wondered.

"Define weird. The EMTs picked him up without even bringing their gear bag inside. They just rolled him out to the coroner, after an out-of-uniform cop snapped some photos on his phone. The cop didn't stick around long either. It didn't feel that official, but I didn't know what was supposed to happen instead. I guess I expected some questions?" Father Jeremy trailed off and shrugged.

"The funeral?"

"Paul," Father Jeremy stopped him. "Be serious. I can't remember right now. I'll think about it, okay?"

Priest funerals were always crowded. Father Paul had been there along with the whole diocese, and he couldn't remember much outside of the main events either.

"Don't worry, Jeremy. Listen, I have a friend who refurbishes computers. I'll have him come out here and set things up so you have a system that will work for you when you're not on campus. Right now, you have to be within range of the cameras to get the signal, but he'll set it up to stream to you over the internet, so you can see live footage on your phone anytime, anywhere. Your internet provider probably has a monthly limit on your total downloaded per month, so watch out for overages," he explained. Then he set to work downloading the app to Father Jeremy's phone and training him on how it worked short-range.

Father Jeremy brought Father Paul an agreement with the internet provider for a translation in layman's terms of how much video Father Jeremy could watch without worrying about the surcharge. The pastor was tired but satisfied that he'd helped a friend, as he filed the agreement away in the secretary's lateral file cabinet. Well, he had helped his friend in one way, at least.

It was hard leaving Father Jeremy with so much more trouble stirred up than he had settled, but Father Paul had to rush to get to Mad Hatter now. He didn't have time to throw a pity party.

"I really appreciate this," Father Jeremy told him on the way out. "Really, this means a lot."

"No problem. Look out for Dominic to come with that computer tomorrow and let me know how that goes. It was good seeing you, man."

Just as the men were moving in for a back-slapping hug, Father Paul's phone rang again. They ignored it and followed their ritual. Then Father Paul crossed the parking lot and checked his missed call log. Some of the earlier ones weren't Father Bob. Luke had been calling.

Father Paul wasn't sure what he was going to say, but a confrontation was in order. Don was doing stalker surveillance, and there were likely cameras in the rectory at Sacred Heart. He was positively boiling at the thought of it, although he thought he was making great efforts to stay calm. Father Paul decided the best plan would be to go into Mad Hatter with as much information as possible. Since he didn't want to trouble Jeremy, he drove away first and pulled over someplace at random to return Luke's calls.

He had pulled over in front of an "Adult Store" by mistake. Realizing that this looked terrible, he drove off again, hoping no one had seen his collar. The second time he pulled over, it was at an innocent gas station. He sighed in deep resignation as he hit the call button.

"Luke?" He prompted.

"Father Paul," the man charmed, "I was worried about you. Anything much happen today?" he asked. On second thought, Father Paul was sorry that he wasn't doing this face to face. He couldn't sense anything over the phone. It pulled him up short.

"I know about the surveillance, Luke."

Silence held for several long beats. "Okay."

That was all Luke had to say? "Is there a reason you called me?" Father Paul asked.

"I was just making sure you're okay. We were looking all over for you," Luke said smoothly. It sounded sinister to Father Paul.

"You were making sure I was okay? Are you threatening me?" Father Paul asked.

"Just settle down now," Luke said in a tone that Father Paul took to be patronizing.

Father Paul pressed "end". When Luke called back, it rolled to voicemail. There was no ping. His voice mailbox was full. It was time to get some answers from the Mad Hatter.

Chapter Nine

The facade of Mad Hatter featured the original animated movie character with his tongue hanging out, pouring—not tea—but beer down his collar, through a sleeve, and into another mug suspended in space just before the establishment's name in a capricious shade of green. Down several concrete steps, the front door was below street level and just visible from the car. Father Paul couldn't see inside from the street, and the great news was that no one else would see him from the street either. As an added bonus, he was mostly sure no one was trying to follow him. He would not run away. He would take this chance. He removed the stiff white collar from his shirt, unbuttoned the top button, and zipped up his black leather jacket far enough that he thought most people wouldn't notice he was wearing clerical blacks.

No tires screeched to run him down in the street. No footsteps echoed his own long stride. He wasn't eager to meet in a presumably dim basement with few exits, but he still had the presence of mind to know he was being silly. Following the stairs to the thick wooden door thumping with a powerful drum beat, down the rabbit hole he went.

Bouncing Irish folk music washed over him. In the

warm, ambient glow, a mix of framed photos covered every available wall, ranging from original book illustrations to stills of the animated movie to modern photos of Johnny Depp as the Mad Hatter. There were tastefully few photos of the actor, while there was a delightful photo collage of locals dressed in Wonderland costumes. Whoever arranged the frames knew a thing or two about balance, color, and how to use a measuring tape, too. The variously sized photos crammed the walls, but even Father Paul could tell there was method to the madness. It was downright charming.

It was also deafening in this place. As he sat in a booth, he felt the music vibrating his seat. He would have to shout in order to be heard by a person directly in front of him, and there was no way someone in the next booth would hear his voice, much less make out the words.

Father Paul settled under a large, framed portrait of the cartoon Cheshire Cat standing on his head—literally, the detached head smiled at the priest from beneath the front paws of the cat. Father Paul decided he could identify with that. He tried to act natural, ordered a beer, cheese dip and wedges, and he disciplined himself to stop looking around. He was late by about ten minutes, but he didn't know who he was looking for. He just had to be patient.

Company arrived after his order, and it brought its own mug of beer and mostly eaten dinner from the bar. It looked like the bear-sized man had eaten a burger while he waited for Father Paul.

"Detective Dzielski," the man introduced himself with a nod. He pronounced his name like the words "gel" and "ski" combined, finally sparing Father Paul from struggling to pronounce a "z" sound immediately after a "d" anymore. It must have been close enough, the way he'd pronounced it for Angela at the station front desk. He had picked it up from his mother, he realized with mild chagrin.

"Brave," the cop observed aloud about Father Paul, surprising him. He looked the cop up and down wondering how he'd come to that conclusion. The detective had presumably been wearing a suit at work as Knaveson had been, but Dzielski had changed into a plain black t-shirt and black jeans before waiting here. Disheveled, wavy brown hair and a handlebar mustache offset observant blue eyes.

"What were you trying to do at the station today?" Dzielski opened bluntly. He did not seem impressed by Father Paul's tactics. He turned his attention back to his fries after reading Father Paul's reaction.

"I wanted to shake things up, find out what's really going on."

Father Paul wasn't sure what he might have added had Dzielski not cracked out a single "HA!" The detective continued to sniffle out snickers through his wide nostrils, shaking his head while he squirted a nice pile of ketchup for his fries. "You kick a hornet's nest, that's maybe okay. Run fast, maybe nothing happens to you. You don't squat over a rattlesnake in hibernation and take a crap on it just to shake it up, find out what it's doing there. That's what you did today. You'll be dead before you find out what's going on, if you keep up the stupid stuff." He continued to sniffle out those soundless—in this din—snorts of laughter. Father Paul found the behavior disgusting around food. Dzielski grabbed a couple of fries, dipped them in ketchup and chomped down on a good mouthful of them. He quickly chased that down with a swig of beer.

"If that snake is the same one that hurt your kids, what do you do with it then?" Father Paul asked. "Let it sleep? I'm not walking away."

"*Your* kids?" the detective huffed around a mouthful. If a wet clump or two fell out at that question, then Father Paul studiously ignored them.

"They call me 'father' for a reason. They're all mine, regardless of age or biology," Father Paul answered.

Dzielski gave a professional assessment of Father Paul's face and general appearance, then he grimly faced his fries again. "I believe you, Father, but that only helps you so much."

"How does that help me?" Father Paul was ready to call the meeting adjourned if there wasn't a satisfactory answer. The detective seemed more like a huge, slow—in more ways than one—nutty professor than a hardened cop.

"It means I trust you, so you have a lot of people on your side, some of them very close. It only helps so much because you ditched them today."

"What? Who?" This was seriously irritating Father Paul.

"Your posse from Limekiln," he winked at Father Paul. "The neighborhood watch or whatever you want to call them." Dzielski was gesturing the way a wheel rolls with his ketchup-covered fries. "Luke called me. I know you ditched them on purpose."

Well, that explained everything and nothing. "How the—," Father Paul stopped himself and regained control. "How do you know Luke?" He stated the question monotone, struggling not to hit the obnoxious man.

"You really have no idea what's going on, do you?" Dzielski asked. At Father Paul's silence, he nodded and seemed to gather his thoughts. About to launch into a story, he had a new thought and asked, "Where were you today?"

"Visiting a friend from seminary, Father Jeremy Muller," Father Paul answered, figuring that he wasn't giving much away. He really didn't want to share information. He wanted to get information in this meeting.

"Oh yeah, Father Tom's replacement. I'm glad he's okay. So, you know what happened to Father Tom," Dzielski stated.

"Why don't *you* tell *me*?"

Dzielski chewed on that, swallowed, and started his story there. "Okay. There was another undercover working the case, and Father Tom was helping him. Priest was a high-class snitch, if you want a name for it. That cop is dead, too. Shot like he was just a random victim of a mugging, off duty. Not sure how they caused Father Tom's heart attack, but it's too coincidental for me. They died on the same night."

"Why haven't you told Father Jeremy that?" Father Paul was astounded.

"He doesn't need to know." Dzielski locked eyes with Father Paul. "Look, I'm sorry, but this is a need-to-know kind of thing. Everyone who gets close to this case dies. We know we have a mole at the station. We know Knaveson sucks, so he's pretty safe. Hey, he's so bad at his job, he might be working for the bad guys! He might as well be! But he won't die, and he's a nice placeholder to make it look like we're investigating the case in an official way. They'd hardly believe we stopped investigating. If he wasn't there, they'd be looking for the new undercover and me."

Now Father Paul was getting somewhere. "Father Jeremy is too close to the case. I am afraid he'll die, and you're not meeting with him," Father Paul stated brutally. "Are you telling me that you're doing some kind of undercover job now? Because it doesn't seem to be going well."

"He's going to die?" The cop got another snicker out of that. "Something going on with your priest friend?" The detective sounded interested in a provisional way, by Father Paul's radar. At least he could rule out one suspect in Jeremy's case.

"There are cameras over there, and I don't think Father Tom set them up." Father Paul debated whether to say anything further. He had a short history of being blown off after telling people about his intuitions. Most people would blow off everything else he had to say, too, if he mentioned something so unbelievable. He took too long considering it, though. The detective could see that Father Paul had more to say, so, taking a leap of faith in the cop, he supplied, "It feels like someone is watching you over there. It's hard to breathe. We opened the windows, and it started to feel better. It's wasteful, keeping the furnace working hard like that, but that's how it is. Maybe this whole thing is so evil, there's a call for an exorcist over there." He shrugged as if maybe he was joking, maybe not. He hadn't needed to cover up, though.

Dzielski had paused thoughtfully in his booth seat at the comment about opening windows. In fact, he had stopped chewing for the first time since ketchup hit his plate. Deciding something, he quickly swallowed and pulled out his phone. "Hi, I'm reporting a possible gas leak. Get someone inside the pastor's residence at …" he rattled off the church name and address twice.

The detective hung up without giving his own information, probably annoying the dispatcher.

"What was that?" Father Paul asked. "You know they can see the caller's ID."

"Not from my phone, they can't. Firefighters with a carbon monoxide detector will check it out, see if it's anything. Before you call an exorcist, Father, think about a furnace, oven, or water heater ventilation problem. Some of the symptoms of carbon monoxide poisoning include rapid heart rate, increased respirations, paranoia, hallucinations, and possibly—heart attack." Father Tom's death suddenly made more sense. "If my theory doesn't pan out, we can call in the exorcist later." He smiled chummily to himself and dug into the fries again.

Thinking back over the details, Father Paul decided that Jeremy was symptomatic from the furnace, but he actually complained about the soup kitchen volunteers. He wondered, "Is it possible that it's all three or at least two of those things?" Getting a blank look, he clarified, "The oven, the furnace, and the water heater?"

"Sure, if they're all on the same flue. You just block the flue," the cop answered. "You notice anything else over there? What was that about cameras?" The question came out lightly, but the cop's gaze was now solidly in work-mode.

Father Paul, once again, found himself giving more information than he was getting. "Are you saying they weren't yours? You had the address memorized," he accused. Meanwhile, he thought to text Jeremy about the incoming fire engine.

Why? Jeremy typed back.

Just let them look around. Inside. Father Paul responded.

OK, Jeremy replied.

"Didn't need cameras. Father Tom was working with a detective, like I said. That detective died, too. Were the cameras recording anywhere on the premises? That might be useful, but nothing else about them will be." The cop was completely focused, staring Father Paul down for his answer. Father Paul decided he was finally seeing a police officer doing his job. It was reassuring after the day he'd had. He decided to let go of the fact that Dzielski had memorized Jeremy's address.

"The way you ask that makes me think you know who put those cameras up, and you know they were recording off the premises," Father Paul established. "How would they be set up? If you can help me find the computer on the premises, the one that's sending information back to Mother Russia or whatever, I'll get you the information you want. Whatever is there. I can tell you the computer we're looking for isn't any of Father Tom's devices or the secretary's computer."

"I'll look into it myself, Father. You need to back out of this mess. Focus on the girls. They're your job," Dzielski coaxed in his gentlest voice, which was still pretty gruff. The cop's confidence level told Father Paul that Dzielski knew exactly how the camera system was set up. This group probably had a *modus operandi*. If only Father Paul knew what it was.

Feeling patronized, Father Paul gave up another point. "Fine. What's Luke got to do with all of this?"

The detective took time gathering his thoughts again, and Father Paul realized with great irritation that the cop was deciding how much to tell, not what order to tell it in. "Girls who work in these hotels go missing. The ones at your parish are the first who have managed to get back to their lives with their families after they're out of the business. The others who came forward two years ago? All gone. Some are dead, and some have disappeared to who knows where."

Dzielski gave Father Paul a moment to process that before continuing, "If your girls had information, we could be talking about Witness Protection Program, and maybe they'd take the offer. But since they don't know squat, that option's not even open. Your boy Luke out there, he formed a little neighborhood watch to keep an eye on things. He's got people at the school, people from the church, eyes on your little rural roads. He makes it hard for anyone to move against the girls. He asks me for advice, but he takes care of everything after that, you understand. My dance card is full already."

This time, Dzielski's pause felt defensive, as though he expected Father Paul to stir up his guilt at not providing more for the girls. When Father Paul remained dumbstruck, the detective carried on, "It works in the girls' favor a little that they really *don't* know anything, so maybe this won't be a problem forever. Maybe they'll be forgotten eventually, even if we don't get evidence to put the bad guys away. But my guess is the girls will never really be safe, unless the case is solved and everyone making money off of it is arrested," the cop stated matter-of-factly. He shrugged, done divulging information, and grabbed up some more fries.

"So why was Don on my street?" Father Paul asked.

Mouth full, the cop hesitated again before answering, "We can bet pretty high that if there's trouble, it'll come at the girls from that direction." Reading Father Paul's face, he added, "It's got nothing to do with the rectory or the church. We know what we're watching for."

Father Paul took in the 'we' for a moment. The detective was in cahoots with an amateur neighborhood watch during an undercover investigation, and he was in such close communication with them, he called them 'we'. "Who else knows about this?" he thought to ask, wondering how far the 'we' extended, leaving him out.

"Bonnie, at the school, obviously, Dolores, and a few others. They just set things up so it's tough to get access to the girls. Even the parents don't know how bad it is. Don't talk to the girls about it," Dzielski warned. "We're on a need-to-know basis here, and the only reason you need to know anything is because you became dangerous today." The cop levelled an accusatory look at Father Paul.

Father Paul grimaced. He didn't like this at all. He had to swallow Dzielski's reprimand with a swig of beer before he could meet the detective's eye without feeling tempted to do him a physical injury. Blame it on the subliminal effect of the thumping music, but at least the temptation to run and hide was absent for a change.

Dzielski started up again, this time with passion, apparently taking offense at Father Paul's sourpuss expression. "You just worry about helping those girls recover. That's the role you're going to play in this. You and your friend, Father Jeremy, you both stay out of the investigation, and we're all better off. Not knowing things is what keeps you safe. It keeps you from saying things you shouldn't say and being places you shouldn't be. You, Father, need to stay out of trouble. Luke and his buddies are spread thin already. Don't push this," Dzielski commanded with finality.

The detective finished his own beer, then resumed his gentle tone. "Now let's say you come up with some information from the girls. You give that to one of the boys down in Limekiln. You don't call me, and you don't stop by the station again. You understand?"

Father Paul decided that Dzielski must regularly play Good Cop / Bad Cop as a solo act. He was good at it. The rest occurred to Father Paul in a prickly flush of understanding. Why would Don be waiting on Father Paul's street? Because Dzielski thought Father Paul was already a target, the first one these thugs would take out, just like they took out Father Tom with the carbon monoxide. But why? What did Father Tom know that Father Paul could find out, too?

Being protected was not what Father Paul had been ordained to do. He liked reading stories about martyrs and had considered being a missionary to dangerous places once. Ultimately, he found joy right here in his diocese, and he hadn't found that same joy as a volunteer missionary the one and only time he'd given it a chance. He didn't even like to travel. In fact, his default mental wiring was to avoid conflict altogether. But the desire to give up his life for his people was still there. There was something romantic in it, like Jesus' love for His Bride, The Church. Jesus' love was ultimate, sacrificial love, and Father Paul wanted to lay down his love in the same way.

Father Paul could imagine facing God after making such a complete offering of his life, and he longed to make God so happy with him. He wanted to imitate what Jesus had done for him. Priests offer Jesus' sacrifice on the altar, and Father Paul had a burning desire to join his own death to it. In a world darkened by sin, Father Paul wanted his life to be offered as a solution, a gift that weighed down the balance of justice and allowed others mercy.

And here was this meddling policeman and his neighborhood watch in the way.

He had some limited options. He could follow the cop. He could follow Luke. He could rush back over to Jeremy's and look for a hidden computer, now that it sounded less likely a criminal had parked nearby with a computer in his car to control the cameras.

The checks came and went with the waitress, filling the dead space, while Father Paul considered things. His phone vibrated.

Going to hospital wearing oxygen mask. Jeremy was texting him.

So I shouldn't call and make you talk, huh?

Right.

What hospital?

Decision made, Father Paul would stay with his friend until he could spring the guy and make sure he felt safe at home. Or take him to Limekiln. "With all the information you're not giving me, do you have a guess about whether someone forgot to unplug the flue or whether they tried to kill Father Jeremy intentionally?" Father Paul asked.

"Carbon monoxide, huh? Tell him to get on the ambulance," Dzielski ordered, looking pleased as the Cheshire Cat.

"He's on it. Are you going to question him? I've got

the name of the hospital," he offered, pleased to know even a small detail before Dzielski, curious to know what the detective would ask Jeremy. This should be a great opportunity to find out something accidentally.

"Yeah, where are we going?" the cop asked, even more pleased with himself.

Father Paul happily gave him the information.

"Now when we leave this booth, we don't know each other anymore. You see me on the street, you don't even look at me, you understand?" The cop had lost his gleeful smile, all business again.

"Yeah," Father Paul agreed, not sure how that would play out in the hospital.

"Go on," the cop said, giving Father Paul a head start. They walked out separately, two strangers going their own ways down an obscure street.

The wily cop used his twirly lights and siren to give himself a head start, but Father Paul thought he was only a couple of minutes behind the man. Panting with the effort of powerwalking down long corridors, he found Jeremy in a curtained "room" in the ER, laid out on a bed with an oxygen mask, already looking as though he'd been abducted by aliens. The cop was nowhere in sight.

Too late, Father Paul realized Detective Dzielski had gone to Jeremy's rectory, and he probably already had the hidden computer he wanted.

Chapter Ten

The hospital kept Jeremy overnight to check his organ function and, especially, his mental status. Father Paul was embarrassed to know so much about what could be wrong with Jeremy now that he'd been breathing in poison for so long. Father Paul made arrangements for a nearby priest friend, someone else from their seminary years, to pick up Jeremy in the morning. He had to tell the story twice before Father Steve believed or understood, Father Paul wasn't sure which. Jeremy was rolling his eyes meanwhile, tired of hearing about it and just plain tired. The patient needed to rest.

The prevailing theory, once Father Jeremy had told the first responders about Father Tom's heart attack and the mysterious cameras, was that someone had intentionally plugged up the flue with cloth, killed Father Tom, and then come back to unplug the flue, removing the evidence of his crime. The perpetrator had missed removing some of the cloth for reasons that were not immediately clear. Obviously, he had also missed retrieving the cameras, so incompetency seemed the best explanation. Then, a starling had managed to get trapped inside the flue and die. Before it died, it appeared that the starling had disturbed the neglected cloth. Cooperating with gravity, the bird's weight stuffed everything tightly at the lowest point in the flue along with the poor stupid bird's remains. This second clogging, more disgusting than the first, was mostly accidental. Insurance agents might call it an act of God, and Father Paul wasn't touching that one. This second plugging was the reason Father Jeremy hadn't been himself lately. This was the reason for his hospitalization. A criminal bungler who failed to completely cover his tracks.

It was all easy enough to remove once a firefighter looked. The decaying bird's body was the first thing to tumble out, solidly thwacking that firefighter on the helmet, and fast behind that came the gray and splotchy stained cloth that gently shrouded the man. He gagged at the stench even as he pawed with gloved hands, first to block the heavier object, then to rid himself of the decomposing rags. His laughing colleagues had then contacted the police, and there was a full investigation underway in the rectory.

One cop suggested that the saboteur hadn't been able to reach all the cloth or had been surprised by someone entering the rectory and had abandoned his unclogging job early. Perhaps the perpetrator hadn't seen the remaining cloth in the dark flue and left it by accident. He must have been flush with cash, since he hadn't returned to retrieve his cameras either. It was a convoluted theory, perhaps, but it was the only theory that fit the facts. "It makes more sense to just call him arrogant or stupid," one flatfoot muttered.

Father Paul didn't have the heart to ask Jeremy whether he realized this meant the killer had probably done something—close windows, clog the flue more fully, or something else—the very night that Jeremy was away at his sister's wedding. Father Tom had been symptomatic long before that night, so it seemed that either an amateur or an expert had to be behind this plan. Still, Jeremy's absence the night of Father Tom's death was too coincidental now. Someone had been watching and waiting, and Father Jeremy had been deliberately spared of that first deadly incident.

At the hospital, Jeremy had to start from the beginning of the story, tell every detail multiple times over again, and even deny suicidality. Father Paul proudly witnessed his friend taking deep breaths and remaining calm during these inquiries. An officer from the rectory investigation visited the hospital with a fresh round of questions, in the midst of which the officer got stuck on the fact that the EMTs' gear bag never made it in the building the morning Jeremy discovered Father Tom's body.

"Why would that matter?" Father Jeremy asked.

The detective briefly explained that the carbon monoxide detector would have been on the bag, and they should have brought the bag inside, automatically discovering that there was carbon monoxide in the atmosphere. Father Paul thought it likely the officer would report the whole ambulance crew for the irregularity. Unspoken was the thought that perhaps one or more of the members had been paid off to leave the detector in the vehicle. Arrogance and plenty of money seemed to fit the facts. The mystery was beginning to come together, Still, Father Paul could see the minutiae of details were beginning to exhaust his friend, so he was glad to see the detective wrap things up and leave.

Father Paul had made the mistake of taking a call from his mother and telling her about Jeremy. Since his mother was friends with Jeremy's mother, he should have known that news would spread to the latter immediately. Judging by the area code, Father Paul was now receiving a call from Jeremy's mother, probably because the unhappy patient's phone was silenced or off. Father Paul had been developing a habit of letting certain calls, usually Father Bob's calls, roll to voicemail, so he nearly silenced this stressful call and tucked the phone away without thinking.

Mentally kicking himself, he received the call and did his best to soothe Jeremy's mother, then forced his friend to speak with her, as she fervently requested the favor. Jeremy did the barest minimum, mostly in monosyllables such as "yes," then perfunctorily informed his mother that he had to go and handed the phone back to his grimacing friend. Assuring the woman that he was keeping a close eye on her son, Father Paul ended that call only to be told by a short and officious woman in scrubs, "Visiting hours are over." No longer able to keep an eye on his friend, at least he had calmed Jeremy's mother in innocence. Jeremy was quite spent, Father Paul could see, and so without argument Father Paul left him to rest.

Father Paul hit the road for Limekiln and took the next call on speaker from his own mother. Again.

"I hate European Starlings. They are the stupidest birds, and they're an invasive species," his mother fumed. She'd really thought this through while he'd been placating Jeremy's mother.

Amused, Father Paul responded, "I have a theory that some creatures fell further than others with original sin, but I would have placed ticks far below starlings."

"Oh, certainly, but as birds go, I really think starlings are the lowest of the low. They're loud and obnoxious, and they can push out lovely native species like owls," she *tsked.*

Father Paul had nothing to add to that. "Mom, I know you're going to want to dive back into this investigation, but please don't. Whatever happened at Jeremy's place, it was directed at Father Tom, not Jeremy. He already told me he's planning to live in the rectory again, immediately after he's discharged from the hospital, which is probably tomorrow morning. The police are investigating it, but this is a cold lead about a cold case. It's not worth disrupting your marriage over, okay?" Father Paul turned his mind to God in a silent, hopeful prayer.

"Of course, sweetheart!" she exclaimed. "You don't have to tell me that! I'm already working on my next project anyway," she said, obviously wanting to be asked.

"What's the new project?" Father Paul obliged her.

"I've started a blog about *Things You Must See* within the four or five nearest counties. I haven't quite decided on the boundaries of the project yet, so the title is in flux. Your father and I will pick places we should visit for ourselves, and then I'll busy myself taking pictures, interviewing people, and writing up my articles afterwards. It's not too messy around the house, and your father gets to veto places. Otherwise, I plan everything, and he just drives, which you know he loves," she explained.

She was a terrible driver, so Father Paul's dad always drove, claiming that he found it relaxing. Father Paul wasn't going to be the one to tell her.

"That's really great mom," he encouraged. "All that since this morning. Wow. Send me the link to your blog once you have it up and running. I want to keep up with you two. Maybe I'll get some ideas for parish field trips!"

She agreed happily, and they were off the phone minutes later. Since she had started several blogs already, she had no questions about how to start one this time—and abandon it later.

At some point, Father Paul would need to apologize to Luke, but it was too late at night to call a grocer. In fact, it was almost early enough in the morning. He considered whether to call Luke about Jeremy's mishap, but he figured that if it was urgent for Luke to know, then Detective Dzielski had already called him anyway. What a strange world he now lived in, Father Paul mused.

The priest managed to pray Night Prayer from memory as well as a rosary on the drive back, and he was exhausted when he sidled the car up against the curb in front of his rectory. He decided that he'd just get a couple of hours of sleep, and then he'd call the Knight to make amends. He didn't even take off his blacks, just flopped into bed after slapping the white collar onto the night table with his cell phone.

The phone alarm went off thirty minutes before Mass. Apparently, he'd forgotten to set an earlier alarm, so he would now have to bother Luke at work. He showered, changed into a new set of blacks, prayed Morning Prayer, and rushed to set up for Mass. He had to remind himself through his foggy headache that he had signed up for this gig voluntarily. Married life was no easier. And plenty of parents out there have had sleepless nights worrying over their children. He was not uniquely put upon, he disciplined himself.

After Mass, he found the kickball flyer at his breakfast table. Yes, he vaguely remembered making that yesterday. He had wanted exercise. That seemed like a long time ago. Too busy for breakfast, he texted Father Jeremy, just to check in, and then he drove to the grocery store.

One cashier line was open with one white-haired woman smelling heavily of smoke perched on a stool behind the counter. It was not Mandy. Her eyes followed Father Paul without a smile or greeting or spark of recognition, which was fine by the priest. Father Paul waved and wished her a good morning as he breezed by. Luke's office door popped open as Father Paul approached. Luke must have been watching the cameras.

"Coffee?" Luke asked by way of greeting. He had a small 4-cup pot steaming away on his left, and he'd turned his back to the security cameras to face Father Paul warily.

"Actually, yeah, that sounds great. I had a late night," Father Paul answered, trying to be natural. He assumed the only other chair in the office, a swivel desk chair too flattened to sit in for long periods. The priest tossed his fancy kickball flyer on the desk, mildly proud of himself for the design work, while Luke poured two fresh mugs.

"I heard about your adventures last night," Luke opened the proverbial can of worms and handed over a steaming mug of java.

Father Paul wiggled uncomfortably in his worn-out chair, trying to settle into it. There was no cushion to settle into. "I think Detective Dzielski already made his point. My role is one of healing, not investigating, and I understand that. I guess I just needed to know that someone was working on solving the case. The newspapers made it sound like the police were badly mishandling things. I apologize for coloring outside the lines." He finished sardonically and took a loud slurp of coffee.

Luke gave an assessing look that Father Paul interpreted roughly to mean, *We both know that a lot more happened last night, but okay.* "Fair enough. What's this?" Luke asked, picking up the flyer. He read the whole thing once, then his eyes ran back over particular lines here and there, taking a deep breath along the way. Then he set down the flyer and pulled out a red Sharpie. "Who edits your bulletins?" he asked without diplomacy.

"I do them myself." Father Paul really needed to learn how to take charge of conversations, he observed. "I meant to apologize about how badly I misjudged things yesterday and how I treated Don—."

"You want to make it up to him?" Luke interrupted, looking up from the flyer. "He needs help with his marriage. He's been spending so much time on watch, his wife thinks he's having an affair. He only tells her that he's volunteering at church, doing Knights' business. She threw him out yesterday not long after he watched you leave town," Luke narrated matter-of-factly, then resumed intently crossing things out, drawing arrows, and generally rewriting the kickball league flyer. Without meeting Father Paul's eyes, he spun around to face his computer and typed his entirely new advertisement.

In his limited experience, Father Paul had learned to let people express their gifts and passions, so if Luke had a passion for outstanding flyers, he would find himself assigned to this task frequently. A sadistic mental voice gloated, *That will teach him*. He hushed that voice.

Meanwhile, Father Paul knew he had a gift for healing marriages, and Don's was in trouble. It was a very bad sign that trust had broken down. Critical, in fact.

"Why doesn't Don just tell her the truth?" Father Paul asked.

"He doesn't want to place her in danger," was Luke's obvious reply. The avid flyer-maker hadn't paused in his labors to answer.

Of course... Father Paul thought. "You really think people are safer not knowing what to watch out for? You're an army of four," he attacked drily. "I don't know what you're waiting for, but whatever it is, the more eyes you have looking for it, the safer we all are."

Luke did turn around now. “I hear you, but it’s Don’s wife. It’s his decision. My wife knows, obviously,” Luke shrugged and turned back to his task.

Father Paul had to keep reminding himself that Luke and Bonnie were married. He was still having trouble putting them together in his mind. Luke was an usher and money counter, so Bonnie never sat with him at Mass or said goodbye to Father Paul after Mass with Luke next to her. She was very busy as school principal, so most of the time Father Paul interacted with her, she was in charge of her own domain that had nothing to do with Luke, just as the grocery store had nothing to do with her. These two seemed to know what was going on in each others’ lives without ever spending time together. It was weird or impressive. Father Paul was still considering that.

Luke added almost as an afterthought, “There might be more to it than that, though. Don doesn’t trust his wife to keep quiet about what she knows. Here’s how he put it. In the Navy, there were some guys who could tell their wives everything, how long they’d be at sea and where they were going. Other guys knew their wives wouldn’t stay quiet, so those wives were the last to know everything. Don’s wife was good at hosting, and that’s great for an officer’s wife. He just couldn’t ever trust her with information. Don is nothing if not dedicated to a mission. And I can’t spare him. I wish I could.” Luke said it as though he’d been thinking over the problem and couldn’t find the way out.

“You’re a good friend,” Father Paul observed.

"Your flyer is done. We're hanging it here?" Luke asked, effectively shutting down the compliment.

"If you don't mind, yes."

"Let's do it. I can donate some grilling meat and other food to get us started. After that, maybe we can tell people it's a potluck," Luke reasoned.

Gliding past the use of the word, "we", Father Paul asked, "Why don't we just start it out as a potluck? Put that on the flyer."

Luke shook his head. "No, let them come have fun once first. Once they're hooked, we'll ask for a little more effort."

Father Paul asked whether Luke was sure, and Luke said he was. Something important wasn't being said. Luke was done snipping between the little tear-offs at the bottom of the flyer. He got up, presumably to hang the flyer on the bulletin board out front, where he would dismiss Father Paul. Father Paul stayed in his seat staring straight ahead.

"What kind of thing is Don's wife likely to volunteer for around the church?" Father Paul asked.

"Funeral meals," Luke answered without missing a beat.

Well, Father Paul hoped no one was about to die, so that was out. "Anything else?" He was looking for something regular, at least weekly, for her to do.

Luke paused towering over Father Paul's chair. "There was a bazaar once that she spent a lot of time putting together. Come to think of it, Don and his wife did a lot together that week or two beforehand. She told him where to move things… He's older now, though," Luke thought aloud.

"How much money did you make at the last bazaar?" Internally cringing at the thought of turning a church into a marketplace, having visions of Jesus overturning tables, and not allowing himself to think about the loudness and general chaos of such an event, Father Paul was only considering the idea as a possible remedy for Don's marriage.

Luke named a figure that was a good start on a new roof, and Father Paul was sold. "That was about five years ago, so people probably have more stuff to donate now." Luke was mentally tabulating a new sum.

"That's good enough. Have Don tell her that he's been working on—."

"They're not on speaking terms," Luke cut off Father Paul.

"Right. I'll just ask her if she has the time to help the church out again like she did last time there was a bazaar, tell her it's about the roof…" Father Paul decided.

And that's more or less how the phone conversation went. Maybe Don's wife regretted throwing him out, or maybe she saw an opportunity to prove to Don that she knew he wasn't really at the church. Maybe it had nothing to do with Don, actually. Married couples were complicated, Father Paul realized. Anyway, she seemed pleased at the invitation, and she'd be glad to organize and price things for the bazaar. She had a few ladies who would help her, too.

"Great!" Father Paul exclaimed, genuinely happy to hear that he could have as little to do with the event as possible. "I'm sorry Don's been stolen away from you so often. I'm trying to get away from asking the Knights to do *everything* but they're always here when something new comes up. Maybe this is something you and he can work on together." He was pulling things out of an over-stuffed closet to get access to hula hoops for an icebreaker at the teen's Confirmation preparation class that evening. There was a little crash as an ironing board fell out.

After the briefest hesitation, "Sounds good," was her reply. "I should get going right now, but I'll work on this starting maybe the week before you want to hold it. We need to give people about three weeks to drop off donations and then I need one week to sort and price things. We'll hold it in the basement, obviously, since it's already cold outside."

Father Paul named the date, a Saturday one month out, and they moved forward.

In those weeks, Father Paul focused on the well-being of the parish, especially the girls and their families. Parish routine began to take a defined shape for the priest. Luke took over as editor of Sacred Heart's bulletin, prominently featuring the upcoming bazaar and the need for donations, and the man had created commendable flyers the whole town would see at the grocery store bulletin board. Healing the girls and their families was a tough and fulfilling job, and yes, Father Paul had found his stride.

As the weeks went by, Father Paul made a point of

giving Don and the other Knights little jobs to do around the church, making it easier for them to do guard duty. Only one or two Knights would ever be available at a time, and they made jobs last as long as possible so that no one would have to keep watch from a car parked on the street during that time. They preferred to be outside, so they cleaned gutters, did yard work, washed windows, removed a tree stump, and eventually started to find their own projects to accomplish. It wasn't a perfect cover for Don, but since he wasn't living with his wife, she'd hardly know how often he wasn't at Willie's.

Willie was widowed, so having someone live with him was an adjustment sometimes joked about during money counting. Underneath the joke, Father Paul realized that Willie was a little more chipper, as if he'd been suffering from loneliness before and no one had noticed. Something would have to be done for him once Don patched things up with his wife. Father Paul put that on his mental list of things to do.

Meanwhile, Don and his wife were on the same team in kickball. Luke had probably engineered that somehow. He seemed to be keeping an eye on the pair from his station at the grill. Kickball was every Saturday morning, and the league grew each week. Mayor Bartoli visited one crisp morning to see what was what. The mayor wore a purple skirt suit with matching purple pumps. Shaking his hand, her long red nails scraped him lightly and caught his eye. "It's wonderful to see Mr. Coppini here as well. He's someone with whom you ought to be acquainted,

Reverend," the mayor said with precise diction. She had already informed Father Paul that he was an emerging leader, a title that he assumed he had earned by captaining the kickball league, and he didn't care enough to ask.

"Brad is a parishioner at Sacred Heart, so I do have the pleasure of his acquaintance," Father Paul responded.

"Oh wonderful!" Her overly made-up eyes widened in astonishment that her emerging leaders had met without her help. "You are gifted at drawing the community together," she continued with surprised eyes, "and Brad is a pillar of generosity. Our community is that much stronger, since you two know one another. Did you know that he donated the beautiful Greek sculpture in the town center?"

Father Paul hadn't known, and he hoped that admitting it would help the mayor feel in control again. "Is that supposed to be Midas?" he asked.

"Oh, I don't know exactly, but it is beautiful, isn't it?" she said dismissively.

"It adds a certain touch, yes."

Mayor Bartoli nodded in serious agreement with his observation, and Father Paul noticed that there was glitter in her green eye shadow. At first, he wanted to help her get rid of it, because he hated glitter. Once it was out of the can, it got everywhere, like anthrax. He realized just in time that the glitter was in the eye shadow on purpose.

Mayor Bartoli went on to inform Father Paul, "Mr. Coppini is also on the community action board that allocates money to the women's shelter, the men's transitional housing, and nearly every other local charitable organization that the churches aren't running. It's *wonderful* to see the possibility of a partnership among you. I'm so glad to hear it."

There was little else to talk about besides the game, and that appeared to bore the mayor, who hadn't dressed to play. She simply gazed over the kickball field like a general on horseback surveying a battlefield. Father Paul had wandered too far away to stop it, when a kickball listed the mayor's way and gently bonked her in the eye. She took a step back in surprise, and Father Paul came running to make sure she was alright. The mayor said something was wrong with her contact, so she needed to go home. Apologetically and with assurances that she did not need or want help getting home, she waved off Father Paul, who held the kickball with the glittery slime of her eye shadow across it. The tenacious eyeshadow would not wipe off in the grass. Just like anthrax.

Father Paul wanted to think positive and convince himself that someone important had just affirmed him. She had called him an 'emerging leader', and she encouraged him to work with Brad. Baffled at her total ignorance of Greek mythology, Father Paul decided he was still inspired enough to strike up a conversation with Brad about whatever kind of partnership might be beneficial to the larger community. Maybe it would lead to that long hoped for dinner at his parishioner's house.

The game ended just after ten o'clock, as usual, and Father Paul looked around for Brad. Brad was gone, Lisa was gone, and half the Knights were gone, too. When had that happened? Father Paul jogged home from the village park to shower and get ready for a session with Renee. He already had Dolores' notes from working with the teen in school this week, and Dolores would use this time to work with Renee's parents. The church bazaar would open during that session, and the whole village knew about it. He was not looking forward to dropping in on the bazaar once it was busy that afternoon, but putting in a little facetime was part of the job.

Before he went to the rectory, though, Father Paul jogged up the front church steps and down to the basement to feed the goldfish. Someone had dropped off a huge tank filled with hundreds of goldfish just a few days before the bazaar, thinking people would take the fish home in sandwich bags and buy what they needed at a pet store. Father Paul wasn't sure about the idea, but he was willing to give it a chance. After all, it was a donation, and the parish could expect to make money from it. All he had to do was feed the fish once per day.

He switched on the lights and let his eyes wander appreciatively over a room of perfectly sorted and tagged donations. The bazaar team had done an incredible job. Father Paul more than trusted them to open shop while he was busy with Renee.

Poised to pour the fish food into the tank, he froze and simply stared. Every single fish was floating on the top of the water. *Oxygen*, he gradually realized, letting his arm drop to his side. There wasn't enough oxygen in the water for hundreds of fish to survive for several days. He realized he was learning a lot about breathing lately. Between the fish and Jeremy, breathing was becoming thematic, really. Somehow, he'd have to find a way to use this as an allegory for the spiritual life and giving room for the Holy Spirit to breathe in a believer.

He sighed at his phone ringing. He had actually turned in some work journals to Father Bob, and they were working out an uneasy truce. But the caller this time was Jeremy, to his happy surprise. "Hey buddy, how's it going?" he greeted his friend.

"Hey, not too bad. Listen, I was praying and had an epiphany about Renee that may or may not be useful to you." Jeremy and Paul talked almost every day now, because of the near-death experience. They were using Father Paul's ministry of healing and Father Jeremy's gift of powerful intercessory prayer as excuses, but they were really checking to make sure the other guy was still alive.

"Lay it on me," Father Paul enthused. The dead fish were already behind him. He had priestly work to do. He switched off the light and jogged away to pay better attention to Jeremy, leaving the bazaar in the very capable hands of his volunteers.

Chapter Eleven

Father Paul pulled warm blueberry muffins out of the pan and arranged them on a plate. He had only made half a dozen, one to spare once everyone showed up. He had timed it just right, once again filling the house with the aroma of baking to put his visitors at ease. Dolores was explaining certain notes on Renee's session during school this week, while she poured hot water into the teapot. Weeks ago, she had assumed responsibility for the task of making tea. It was part of their ritual now, three times per week, once per seriously injured girl and her family.

Father Paul's mind was still a little stuck on what Father Jeremy had told him. Jeremy said, "Renee needs to feel beautiful." Father Paul's excuse not to tell her the obvious fact was his scatter-brained assumption that every woman paid for her body must already realize that she's objectively beautiful. It didn't make any sense that she would need reassurance. But of course, the truth was that Father Paul was afraid to say anything, because it could lead to accusations or just plain weird scenarios. What if she thought him interested in her in a way other than fatherly, exactly as Father Max had been? The whole thing was too risky.

Give me a sign, he prayed, as he retrieved the floral butter dish from the refrigerator placing it alongside the matching plate of muffins.

"Oh, and just one other thing, Father," Dolores interrupted his thoughts with a slower cadence. He hadn't been paying attention, he realized with embarrassment. "Renee's parents thought it was important to mention last time we met here that Renee had pulled her cheerleading uniform out of the closet for a few hours one day. She laid it out on her bed. Then, without saying anything to them, she tucked it away again. They tried to talk to her about it, but she became very defensive and shut down. They felt certain there was something important to it, but they wanted our help to sort it out. She shut down for me, too, in our session," Dolores told him.

'Mysterious ways' just were just a nasty rumor about God, not a reality for Father Paul. He thought he had that cheerleading outfit scenario sorted out already. *Nice sign*, he prayed silently.

Dolores and Father Paul discussed rescheduling one of the girls and her family to later next week. Father Paul handled it patiently, but he really wanted to put his fist through something. The girl's parents were so busy, it actually made sense that they hadn't noticed anything odd about her schedule while she was driving out of town several nights each week. What frustrated Father Paul most was the fact that they still didn't see their part in the problem. Dolores had been right about the girls needing a spiritual father as part of their healing, each girl for her own reason. The knock came at the front door right on time. Renee's parents were ready to do some work.

Renee's parents greeted him first, the teen hiding behind them as per protocol. But she was putting on a show of making eye contact and smiling just a little too brightly. That always meant something was close to the surface and ready to come out, as if her emotional injuries were splinters that worked their way out, giving tweezers a place to grip and pull. Father Paul wasn't worried, since he already had confirmation of the issue he was dealing with. God would help him say what was needed in the right way.

About to close the door behind her, he accidentally gasped instead. She turned to meet his eyes and caught him staring at the top of her forehead just at the hairline. He looked down to read her expression, realizing too late that his own must be horrified. He tried to rearrange it to no avail. Renee's parents and Dolores were watching now, too.

Father Paul cleared his throat and broke the silence. "What happened to the top of your head, Renee?"

She flushed red. "Nothing!" She managed to sound insulted.

"It's bruised black and blue, Renee."

Her father strode over and tilted her head forward so he could see the top of it. She had the mass of dark curls pulled back into a messy bun, so there was no part. Father Paul could only see the sinister bruises at the edge of her hairline where her makeup hadn't quite done the job.

Renee's father could see enough to know that Father Paul was right. "Take this bun out," he ordered in a charged whisper.

Father Paul felt something inside Renee tear open as she sloppily moved to obey. Her face twisted as she tried not to cry. She was emotionally naked to them. All her self-hatred was exposed for them to gawk at as a group. Father Paul gently stepped between Renee and her father, who was forced to take two steps back. He hid Renee solidly behind his back. "That's enough," Father Paul said.

"Enough?" her father asked. "Enough for what? We don't even know who did this."

Father Paul thought it was obvious enough, but he asked without turning around, "Renee, who did that to you?" He gave her a pause, but he didn't really expect an answer before he pushed her a little. "Someone at school? A classmate? Did the men from the hotel come back?"

That got him a warning look from Dolores and equally strong reactions from Renee's parents. Dolores shook her head to warn him away from that subject.

Since there was more silence behind him, he continued, "Should we be looking for a new boyfriend? A teacher at school? Who?" He figured she would fold at the threat of a witch hunt. She never thought she was worth the trouble and wouldn't want to call more attention to herself.

"I did it myself,' she admitted defiantly.

Her parents gaped at that by staring at Father Paul's sternum as if to see through him. Father Paul was very grateful that Renee couldn't see them, while they recovered their senses. Her anger was protecting her for the moment, but she didn't need this image of their shock in her mind.

"Why would you do that?" her mother asked, truly baffled. She hadn't seen the bruises yet. Her foot wavered, as she assessed Father Paul's seriousness about hiding Renee from her. Underneath all that reserve, there was a protective mother wanting to do something, and unsure of what to do. Father Paul wondered what was keeping the woman from just being herself. Humans were mysterious, and God was the straightforward one, Father Paul observed.

Renee sniffled, and Father Paul was sure she was putting her response into words that would hurt her parents. He quickly exchanged a glance with Dolores. She nodded in return.

Father Paul offered, "I'll see if I can sort that out with her. Let's split into our usual groups for now. Be sure to take a muffin and some tea." He gestured solicitously toward the kitchen, as though this was a normal day in the woods for him.

Renee's parents accepted his calm facade as reassuring. They followed Dolores, leaving their daughter in professional hands. They picked up a muffin and a little teacup each. It wasn't that they didn't love their daughter. They couldn't imagine where to start finding out what she needed or how to help her. Dolores kindly pointed out the couch that faced Renee's parents away from Father Paul and Renee. And for now, that was best.

Father Paul faced the girl, unable not to see the top of her head from his viewpoint.

He could break the ice by making a joke of it, but then she would think that callousness was acceptable. He had to teach her discipline. "A wall?" he asked.

"Door frame," she answered.

He nodded. "Are you hurt anywhere else?"

She looked guiltily at him.

"Other bruises, cuts, burns…"

"Bruises on my legs. That's all." Defensively.

He relaxed. "Okay. What set you off?"

She shrugged.

He sighed, led her to the kitchen, and settled into one of the bar stools at the kitchen counter. As Renee followed suit, the dark bruises seemed to wash away in the warm glow of sunlight through the east-facing kitchen window.

"It is the case that you did this on your own, right?" He had to be sure. Father Paul slid a muffin to her and took one for himself. They both hunched forward over the counter, picking at their muffins, crumbling them over frilly little flowered plates someone's great grandmother probably donated to the rectory.

She nodded, this time as if she were afraid of being rejected, not defiant but vulnerable.

"Did anyone make fun of you? Bring up something they shouldn't have? Did something happen?" he probed and waited. "Lay it on me."

He let the silence stretch on, deciding it was just as uncomfortable for her as it was for him.

Eventually, she shook her head.

Well, that was something positive, he decided. At least people were behaving decently towards her. That alone was a testament to the faculty and students at Sacred Heart's little school.

But then, if nothing set her off, all this rage was residual from her time in that hotel room. Beating your head against a wall—or a door frame—was supposed to be a figure of speech. What had to happen to people for this to become a potential relief to their rage?

Somehow, the story about these girls had lost its depth for Father Paul. In the weeks of talking about it, it had become routine. Life had happened, and everyone's lives produced scars along the way, some deeper than others. These had come to seem like admittedly deep scars, but not so deep as to be categorically different from what everyone else was going through.

This was all the reminder Father Paul needed. What these girls had been through was in a category all its own, and it had driven Renee a little bit insane. It had broken her. His own rage surged like a mushroom cloud. He used the anger to help him focus on Renee.

She was studying her fingernails, face puckered up as if she had swallowed a lemon. Her muffin was destroyed past the point of being fun to pick at, and none of it had made its way into her mouth.

"Feeling a bit depressed?" he asked, trying to get her to talk. Maybe she would talk about depression instead of anger.

Yes, she was depressed, she nodded, but she would not be talking about it. She didn't even look up from her ripped fingernails.

"You know depression is just anger turned against yourself." He let that sink in. "You were right to be angry at every man who sold or bought time with you. They were committing a crime, and what they did was abusive. But at some point, you must have decided not to be angry with them. You decided that it was all your fault instead. All the anger you should have felt toward them, you turned against yourself instead. Now why would someone as smart as you do something so silly?" he wondered aloud.

"That's not what happened," she said loudly enough that Dolores had to redirect Renee's parents back into their conversation. Renee stared down Father Paul. "That's just stupid."

"Fine, that's not what happened," he allowed. "I was wrong."

"You're only saying that because you think I'm going to agree with you eventually. You think you're so smart," she accused.

"I don't know what it's like to go through what you've been through. But I am listening, if you want to tell me about it."

She thought about it and puckered up with her lemon-swallowing expression. "Nope, I don't."

Great, he thought, realizing he was going to have to push her again. He tapped into how she was feeling and made an educated guess about what she was reliving in her memories. “It seems like being forced into having sex with men at random would be infuriating. Maybe you felt so angry you couldn’t think in words anymore. All you wanted to do was spit and bite and claw like an animal.”

One of her eyebrows kicked up in disbelief, maybe because his imagery was a little over-the-top. It was, in fact, exactly how she felt though, according to his emotional radar. *Emo-dar!* Father Paul was proud to have a name for it, finally. So, he reasoned, maybe Renee couldn’t believe he’d guessed right once again. Or perhaps she wanted him to doubt himself and stop picking at the wound. Her eye roll was the convincing gesture. He was so close to the truth, so close to blowing open her anger and helping her get it out, she was desperate to stop him. No one wants to know what their anger will do when it comes out.

“So, what happened? One night some guy noticed how angry you were and said something to your handlers? Did you get hurt because of that?” Now, he was blindly guessing. She took the bait anyway.

“No, my best friends got hurt. And he decided he didn’t want me, because I threw up on him. He reeked like burned Doritos, alcohol, and something plasticky. I remember it exactly. The smell was coming from his skin—I kid you not. And he stank so bad, I threw up. You know what? I was so pissed at... where I was in life and what I had to do, I aimed for him.” She giggled a little maniacally. “I actually aimed at him. I think he knew I did it on purpose. He made this huge deal out of it, like he was any dirtier." She turned her face away in disgust. Perhaps she realized she'd said more than she'd intended. She had in fact paid for being angry.

"Then what happened?" Father Paul asked.

"They gave him two freebies to make up for it. My *friends.* They both had to sleep with him, and I got to watch the videos," her voice hauled an armload of sarcasm. "But first, they made me lick up the vomit that landed on the sheets. I hurried to eat it. They threatened to burn the others. I guess they were probably lying. They threatened to burn me first, but I guess I didn't mind that as much. Maybe I wanted to die. Maybe I hoped they would get carried away and just kill me. I think I laughed at them when they threatened me." She shrugged to punctuate several of those thoughtful comments. She was completely calm, detached.

"What did you tell yourself about all of that? It's important that you try to remember it precisely, whether it was words or an intuition. Take your time," he coached her.

"What do you mean?" she asked.

"Did you … learn anything new about... how you rank in the world?" He struggled to find a way of wording it that would make sense to her, even though it was wrong. It was exactly what he wanted her to unlearn today.

She did her best to answer. "My friends were good at this, professionals. I was just trash, made to eat my own vomit. Dogs do that sometimes, you know. Eat their vomit," she clarified.

He nodded. He was pretty sure that was in Scripture somewhere, and that was the only reason he knew about dogs eating vomit. Proverbs? *Typical Catholic*, he chastised himself. Getting back to the young woman in front of him, he tried to sum it up, "So you thought you weren't even good enough to be a prostitute. Subhuman. More on the level of dogs."

She closed her eyes and tears rolled out. "It's true."

"No." He was firm, not accusatory. That got her attention. "It's what you had to tell yourself to get the anger under control and keep going. You *always* knew it was wrong."

He could almost hear her wondering, *Did I know that was wrong?* She stared at him sidelong, her eyes were locked on his. There was a burst of laughter from the other room, but even that didn't disturb Renee. The volume from that room had been gradually increasing to a loud rumble. Dolores knew this was going to be a heavy session, so she kept hers lighter and distracted. Renee's parents would be emotionally available to support her when this was over. Dolores really was a great teammate, Father Paul recognized anew.

He started in again. "You couldn't afford to be angry anymore, not at your handlers or at any man who came to you afterwards, ever, because your friends were threatened. You turned your anger against yourself on purpose to protect your friends. You even elevated those girls above yourself while you were at it. They were 'good prostitutes', and you were below them. You protected them even within your own thoughts. You destroyed yourself for them." He let her think about that for a few seconds. "There's something noble in all of that, something very good and heroic." *Even though it was twisted and horrible and very, very wrong,* he finished in his mind.

Even in the most evil circumstances, people were always trying to sacrifice themselves like Christ, Father Paul mused to himself. *Our hearts are restless until they rest in You, Lord,* he prayed while he waited.

He knew the moment the weight lifted from her, not just because of his sixth sense. Visibly, her shoulders straightened, her eyes brightened, and she was ready to do some more forgiving. They'd been at this for weeks, and she'd already learned the joy of letting go. She was going to have to forgive these men many, many times, but she was healing deeper each time she dug in and decided that they didn't owe her anything. The debt was behind her, not on her shoulders. Those men could not repay what they had taken from her anyway. He walked her through the familiar process, and she followed step by step. There was no more resistance this morning.

Forgiving herself naturally led into asking God's forgiveness in the sacrament of Confession. While she recited the Act of Contrition, Father Paul catalogued what to tell Dolores of the session—omitting the confession, obviously—so that she could follow up on Renee's mental health. A doctor's visit for medication might be helpful. He would leave that problem for Dolores.

At the end of their time together, Father Jeremy's

epiphany pushed itself to the forefront of Father Paul's mind. He had to say it, but he really didn't want to. The words burst forth from him when he couldn't hold them in any longer. "You know you're a beautiful young woman, Renee. I hope that you'll find the perfect man for you when the time is right. Later on, when you're older," he added nervously.

She cocked her head to the side. "How did you know? I didn't tell you they said that."

"Said what?" he asked. She was looking at him as if he had three heads.

She swallowed. "They told me I was ugly that night. That was the worst part," she said with a dismissive hand gesture and diverted her eyes to the floor. Clearly, she was serious, but Father Paul couldn't believe it.

"Not eating vomit?" he asked and wished he hadn't.

"Really." She met his eyes again. "I was naked and sitting in vomit, and then they made me eat it. That was so disgusting, I nearly threw up again. They taught me how to hold it down, though. That was the point, I guess. You can control whether you throw up, you know," she informed him.

He was speechless. Teens thrive on shocking adults, he reminded himself, unable to discern how she might be exaggerating this particular story.

"You can, even if someone smells like burned Doritos and a whole lot of other nastiness, you just swallow it back down and move on. They only threatened my friends to make me learn that." She took a moment to find her bearings, since she had veered off the topic. Remembering where she'd been, she continued, "Anyway, it just seemed so obvious when they told me I was ugly. Even now, I feel like that's what people see when they look at me. The kind of girl who sits naked in her own vomit and eats it, because that's what she deserves. Stupid, right? They were wearing masks, so they might be ugly, too. I shouldn't have listened to them, but I can't get it out of my head. Their little snickers—the whole thing just keeps playing in my head. Sometimes I can't get it to stop."

"Well, I want you to know you're beautiful. You can jump back into that cheerleader uniform anytime you want to. If you want to. You're the same young lady who wore it well before this happened to you."

She was thinking about it. Father Paul could practically hear the gears churning in her head. She only ever believed she was ugly because she had turned her anger against herself. Now that the anger was gone, there was nothing holding this lie in place. She didn't have to bother staying stuck in that moment anymore. Her unraveled mind reknit itself a little more, honestly perceiving the world and herself and her place in the world. She was going to be alright eventually. Stronger than before.

"Take a look at photos of yourself from a year or two ago, especially when you were dressed up for a dance or something. I think you'll see that you were always beautiful. But the way you feel about yourself does change the way people see you. Take an honest selfie before you start looking at those photos, and then take another afterwards.

You'll see the difference without trying to smile for the camera. Will you do that sometime this week?"

She was curious, and she nodded that she would. "Thank you, Father."

"Of course." Father Paul called out to see whether anyone wanted the last muffin. No one did, as usual, but this was as good a signal as any that the time was up.

At the door, Father Paul delicately suggested, "Will you be visiting the hospital next, perhaps for a head CT or something?" Renee had seemed coordinated and coherent, but he hadn't asked much about the timing of the injuries or her symptoms afterwards. And it would be good for Renee to see how much her family cared, even if she screeched about not wanting to go.

Her parents consulted one another briefly, all comments in the affirmative. They turned to Renee. "Fine," she shrugged at them, feigning indifference. If he hadn't had his sixth sense, he'd have no idea she was flattered. She needed this attention so badly, he'd have to plan something to prevent her making a habit of seeking attention this way.

Father Paul gave the parents a warm, approving smile and nod. They had done well. This had been a homerun of a session, even if there was so much more to be done.

Chapter Twelve

"I NEED TO TALK to you." A female voice from nowhere pierced through Father Paul's distracted thoughts and brought him back into the loud, crowded church bazaar. Father Paul found it frankly awful, and if it wasn't his job, he wouldn't even be standing here. Who thought these events were fun?

Every single person around him did. They haggled over prices. They carried armloads of used clothing for every member of the family or boxes of books or little glass decorations. And still, they *ooooohed* and *ahhhhhhed* over more newfound treasures. These people were crazy. *Why didn't they just shop online like normal people?* Father Paul wondered. Maybe he was irritated about something else, though. He couldn't hear himself think. He would never sort out any thoughts or feelings while standing in the midst of this cacophony.

The woman caught his jacket sleeve and led him out the side door and up the concrete stairway to ground level, away from the door. Thankful for the relative calm as well as the cool, crisp air, he pulled himself together for confession or counseling or whatever this was going to be. Tuning into her, he quickly realized that this woman was angry. She appeared to be scowling *at* him, and for the life of him, he couldn't especially remember interacting with her before. What on earth could he have done?

"I just want to tell you something about how you come across. Do you know I just waved at you? I was standing right in front of you, and I said *hello* three times." She waited.

Father Paul took a deep breath in preparation to say something and shake his head in the negative. The short, raven-haired, provocatively dressed, and entirely too energetic woman cut him off first. Father Paul didn't know her name, but he'd seen her often since he'd moved to Limekiln, as though she'd been waiting for the perfect moment to attack.

"Okay, so I've been talking to other people, and there are a lot of people besides me who have noticed this about you. Maybe you have something against all of us or you just think you're so much better. I don't know. Whatever it is that's wrong with you, you need to get it under control, because it's not *welcoming*. I can't 'invite friends' to this church," she made finger quotes in the air with shaking hands, "because they'd have to face you at some point. What would I tell them if they asked me why you didn't notice them saying *hello*? I just simply wanted to say *hello*. Can you hear how sad that is? And it's not just me. Everybody is talking about it."

The fact that she'd talked about him behind his back and stirred up trouble beyond this confrontation did not endear her to Father Paul. Still, this was a complaint

Father Paul had gotten before, and it was a problem for people who didn't know him. He was about to ask her forgiveness and ask her to presume innocence in people generally, when she cut him off again.

"People were looking at me just now, wondering what I was going to do about you. I told them I'd straighten this out. So let me tell you, it's not just that you ignore people. Your homilies are *so* insulting. I'm a good person, okay?" Her face had been flushed with anger already, but now she began to pace like a lioness trying to escape a cage. "Sometimes a walk in the woods is just as spiritual for me as going to Mass." Finger pointing. "I do what I need to for me. Your comments about 'serious sin'," more finger quotes in the air, "are not appropriate or in touch with this town. You don't have kids. You have no idea what it's like to have things going on outside of this building."

He trained his face to go blank at that last comment. According to Father Bob, he'd been neglecting this building and the people in it. A teenager, not bone-thin like her mother but slightly heavier set and somehow permanently pouty, barked out from a van parked down the street, "Mom!"

Completely ignoring her daughter's tone of voice, the woman sighed, resigned that Father Paul was incorrigible. "My daughter is waiting for me. I guess this conversation will have to wait. For another time. Or whatever." She seemed so put upon and tired and perhaps enslaved to her daughter, Father Paul truly did feel sorry for her. Another person for his prayer list. He didn't know her name, but he wasn't going to ask. God would know who he was praying about.

As she stomped off, he realized he was outside! And alone! Hooray!

The heavy metal door popped open again. "Father, have you got a second?" It was Luke this time, and Father Paul wasn't sure he could take any more. "Are you okay?" Luke asked. Father Paul's face must have given something away.

"Of course," Father Paul corrected himself, assembling his warmest, most paternal facial expression.

Luke's glance swept in the direction Father Paul had been facing. He zeroed in on the woman snapping her van door shut and snarling at her daughter. "Oh, Tina blew up at you?" he guessed.

"Yes, it appears that I'm arrogant, and she had had her fill of it," Father Paul said blowing out a sigh. Some of the words she had spat at him started to niggle at his brain, making him wonder how much truth there was to them.

Luke shrugged. "I can't remember what she called me, but I made her mad once by refusing to put the Knights on parking duty for Christmas and Easter."

"It's street parking," Father Paul said stupefied.

"Exactly. But she heard of a church in Maryland where the parking lot was *the* big issue, and they flourished after getting parking lot ministers. Lazy! That's what she called me!" Luke smiled with amusement at the memory, just as the woman jerkily backed into the car behind her with the van's plastic bumper. She did not seem to notice. She was still bickering heatedly with her daughter.

"Anyway," Luke started again, "I wondered if you wanted to get away and do something this afternoon with the guys. The Knights have a real adventure planned, and we could use the extra hands. It's time-sensitive."

Father Paul's excitement was instantaneous. Echoing Luke's usual phrase, he said, "Let's do it." He couldn't wait to do something about this case! The anger stirred up during Renee's session was still smoldering hours later. He didn't want it to abate until he had done something productive with it. He felt like being a little reckless, actually, and he couldn't wait to find out what Luke's plan was. Father Paul didn't have one.

An elderly woman cracked open the side door and called sweetly for "Luke darling," who put on a charming smile and immediately began taking backwards half-steps in her direction.

"Okay, Ethel," he shouted to her. She beamed back at him and waited in the doorway.

To Father Paul, Luke stage whispered, "Great! We're meeting at Don's house. Two o'clock, assuming the bazaar ends on time. We'll get you back here just in time to hear Confessions."

"What?" Ethel asked, obviously hard of hearing.

"What do you need, Ethel?" Luke shouted. He looked to Father Paul while Ethel went on about needing a big strong man to move something.

Father Paul sneaked into the empty sanctuary and prayed before the Blessed Sacrament in the tabernacle. His eyes wandered, though, to the newly restored statues of the Sacred Heart of Jesus and the Immaculate Heart of Mary. One by one, the Stations of the Cross were returning to their spots, vibrant and intense again. The artist was doing a phenomenal job. Father Paul remembered Brad, the donor who made this tabernacle possible, and his troubled marriage. He thanked God for this time of intimate prayer, and then he started his list of petitions beginning with Brad and Lisa, then the crazy lady what's-her-name—oh yes, Tina!—with no driving skills, then Renee and the other two girls, their families, the police, and on and on and on. He placed each burden solidly on Jesus' shoulders. Each one was too heavy for Father Paul to carry, and the load of them had been crushing.

It occurred to him that the nasty confrontation at the bazaar had been a favor to him, spurring him to unburden himself in prayer. It also occurred to him to wonder why Luke was suddenly inviting him to help investigate the case. There was something fishy about that, and Father Paul wasn't entirely clear about who to trust yet. He asked God for help discerning that, too. Receiving no answer in prayer, he decided he would ask Luke about his change of heart.

He got his answer some hours later, huddled with the Knights in Don's attic—his wife hadn't changed the locks or filed any paperwork to keep him out—for the Halloween decorations.

"My wife's birthday is October twenty-ninth, so she loves Halloween, scary stories, the costumes, the candy, all of it," Don explained in a rush. So, the plan had nothing to do with the investigation, Father Paul realized. The attic was crammed full of boxes and boxes labeled "Halloween" to carry down to the porch. There were also some new items in Don's car, and finally there would be reappropriated pieces like the wheelbarrow in the shed that became decorations just for the month of October. "I'll show you where everything goes. We just have to be done when Bonnie texts Luke."

Bonnie was with the ladies cleaning up from the bazaar, and her task was to keep eyes on Don's wife in case she tried to slip home early. Father Paul estimated they had less than two hours to do a full days' work. He debated whether to comment on the irony of using something Pope Benedict had called "dangerous" and "occult" to patch up a marriage, but pastoral sensitivity won out. He would point out the pagan qualities of a macabre Halloween celebrated sans hallowed souls some other year.

His first task was arranging a broken plastic skeleton so that it looked like it had been buried in a wheelbarrow that was filled with dirt. Presumably, the skeleton was digging its way out now. It grinned up at him, limbs splayed everywhere, looking uncertain but happy. Father Paul asked for and received from Don a plastic flower that belonged in some other holiday's decoration box, which he set upright in the dirt over what would have been the skeleton's heart, and he arranged the skeleton's hand around it. The skeleton's grin took on new meaning. *Yes!* Father Paul was thrilled to have repurposed just one decoration.

Josh and Willie were stretching a web over the porch

railing. A huge, wiry-legged spider with purple sequins covering its posterior waited to be tangled up in it. Father Paul asked Don to get him some letters, and Don had the good fortune of finding a string of "Happy Birthday" letters in purple. They arranged the letters across the web, and they worked the corners of a few letters into the webbing. The spider sat so that it peered down at the letters. It looked good. Father Paul nixed the notion when they tried to add paper bats to the webbing. He was still traumatized. "Just the spider is perfect," he assured them. They pretended to believe him and moved on.

Encouraged by these feats, Father Paul made it his job to create a sweet, loving scene of morbid decorations, and he largely succeeded. He vetoed several disgusting decorations on the grounds that they couldn't be made to fit the theme of scary sweetness. "How is that going to fix Don's marriage?" he asked the Knights until it became a mantra that kept them on task. Eventually, they grumbled it with him in the style of mumbled prayer responses at Mass. Father Paul took that as a sign that they completely understood and agreed.

Luke's phone buzzed with a text. He finished packing away the sneering witch-zombie for another year before checking his phone. "Good news!" he announced. "The ladies are doing the heavy lifting. There won't be anything for us to do after counting money tomorrow afternoon." He texted something back to Bonnie as the men on the porch soberly nodded and expressed appreciation. One of them said something wryly approving about women's rights. They were getting tired.

"Would anyone like a glass of water, coffee, or something stronger?" Don offered. Everyone wanted water, and Father Paul followed Don inside to help him carry the glasses.

Something odd on the stove caught the attention of both Father Paul and Don, immediately sidetracking them. They walked over. There was a pot half-full of water with a votive candle standing tall, glowing inside it. The candle's glass casing featured a picture of Our Lady of Guadalupe on it, and there was an index card on the counter nearby. Both men shouldered in to read it.

"Blessed Mother, please pray that Don will show some sign of fighting for our marriage before this candle burns out. I will not file for divorce until then. Please show me whether my marriage can last. Amen."

The candle was about seven inches tall, and it had about one inch left to burn.

"How much time do I have to replace this one?" Don asked. Father Paul was a professional with candles, so obviously he would know.

"You don't need to, Don. The Blessed Mother is already answering this prayer. Take a look at what we just did," Father Paul said.

Don looked around, apparently gathering Father Paul's meaning from the windows. "Will she see it that way?" Don asked, unsure.

"Yes. As your parish priest, I assure you, that is exactly how women think." And that settled the matter. Neither man mentioned the candle or the amazing fire prevention techniques Don's wife had utilized when they brought the glasses of water outside.

The men made some self-congratulatory remarks. Josh received some heavy backslapping for his work setting up Cinderella's midnight scene on the roof. The carriage was a pumpkin again, and the rest of the entourage glowed in various stages of shifting back to normalcy. The extension cord reached to the porch outlet, so Don's wife would be able to light it up with ease. The ladder and a few other items still needed to be put away, but Father Paul would have to leave soon to hear confessions.

Don stammered out with difficulty, "I just want to thank you all for doing this. My bride will be so happy." Face red, he was done talking. Tears formed in his eyes. He clenched his jaw and gripped his water glass for control.

"We're all in this together," Luke told him.

With surprise, Father Paul realized that was true. "How is it that we're all here together? Who's keeping a look-out?"

Luke blinked at him for a moment. Carefully, he answered, "Someone else has it today. The person we're watching isn't in town. I'll hear about it if he leaves work early," he said pointing at the phone on his belt by way of explanation.

Father Paul racked his brain. It wasn't as though he knew everyone in town, but it certainly narrowed down the possibilities, knowing that the suspect worked out of town on a Saturday and lived in Limekiln. And it was confirmed to be a man. He should spend time with the Knights more often and see what else slipped out.

Luke might have realized his mistake. "Let's put these things away." He gestured with his eyes at the things laid out on the lawn. "Father, I know you need to run off for confessions. Thank you for coming," he said. The rest of the men said something similar, and Father Paul obeyed the dismissal. He'd found out as much as he was going to today.

Sitting in the darkened box of a confessional, praying the Divine Office and wishing someone would come to confession, he accidentally shouted, "Stupid!" His eyes shifted left and then right, as he confirmed by listening that there was no one in the sanctuary yet. No one had heard his outburst.

Who lived in Limekiln and worked out of town? The guy who owns several hotels. This wasn't new information, and he could have investigated that a long time ago. Why on earth didn't he already know the man's name? His *mother* did. He reminded himself to run a search on Father Tom's research notes instead of asking her.

Immediately after the vigil Mass, Father Paul searched for a name. When he found it, he stared at it. He searched some more and found the same name. He did a Google search for property ownership and managed to find the same man's name. Not allowing himself to feel anything yet, he put together a list of the hotels and addresses. The question was which one to visit tonight and how best to stir up trouble until it came to find him. He wanted to face this head-on. Inspiration struck.

He called Luke, found out Luke was at home, and told

Luke he needed to talk in-person. He was at Luke's door five minutes later.

Ignoring Luke's gesture of welcome to enter, Father Paul asked, "I just wondered, was it Detective Dzielski who was keeping an eye on things for us today?"

Luke's emotional response was all the confirmation he needed. Fear, protectiveness, the too urgent need to cover up something. Father Paul knew which city he was visiting—the one Dzielski worked in. There was only one affected hotel in that city.

"Tell the detective I said 'thank you'. Oh, and it was really great getting to spend time with you guys today. Thanks for having me along for the adventure," he said backing off the porch. He waved a friendly goodnight, and he was off.

"Hold up now, Father. What are you about to do?" Luke asked. "You do the wrong thing, you expose all of us."

"You don't believe that. You're trying to keep me out of harm's way. I don't want to be kept!" He had the presence of mind to stage whisper instead of shouting, but his anger was clear. Luke appeared shocked by the intensity of it. He was seeing a whole new side of his parish priest. "I'm not listening to any more hurt from those girls until I've done something about it. No more!"

"Then we go together," Luke responded simply.

"No, we don't," and Father Paul might have actually curled his lip delivering the surly response. "You have a wife and people who count on you. I'm a priest for a reason. I'm completely free to do what's needed for my people whenever it's needed. I'm going solo."

"You're wrong. Your people depend on you just like my wife depends on me. You are not going alone." Luke was immovable. "Are you going to try to leave without me, or do I have a minute to tell my wife where we'll be?"

Father Paul huffed. "Go ahead." And Father Paul waited on the porch.

When Luke reappeared with a jacket, Bonnie came to the door. "You know this is not a good choice," she stated, giving Father Paul one last chance to change his mind.

"Luke doesn't have to come, if he doesn't want to, Bonnie. I didn't ask him." Father Paul was tired of defending himself.

She nodded, as if his answer confirmed her suspicions, and she gave up. "I expect you to be back by midnight, or I'm sending out a search party," she warned, her gaze so direct as to be threatening.

Father Paul believed her. "Thank you." As she kissed her husband goodbye, Father Paul had second thoughts about the wisdom of stirring up trouble just to see what would happen. Recklessness no longer seemed such a fine idea, not when a man had someone waiting for him to come home.

Luke might have sensed his hesitation. "I'm tired of waiting, too, Father. Let's go stir up some trouble." He put his arm around Father Paul's shoulders and led the priest to his own car. Father Paul, in response, slapped Luke's back like they were headed into a football game. Glancing back, Luke called to his wife, "See you soon, hon." She was watching them through the screen door, worried.

She was arm candy, she realized with a smile. She had attended an award dinner for his exceptional generosity towards various charities in the maroon dress a few weeks ago, and tonight it was a banquet to honor his service on some volunteer board of community businessmen and women. She understood they did a lot of good for a lot of people who are usually forgotten. Her dress tonight was a vibrant green with silver trim and rhinestones. She felt so alive, so hopeful.

Maybe someday he would be her arm candy. Her smile renewed itself at the thought. She would have to keep studying and working hard in school, but she was hopeful that she could do whatever she set her mind to do. Besides, her parents were keeping an eye on her from heaven. She couldn't believe the luck they'd given her.

Dishes tinkled in a delicate way, hushed by the air conditioner in the hotel ballroom. She wasn't bothering to follow the polite, restrained conversation, and she didn't think he was either. It didn't matter, except that he had the networking he needed in order to keep doing charitable work for the community. He was such a good man.

To think, they happened to run into one another when he was visiting a professor friend on campus. Now, he was asking her to marry him. This man had effected surreal changes on her life. Just before this banquet, she told him that she needed more time, but now her finger felt bare. She thought he'd been insulted by her hesitation, too, and she never meant to hurt him.

He was a good man, and she wanted to belong somewhere. She wanted to be in a family again. It just made a lot of sense to wait until after school to get married, and that would only be a couple of years. She was a sophomore already. The timing was almost right. That thought warred with her fear of losing him. If only she'd had her mother to talk to then.

"I should get home soon and study," she reminded him demurely. An expression she couldn't quite identify flashed over his features and was gone.

All business now, he answered, "Of course." When this man made up his mind, he did whatever he had decided on. It was just one of the things that made him so amazing. He even looked amazing in his tuxedo. Elegant. He looked tired right now, too. She supposed she was doing him a favor by helping him bail out of this dinner early.

The shiny black SUV purred the whole way to her apartment. "Let me get your door." His hand on hers, he had her full attention when he ordered that. She couldn't deny him this time, even though it made her feel small, controlled for some reason. Why didn't it feel charming? What was wrong with her?

He was being very serious tonight, she thought, as she took his hand and let him help her down from the SUV. He walked her up to the apartment, and she fumbled for her key. She debated knocking, so her roommate would let her in. "Couldn't I help you study?" he asked. He looked sincere, as though he actually intended to help her study. She found her key and let him in. Her roommate wasn't home.

In hindsight, it was difficult to say where she should

have drawn the line. Was it when the circles he rubbed on her back shifted to her arms? Or should she have just known that he had no business rubbing those same comforting circles on her calves? She had changed into yoga pants, and he had undone his bowtie, kicked off his shoes. He reached up her pant leg seeking skin contact. Where was the boundary? When she decided he had crossed it, he was scornful. "I'm just rubbing circles," he laughed at her, wide-eyed as if wondering at her overreaction. He toned down the behavior, rubbing her calves through the thin material again, smirking in an odd way, as though there was something she didn't understand yet. It was humiliating. What was wrong with her?

She had already decided he was "The One". She trusted him. He would stop before they went "too far". Deciding she didn't want to seem immature, she let him push the boundaries. He really was just trying to comfort her, rubbing circles, she told herself. And he really was helping her study. She was getting this. Sort of.

Part of her had wanted to wait until she was married, not that they had had this conversation yet. She wasn't religious or anything, and she wasn't sure what her parents would have said about it. They were gone before they'd had this conversation. She imagined—hoped even—that her parents had waited until they were married just because it was romantic. For herself, she had wanted to wait because that was what princesses did. It would have made her feel cherished.

But she was all alone in the world, except for this man,

and without asking him, she knew he would think that was silly. He would tell her that princesses did this all the time, because princesses did whatever they wanted to. She ignored the rock in the pit of her stomach. She was simply growing out of some vestige of childhood finally, she told herself, and she was a little nervous. This was nothing to get worked up about. She was fine.

Chapter Thirteen

Father Paul drove Luke in silence that was punctuated by the occasional Action Item. None of those actions seemed likely to produce any good result, so the men took turns shooting down each idea, one by one.

"Look, Father, we're not just going to sit at the hotel's bar and hope that someone who looks like they're involved in trafficking sits down next to us," Luke said in exasperation, rubbing his hands over his face as if to wake himself up.

Father Paul realized that the stake out, the early mornings of a grocer, keeping his own marriage together despite the long hours, and leading the other Knights through their troubles was taking a great toll on Luke. "But if we did," Luke commented dryly, "that would mean keeping you out of trouble for one more night. I'm not sure why I'm trying to help you come up with a better plan."

"You need some sleep," Father Paul explained. "You need this to be over more than I do. It's time."

Luke, weary but alert, seemed to accept that. "Let's do it. How do you want to play this?"

Father Paul saw no way around it now. He was going to have to trust Luke. Starting out hesitantly, "Well, actually, if we sat at the bar, I could figure out who's there for trafficking, and we could follow them. If we look like we know where we're going, we could get pretty far. We would definitely get the attention of the people we're looking for. Unfortunately, that's as far as my plan goes, and I realize it's dangerous."

"You'd … sniff them out? What?" Luke asked, interested but right on the edge of scoffing.

"Something like that, yeah." Father Paul chuckled. Luke was still waiting for a real response. Scared and ready to be laughed at, Father Paul put on his most serious face and stared at the road straight ahead, flexing his hands on the wheel. "The reason I'm good at healing and working with the girls is that I'm... highly empathic. I pick up how they're feeling, and I know. I know when they want to avoid something, what they can talk about more deeply, and whether they're being honest with themselves. I can also sift through a crowd and look for certain emotional mixtures. I want to try to find the, uh, customers as they walk in, and then just follow one to wherever they go next. We'll do what they do and crack the place open." Before he was done, he knew that Luke believed the first half of what he'd said. The second half sounded shaky, even to him. "Why do you believe me?" Father Paul blurted, surprising himself. He wasn't sure he wanted Luke to answer.

"Dolores suspected something like that. Said she thought it was supernatural. She told Bonnie, Bonnie told me," Luke said off-handed, distracted. Before Father Paul had processed how he felt about all of that, Luke continued with the plan. "There are cameras in the rooms, so they'll know we haven't touched the girls," Luke cautioned.

"As long as we pay and don't mark up the girls, do you think they'll care?" Father Paul asked. "Besides, you're jumping pretty far ahead of where I ended the plan."

"Just following it through to the next logical step, Father. That's where you're putting us, and they'll wonder." He seemed to bite his tongue rather than say, in front of a priest, what the men would be wondering. "I guess it all depends on whether we happen to be dressed like the average customers—," Luke broke himself off with a humorless laugh, "They're called *johns*, Father—who come knocking on their doors."

Father Paul did a quick mental search for a picture of a john. Upon finding one, he had a further realization and pulled over to concentrate. "We might need a swipe card I just remembered. It must let you into a wing of the hotel where this kind of thing happens. I don't know where the card is anymore. It has to be in the rectory somewhere," mentally tracing where he had put the swipe card after anointing the dying man so many towns away from Limekiln. Renee had described the man as dressed like one of her schoolteachers in khaki pants and a button-up shirt, just an average guy, not someone you could pick out of a crowd.

Father Paul recalled he had been upset about all the Catholic churches he had driven past on his way to Frank's sick bed. He'd been hit by a deer on his way there. Then, he'd been so tired on the way home. He remembered putting the card in his shirt pocket—he'd been wearing clerics that night, and he didn't have *that* many clerics. They're expensive. Could the card be lost under his bed, with or without a clerical shirt? He didn't think he was missing any clothes.

Luke interrupted Father Paul's frantic mental hunt. "You got a *swipe card*? The undercover guy doesn't even have one yet, and he's running out of administrative leave for this stint. His cover's almost blown. You have to be a *long-standing* employee or customer to get a *swipe card. Who* did you *meet?* And *how? Where?*" Luke was more agitated than Father Paul had ever seen him. "And how did you *lose it??* I'm sorry, did you actually forget you had one?"

"I'll find it. That settles things. This is just a scouting mission to survey the territory. Next time, I'll have the swipe card on me, and we'll see whether we can get inside. We'll have a plan and everything. We're just going there to have a look around tonight. Agreed?" Father Paul waited for Luke to respond, but the man appeared stunned. "I'll find the swipe card. I promise."

"How? Does the swipe card carry some residual emotional energy or something?" Luke asked, genuinely trying to understand.

"Uhhhh, no. I was going to ask Saint Anthony to find it for me. That always works." Father Paul realized they were still parked on the shoulder, checked his mirrors, and got the vehicle moving again. "I think I only pick up on emotions in the moment, and I can usually get a reading on someone's emotional range, I mean the range of likely responses within their personalities. I call it an emotional signature. I sense whatever is nearby, but it's usually just white noise to me. Only an extreme emotion or a wild change of emotion jumps at me and grabs my attention. Everything else passes under the radar until I bother to look. Normally. I don't actually know how this thing works, and I don't know anyone else like me."

"Does it go through walls, around corners, that kind of thing?" Luke asked, grasping for words. Father Paul knew what he was getting at.

"I don't have to see the person to know how they feel. My range goes up to … no more than a quarter of a mile, I would think. I'm not sure," he thought aloud.

"Then we don't need to follow anybody tonight," Luke smiled sagely. Father Paul had no idea where he was going with this, but Luke coolly explained, "You'll know where in the building girls are being abused. Just put up your radar. We'll walk there like we're right on time, give them your friend's name, and get ourselves some time. Things will go down much smoother tomorrow night after we have the layout of the land and extra people on the inside. Dzielski will finally be able to pull in some extra resources and bring the whole place down red handed. Piece of cake. Now who's this friend who *gave* you his swipe card?"

Father Paul was almost sure it wouldn't work like that.

Belatedly, he remembered to tell Luke, "I can't give you the name. Didn't say there was a friend anyway."

Luke scowled suspiciously but said nothing.

Father Paul spent the remaining time in the car frustrated, unable to say why he had a bad feeling about the plan. Part of the problem was clear as soon as they arrived. "Interference," he sighed. "There's too much interference in a public place. It turns everything into an emotional wash." Father Paul and Luke headed for the bar, throwing into motion Plan B.

It came out of nowhere, and when he saw it, Father Paul's knees nearly buckled. He managed to rip his eyes away and keep walking. Luke hesitated a step, allowing Father Paul to keep up with him. Father Paul was fairly sure Luke also saw what caught the priest's attention, but it was no surprise to Luke. Nonetheless, that smirking, smarmy image would burn itself into Father Paul's brain like a scar.

Brad Coppini, owner of Gilded Swan, leered gleefully out of a photo ornately framed. He looked sharp in a coat and tie. And for the first time, he looked demonic. There was a presence in his eyes that was invisible in-person, but in the photo, it was plain. It was so apparent to Father Paul, he wondered why anyone would hang such incriminating evidence.

"I thought you knew," Luke said softly. The hotel carpets and high ceiling served to both mute and mix most conversations. "Didn't you already know?"

"That the man is possessed? No, I just saw that for the

first time, and I have no idea whether it's better to call for an exorcist before or after he's been arrested. They didn't cover this in seminary," *like so many other things*, he grumbled mentally. Father Paul was in over his head again.

A simple reconnaissance mission, a little scouting, some looking around. And it was completely out of control. He should have known nothing would be simple. God was trying to get him ready for heaven, full of virtue and grace. Grace! Father Paul quickly prayed that God would protect him and Luke on this foolhardy, half-baked mission, then prayed the Saint Michael Prayer.

> *Saint Michael the Archangel, defend us in battle. Be our protection against the wickedness and snares of the devil. May God rebuke him, we humbly pray, and do thou, o prince of the heavenly hosts, by the power of God, cast into hell Satan and all evil spirits who prowl about the world seeking the ruin of souls. Amen.*

"I meant that he owned the hotel, but I think you're being fair enough." Luke said. By that time, he had led Father Paul to unoccupied bar stools. Luke questioned the barkeep about beers. If Father Paul's "emo-dar" was working right, the short list of options had induced a new wave of aversion from Luke, invisible to the barkeep since Luke had adopted a fixed, placid expression for the evening's activities. Luke ordered two beers that were probably less to his liking than anything in Limekiln. As soon as the server walked away, Father Paul let out a snort of amusement.

"Having a good time?" Luke was wearing an amused grin, too, knowing he couldn't hide his distaste over the beer selection from the empathic priest. Perhaps they were both attempting to keep the conversation light, considering what they were doing here. The situation was too intense without an inside joke or two.

"Tell me who got you the swipe card," Luke requested as though he were indifferent. It was obviously bothering him. The light, joking moment was already over.

"I can't tell you," Father Paul said regretfully. "I know that doesn't look good for me, but there's nothing I can do about it. I can't tell you."

"You *can't*?" Luke lingered on the second word. Father Paul kept his face blank. "Ohhhh," he drawled, amused at what he probably understood as Father Paul's expression of innocence. "This is nothing illegal. It's a sacramental thing, right? But how could you have gotten the swipe card during someone's confession? Was handing it over part of his penance?"

"I can neither confirm nor deny your assumption. However, you'd be surprised at how easily a situation like that could possibly come up. Not that it did. Can't we just say I picked it up on the street?" Father Paul asked.

"Not really, not if you're sure it's connected to human trafficking," Luke responded neutrally.

Father Paul had nothing to say to that, so he glanced

around, taking in the hotel decor, which constituted an elaborate attempt to live up to the name "Gilded Swan." The scene was cringe-worthy. At the end of the bar, someone aesthetically deranged had placed a monstrous golden compote filled with golden eggs nesting on gilded little pieces of straw that Father Paul supposed to be spray-painted. When the barkeep returned with the beers, Father Paul looked down, and his eye caught the swan-shaped water taps, designed so that the keep would have to twist the swan's gilded neck to turn water on and off. His gut wrenched with the imagined pain of those abused inanimate creatures. The bar stools were upholstered in a gentlemen's club shade of dark green and set on gilded bases. Glass chandeliers—doing their best to appear crystalline with gilded metal work—dimly lit the place, setting an ambiance that screamed for cigar smoke of a bygone era. Of course, Brad's photo frame had been gilded, too.

Luke seemed to be quietly sizing up the patrons. Father Paul thought he and Luke looked roughly average among the men scattered about the bar. Some wore business suits, while others wore clean jeans and t-shirts. Luke and Father Paul had both opted for polo shirts and slacks. There was only one other man in the bar dressed like that. Perhaps they did stand out but not by much.

Father Paul stretched out his radar to filter through the patrons, while Luke chatted up the barkeep, presumably digging for information. Father Paul paid no attention to their conversation. He stretched himself to reach farther, sifting emotions as he'd never had a reason to before. There were lonely people, stressed-out and angry travelers, excited tourists. A surprising amount of loneliness kept cropping up. Was it something about hotels?

Hot spots of emotion grabbed his attention, and he sifted through what he found there, patiently waiting for something that matched the emotional signatures of the girls he knew. He thought he knew the kind of brokenness he was looking for. Exhausted, he downed the last of his beer, and then realized he must have been sitting here spaced out for a while. Luke assumed they were moving, took a final swig of his beer, and looked to Father Paul for direction. Father Paul gave him a head shake. Luke looked away, undoubtedly searching for a Plan C they hadn't made up yet.

That's when it finally occurred to Father Paul that he'd been searching for the wrong thing. He should have been looking for voids of emotion, places where people were blocked off entirely.

"Wait a second," he said to Luke. He shut his eyes to focus what energy he had left back to the several pockets of selfishness and loneliness and lust… to find those who were not emotionally present to anyone else. They felt isolated and perhaps even vacant within themselves. Target acquired. They were almost translucent to his radar, like ghosts or apparitions. This is what Renee and her friends would have felt like *before* he met them, and this was as good a trail as they would get to follow tonight.

Father Paul excitedly nodded. Luke gave him a *calm*

down look and set a leisurely pace away from the bar. There was cash left behind, and Father Paul realized belatedly that Luke must have paid. The priest would pay him back later. He had to focus on this thin thread drawing him to the back of the first floor.

Father Paul mentally kicked himself. He could have figured out that it was the back of the first floor from the girls' stories. Come to think of it, Dzielski must have known, and for once, oddly, it seemed that Luke didn't know something that Dzielski knew. But no one could have drawn a map of this circuitous route. Father Paul and Luke double-backed more than once, gradually winding their way to a door with a security camera and a card reader. Father Paul and Luke exchanged a look, *now or never*, and then Father Paul knocked.

A large man with a bulge beneath his jacket opened the door. Father Paul was tongue tied.

"A friend recommended this place to us… for some company," Luke smiled slyly.

Luke's eyes shifted to Father Paul expectantly, but there was no way Father Paul could reveal the name. The "friend" was protected by the seal of confession. How incredibly painful. Father Paul quickly dismissed the idea of dropping Brad's name, since that might attract the man's presence. Father Paul hedged, "My friend was pretty adamant about me never mentioning his name to anyone. He didn't give me any exceptions, and I didn't ask for any."

The man with the obvious gun bulge, however, cocked an eyebrow. "Well, maybe you're discreet, and that's a good thing. But how do I know you're not cops?"

Father Paul answered dryly, "I'm sure cops would have come up with a better story."

The burly man laughed from his belly. "Okay. We don't have any openings for an hour or more, depending on what you want. But come on, get in here so we can talk," the thug urged, mirth still evident on his edgy visage.

Father Paul didn't want to go in, but Luke stepped past him during Father Paul's moment of hesitation. Father Paul had no choice but to follow. It felt just as if chains were wrapping around him, when the heavy door clicked shut at his back.

"What kind of action are you guys looking for?" The man's muscles bulged through the jacket so much when he crossed his arms that the muscles cast shadows. Father Paul tried not to think about whether this man had murdered people often or just once in a great while.

Luke supplied Father Paul's lack again. "I'm looking for a brunette, a sweet little girl," Luke said. Father Paul could *not believe* the things coming out of his friend's mouth. With surprise, he realized that Luke was indeed a friend. The very best, considering the risk he was taking on Father Paul's whim.

"The same for me," Father Paul managed barely. He nodded, and he guessed that he looked like he was out of his mind. He certainly felt that way. Then he started babbling. "Not that we're looking to be with the same girl. Different brunettes. If you have two tonight. Who are sweet...? You know." Not sure anyone knew, he stopped there.

"It's his first time doing this," Luke explained, as if he had done this before. Father Paul thought Luke was one cool talker. He was grateful for the Knight's presence.

Muscle Man gave a single shake of his head. "Did your anonymous friend tell you our rates?"

Luke and Father Paul shook their heads.

The rates were astronomical. No wonder they could afford bouncers and cameras and payoffs to the police. Especially since the girls got so little of it.

"Cash," the man emphasized, as if waiting to see proof that they could pay. And they could not. Who carried cash these days? The man lowered his chin as if to stare at them over the top of bifocals he wasn't wearing. The look was intended to be intimidating, but it didn't work for Father Paul. Muscle Man got his looks from a gym, not from doing any practical thing. He might not have any skills at all, just a gun, and guns were easy to take away at this proximity. Father Paul felt himself getting his equilibrium back.

"We'll just hit the ATM across the street and come back," Luke said.

They would come back the following night, Father Paul thought, because there was no way they could lay out that much cash twice. They needed backup and a real plan.

Weirded out and newly aware of walking past a great number of security cameras on the way out, they talked and headed straight for the parking garage. Before they belted in, Luke dialed up Dzielski. From where he sat, Father Paul could hear the man shouting through the phone.

"What the hell are you doing in there?!" Father Paul imagined the cop's mouth full of fries and spewing bits as he bellowed.

"Relax," Luke commanded. "We stepped out. We know where to go tomorrow, and I think we'll have a swipe card."

The same guard from the door peered out at them from a stairwell. He had followed them, wondering why they headed for a car instead of the ATM no doubt. Luke moved as though to hang up the phone, but he placed Dzielski on speaker phone, then darkened the screen. He turned to speak to Father Paul. "How fast can you get in touch with your man on the inside? Get us some backup?"

Father Paul did not understand, but then Dzielski responded. "Why?" Dzielski snarled out of the phone on Luke's lap, "You aren't going back in there."

The thug knew they had spotted him, and since they were staying in the car, he was coming to them. Father Paul hoped they would just talk. Luke could talk them out of anything. This would be fine. With admirable calm, Luke told Dzielski what he was about to hear, all the while making it look like he was talking to Father Paul.

Dzielski let out an expletive, and Father Paul imagined him poised to call his undercover man, if the situation heated up.

Muscle Man motioned to him to roll down the window, which Father Paul had to turn on the car to accomplish. Running the engine was a plus, he decided. Muscle Man was at Luke's window, not the priest's. Probably another plus.

"Do you guys need a group rate or something? As long as you only take a half hour combined, I can give you a room with your fantasy brunette, no problem. Sorry if I spooked you with the price there."

Father Paul was lost for words.

A smile spread across Luke's face. "Oh no, we'll each need our own time," he drawled. "Should we make appointments for tomorrow night? We'll have the cash ready then."

All very civilly, the two of them made plans for Sunday night—The Lord's Day, for the love of Saint Mike—while Father Paul attempted not to gape. Muscle Man pointed at his own temple and said, "Got it." He patted the hood of the engine, signaling that Father Paul could drive now. Unaware until that moment that he'd been pinned by a predator, Father Paul exhaled and forced himself not to speed away. Muscle Man gave them a big wave from the door to the stairwell. Luke and Father Paul gave little waves back.

"Did you get that?" Luke asked. Father Paul again did not understand until Dzielski answered.

"Not recorded, no. I'm sorry," and he did sound genuinely grieved. After a brief exchange, during which Dzielski acknowledged that Luke and Father Paul had nearly gotten results, though he was still very, very angry with them, Luke ended that call. Then, it stopped seeming surreal to Father Paul. He was really driving the car away from a hotel that trafficked minors, and he would risk his life again tomorrow to end the trafficking ring. The same trafficking ring that had deeply wounded Renee and so many others.

At a gas station, Father Paul stopped and just managed to get his head out the door before vomiting. He was still tangled up with the seat belt, though. It kept catching him and making the whole activity more difficult than necessary. He hung out the door heaving a little alcohol and a lot of gastric acid, he realized with some chagrin. If only he were wearing his collar, he would paint the stereotypical picture of an alcoholic priest. Meanwhile, he heard the glove compartment open, the center console, some more rummaging around. Luke left the vehicle wordlessly and minutes later stood before Father Paul holding baby wipes and a travel-size bottle of mouthwash from the convenience store. Father Paul was still hanging out the door, trembling and sweating, finally unbuckled and with both feet on the ground. He wasn't sure that he was done.

Father Paul was somehow offended by that little baby wipe. "How can you stand it?! We were so close! How can you stand it! You know what they're doing in there! How did we walk away? Why aren't we still there? We should be fighting for whoever those girls are in there! I can't even feel them. They're *dead* inside, but we *know* they're there!"

"They stumble that run fast." Luke didn't blink. He was still offering one baby wipe from the little pack.

"Shakespeare? Seriously? What is *wrong* with you?" Father Paul roared.

"The man was right. I quote him. Give me credit for

quoting the cleric character in the play." Luke waited for Father Paul to get control of himself. "We go home tonight, and we come back tomorrow with a plan and backup. We never should have gone in tonight anyway. With a little luck, we can surprise those people by coming in with the swipe card. It took that guy almost five seconds to respond to a knock, which means he was in a room, probably that office to the right watching the cameras. If we keep our faces down and move fast, we could get a jump."

Luke waited a beat to let Father Paul process the information. "That card means everything. Backup means everything. Contacting the man inside, especially since you and I don't know his face, means everything, and Dzielski says that will take a day, since it's only safe to contact the undercover when he's not at the hotel. We can fix this, Father. But we need one more night to make sure we make things better instead of worse. That's how I can walk away. I'm coming back tomorrow, and this will be over. One more night," he coaxed. Father Paul belatedly realized he must have tuned out some of the conversation Luke had with Detective Dzielski. They had been arguing, but Father Paul couldn't recall the topic. Luke proffered the baby wipe again.

Father Paul took it, but he hung his head. This was not a proud night's work. A tear or two might have fallen onto that baby wipe. Luke rounded the car and slid into the passenger seat. Giving up, Father Paul decided it was better to be angry than it was to sob with a little baby wipe in his hand. He felt ridiculous. Resolved, he quickly rinsed with the mouth wash, walking over to the grass to spit it out. Then he tossed the used wet cloth into the trash can by the pump, snapped the door shut, belted in, and drove away. Each step took concentration to accomplish. Another tear or two might have escaped on his way to dropping off Luke, but he mostly managed to drive home angry. "Hell is empty," he decided, "And all the devils are here."

In just a few tries, she got pregnant, not that she *had been trying. She accepted his marriage proposal, reasoning that she would finish school part-time. She even went to confession, inexplicably gaining religiosity, only God knew why, and the priest commended her on making the situation right by marrying and by not considering abortion. He urged her to abstain until the wedding, and she somehow found the bravery to ask that favor of her fiancé. The priest was only asking her to do what she'd wanted all along, and she did feel guilty of something. She had asked very gently, giving herself room to take it back, as though she had been joking. Her dashing fiancé didn't even mind. He was happier, since the engagement. That really had meant a lot to him, she realized.*

That, and the church had hurried the wedding in consideration of the child's life. The priest confessed remorsefully that he had made a couple wait once, insisting they go through all the premarital preparation and a retreat, a minimum of six months waiting period to get married, as if they were buying a gun. That couple had really been in a hurry, and the news had deflated them both. The next time they visited him, they weren't in any hurry at all. She thought there was a tear in the minister's eye as he told the story, but he changed the subject and set a date acceptably soon. They promised to finish the marriage classes in good time after getting married, and her groom left a substantial thank-you. Was he trying to buy his way out of purgatory?

The wedding night came. They arrived at his father's hunting cabin, so romantic, where they would not be disturbed. He had never been interested in hunting—or in the outdoors, for that matter—and his urbane wardrobe showed it. She entered first taking in the vaulted ceiling and open floor plan of the log "cabin" finished with an incongruous marble kitchen and chrome appliances. She turned, aware of him watching her, and let her puffy white skirt swish prettily around her. Smiling at him, it was her turn to watch, as he set the two suitcases down and locked the front door behind him.

Something was wrong with him when he prowled toward her. Too late, her eyes interpreted the movement of his shoulder. She had no time to avoid the first punch to the gut nor the bearings to avoid any thereafter. Once she was on the floor, he kicked instead. She tried to defend her baby more than herself. Her insignificant arms were meager defense against him. He kicked her until she thumped up against his father's gun cabinet. He grew tired of the noise of the guns rattling behind her at every kick, so he dragged her by the hair to the kitchen. She scrabbled her feet to help him move her, trying to avoid the tugging pain in her scalp when he was forced to drag all her weight, trying to get back on his good side, soothing him with nonsense words to help him calm down and talk this out. Then he used the kitchen cabinets to hold her in place for more blows.

He kicked until she knew her child was dead. He knew too, heard the change in her cries. No longer begging, no longer afraid for her child, she wailed in defeat. She wanted to be dead, too, this lost princess. Blood had dripped from somewhere on her face into the white, fairy tale gown. That sight finally made the situation real to Lisa. She could not talk this out with Brad.

He kicked skillfully several more times, no longer angry but precise. Lisa lost count. Perhaps Brad imagined that she could act as well as he could, and her change of tone was a ruse to save the baby. Or perhaps she had inconvenienced him in other ways besides holding out very briefly against his marriage proposal. Perhaps he was punishing her for those unknown offenses. Lisa was never able to figure out why he kept going or why he finally quit, though, in the future, she would have plenty of time to think it over.

He walked away unconcerned while she choked on her saliva and tongue, struggling for air. He left the cabin for a time, and she only dared to splash water on her face, staying exactly in the spot he'd left her. Maybe he took a walk to calm down, or maybe he went to make an important phone call. She was still sitting in that spot by the kitchen sink hugging her knees when he returned.

When the stillbirth happened the following morning, she went down to the lake. He'd left to get supplies, stranding her without a car or phone. Her poor sense of direction would have gotten her lost before she found another living soul, and she was truly afraid of her new husband discovering her where she shouldn't be. She could think of easier ways to die than being beaten to death, now that she'd had a lesson in it.

Lisa felt more than saw that it was a boy. She named him Matthew and hid the body from her husband. Carefully, she removed some sod, including a patch of daisies, buried him deep under the earth on the shore of the lake. She feared that an animal might discover the body, and she would not be able to live with that. The baby needed to be safe from now on, never to be injured again. She was careful, even watered down the spot with handfuls of lake water to disperse the smell of blood. There was no stone to place over the grave, but she replaced the patch of daisies and could always find that spot, even years later.

Lisa could not imagine what to pray right then, though she would pray desperately later on. All she could do then was cry. She thought about God, though, and hoped that counted. Since the grave remained undisturbed by animals, her hope grew that God had indeed heard her.

Recovering on the couch in the cabin, her mind began to clear and to function normally again. Nonetheless, almost all of the options she could think of ended with her dead. Of course, he knew the addresses of the women's shelters he had funded from the ground up. She suspect-

ed he could find out the addresses of any shelter in the country through the national contacts he had. He didn't give her cash, only credit cards, and she had signed the papers to combine their accounts before she'd even gotten married.

She convinced herself that she deserved the hell she was in. Her child was dead because of her incalculable stupidity. Brad didn't have to threaten her to make her behave. She had nowhere to go, no will to move there, and no faith that she could have her life back. Had she ever had one? She wondered now. Doubted it. Didn't care.

In desperate moments, she imagined physically confronting him, but even in her wildest dreams, she lost. In her bravest moments, she imagined that she was saving some other unsuspecting young woman from this fate by occupying this single spot herself.

"You're here to make me look good. If you ever stop doing that, you will have outlived your purpose," he told her once.

They had been dressed for a black-tie event, some charity dinner or other, and she really had not wanted to go out that night. They had just fought about whether or not she should be "allowed" to work a part-time job that wouldn't interfere with their time together, and she was feeling hurt. He gripped her arm hard enough to bruise it, she realized the next day, and he had growled the words at her. It absolutely was intended as a death threat. Her life hinged on whether she made him look socially correct. And if she died, then some other woman would be manipulated into taking her place. Staying was as heroic as she could be.

Gradually she observed that Brad was using her as camouflage to blend in with normal society, because nothing about him was normal. There was something wrong with his business associates, and he hid certain phone calls and text conversations. The one plan that persisted through all her quiet vetting was the plan to put him in prison. Not for domestic violence nor for the murder of their son. Lisa needed to be smart and bide her time until she knew what was happening, she decided. Eventually, she would make the world a safer place by putting just one evil person in prison.

Chapter Fourteen

Counting his blessings after dropping off Luke, Father Paul thanked God that he hadn't visited the hotel on his own. He felt there was strength to be gained by keeping up his hope in God, so he did his part to maintain a good attitude. The priest reasoned that the Holy Spirit would do the rest, so long as he did his part. He reminded himself that God had provided a team of people to help with every aspect of this assignment from healing the girls to ending a major crime scheme. And the girls were healing, rather quickly considering everything they had been through.

So what if Father Paul lived a couple of houses down from Brad Coppini and hadn't known the guy was a crime boss? Everybody misses a detail here and there. Of course, Father Paul had also missed the fact that Lisa was being held hostage by thugs, not male nurses. Okay! It was going to turn out all right. God was providing what was needed in *God's* good time. This whole story was going to turn out right in the end… he hoped.

Most of all, Father Paul was grateful the guard at the hotel hadn't pulled out any of his weapons. Luke was one smooth talker, he reminded himself. Still, when the guard had followed them to the parking garage—now that had been scary! Whew! God was good.

He pulled up tight to the curb in front of the rectory, turned off the lights, then the engine. And he simply sat there with his hands on the steering wheel, letting himself come back down to reality again, breathing. Remembering the swipe card, he popped open the door and headed for the rectory. He had to find that by tomorrow night. Luke thought it would be critical to getting a jump on things, though Father Paul wasn't sure why the cops hadn't just come up with an arrest warrant and stormed the place. Everyone knew what was going on in there, including Father Paul's mother. Father Paul always thought of these things too late to ask about them. Mentally, he kicked himself.

Deciding that he would find out more after the case was closed, he set his mind to retracing his steps after that sick call weeks ago. He was now roughly following the same path from his car to his rectory as he had after the sick call. But if it had fallen out of his shirt pocket and into the grass, he would have found it the next day. Now that he was thinking about it, he was fairly sure he had done something with it just before falling into bed. He had pulled it out of his shirt pocket and put it someplace safe. He'd been sitting on his bed...

He froze with his foot mid-air, almost touching the first step up to the porch. There was an emotional signature inside the house. The rectory was completely dark. Not a sound emanated from the place. He stepped back and listened. Father Paul was absolutely sure he was being watched or listened to by someone in the kitchen. Just one person through the open window that looked out onto the porch. One threatening person.

Father Paul considered his cell phone and who he could call. He was about to run back to his car for safety, when the man in the kitchen called out, “Come on in, Reverend. I’m only here to talk.” The voice carried a strange mixture of amusement and gravity. Father Paul found something familiar, not in the person’s voice, but in the attitude. It was as though disobeying would have made him childish and the whole conversation more aggravating for the speaker than necessary. His feet moved again of their own volition, conveying him inside. The tone reminded him of his father’s voice, he realized halfway there, the tone his father would use when little Paul had been caught with his hand in the cookie jar—amused but not enough to tolerate disobedience.

Disgusted with himself, Father Paul flicked on the lights in the kitchen, hoping the man in the dark would be stung by the brightness. The kitchen was in total disarray, as though a gorilla had gone wild and thrown around, dumped out, and generally ruined whatever he found entertaining. A man with apish hair everywhere except the very top of his head sat at the kitchen table. His brown suit jacket stretched at the shoulder as the man rested his elbows on the table and tented his hairy fingers in a gesture more scheming than prayerful. Father Paul thought the man’s craggy features made him seem sort of dried up, as if he had been imposing once and hadn't figured out yet that his potency had evaporated. Father Paul let the awkward silence drag on, impatient for this man to deliver his message and leave.

"Would you like to know why I'm here?" the man asked, amusement dripping from his tone.

"I imagine you'll tell me whatever you waited here to say, whether I want to hear it or not. Hurry up. I don't have all night." Maybe the man was too impressed with himself to have ever been menacing. Father Paul was too deflated from the last adrenaline rush to really care. What was the use in worrying anyway?

"The way you're staring at me makes me think you're not as smart as I thought you were, Reverend." The man cocked his bald spot to the side, appearing to reassess Father Paul.

"Are you the one who killed Father Tom, gassing him with carbon monoxide?" Father Paul made the guess based on the fact that the man had broken into his rectory. And the guy was obviously not nice.

Disappointment plain on his face, the man answered, "Not even close, Reverend." Now convinced that Father Paul was stupid, he asked, "Where did you put the swipe card? And who did you get it from?"

"How did you know about that?" Father Paul figured the swipe card was the reason his kitchen, and probably the whole rectory, was in disarray.

"Where is it?" The man spoke very slowly and very clearly, biting off the final consonant. The intended effect was quashed entirely by the man's languid body language. If he was a thug, he was no match for the guard at the hotel. Muscle Man would squash this guy like a pesky mosquito.

Unmoved, Father Paul answered, "I can't remember. Seems like it will be a little harder to find now," openly surveying the damage. It turned out that Father Paul was in fact brave enough to take a few steps forward and even taunt the stranger in his kitchen. "Oh no," Father Paul joked, "this belonged to the parish, not me. You owe Sacred Heart a new coffee maker." He held aloft just the handle of the shattered carafe, glass shards and the lid still littering the floor. "Did you think the swipe card would be inside?" Father Paul asked incredulously.

The man still hadn't moved, but he seemed to be reconsidering his strategy. "We got off on the wrong foot, Reverend. My name is Agent Ben Miller, F.B.I." He emphasized each letter of the acronym in the style of spelling bees.

"I hope you have a search warrant," Father Paul said with mock concern.

Miller huffed. "Oh, you think I did this?" He openly surveyed the wreck. "I thought you were just a messy housekeeper. Your door was open, so I let myself in. No need for a warrant." His eyes impotently dared Father Paul to question him further. Father Paul bit his tongue and let the man continue. "You hold an important tool to solving a case we've been working on for months. Now if you'll just hand it over, we'll take it from here, and you and your friend, Luke, can take tomorrow night off." He held his hand out expectantly.

"I'm afraid I don't remember where I put it." Happily, he wasn't even lying! "And since you obviously keep a close eye on me, I don't think you have to worry about missing the moment when I find it. Are we agreed?" At first, it seemed most likely that Father Paul's car was bugged, but he was going to check his phone for new, unexpected apps as soon as this character left. He would have to check Luke's too, he realized. And maybe Dziel-ski's. Bugged cars seemed less and less likely as the list went on. Someone was a moron and didn't realize their phone battery was draining too quickly from an app that transmitted every time they talked near it. He hoped for pride's sake that it wasn't him, but he was so sleep deprived lately, he really wouldn't have noticed something so trivial as how often he had to charge his phone battery.

"You're absolutely right," Miller said, getting up to leave. He was a match for Father Paul's height. He probably needed that height in order to feel impressive. As he shouldered past Father Paul, he poked a finger into the priest's chest and added, "so you'd better not try to hide it from me when it turns up. And Father, it had better turn up soon. Find it."

Tired of being growled at, Father Paul thought about questioning whether the agent meant "us" meaning the agency, rather than "me", which was really very arrogant, but he let it go. The man was leaving, and there was no point in spinning him up again. It was far more important to consider why the man was so confident Father Paul wouldn't discover the way he was being monitored.

He found the alien app instantly, but he waited to delete it, not wanting to tip off the agent right away. Chances were good that he would find the app on his friends' phones, too, he decided. He watched a stereotypical 'unmarked' surveillance car, a black sedan with tinted windows, sluggishly convey Agent Miller away in the passenger seat.

Mentally, Father Paul retraced his steps the night he came back from that sick call. He stepped carefully around some obstacles that hadn't been there until the place was trashed, but he managed to keep his focus. At the foot of the stairs, Father Paul remembered where he had placed the swipe card for safe keeping. He checked his wallet. Yes, he had had the swipe card in his wallet and on his person all evening long.

How was it supposed to be helpful? With an armed guard a few seconds away from the door in the hotel, this was going to give them a few seconds' worth of an advantage.

Father Paul couldn't call Luke and ask. He couldn't call anyone who knew anything, not until he had checked their phones. He could run over to Luke's house, bypassing the potential bug in his car, but really, what did he have to say? He had the swipe card Luke wanted, and he might lose it if he made a big deal out of it. It would be nice to know whether that Neanderthal were actually an FBI agent, but he appeared not to be on the Good Guys' side, regardless of his club affiliations. The safest, sanest course of action was simply to put the swipe card back in his wallet and go to bed, as if nothing had happened. So, after hefting the mattress back to the center of the bed frame, Father Paul decided to leave the dirty sheets where Agent Miller or his partner had left them on the floor. Putting fresh sheets on the bed seemed like the logical thing to do, since someone had already gone to the trouble of stripping the bed. Father Paul even started a load in the washing machine with the dirty sheets. He forgot to put them in the dryer before going to sleep, and, as his Sunday would unfold, those sheets stayed in the washer for days.

After Morning Prayer and a quick shower, Father Paul started celebrating Sunday Masses. The nine o'clock was sparse and uneventful. He managed to prepare scrambled eggs, toast, and tea despite butterflies—or rather angry birds—in his stomach. He was not surprised to receive the Knights' visit, but they were most surprised to find him drinking tea in the morning rather than coffee. Perhaps they were also surprised at the state of the room. And the entire rectory. Thank the saints his hot water kettle was metal, and his tea bags were individually wrapped. And thank the saints again that Agent Miller didn't think anyone would hide a swipe card inside a refrigerator. He obviously never watched cop shows on TV.

Raising his hand in a "stop" gesture, Father Paul pulled out his phone, turned it off, indicating that they should all do the same, and then waved them over to the table. Astonished, all four Knights pulled out their phones, held down the "off" buttons, and watched as their own phones powered down. They approached tentatively, surveying the damage.

"Tea anyone?" Father Paul asked. Everything was normal now. He couldn't even get excited about everyone needing to turn their phones off before talking.

"Josh, would you go get the coffee maker from the sacristy?" Luke requested.

Josh identified what was left of the rectory's carafe in the mess. His eyebrows popped, he stared for a moment, and then he strode out the front door without a word. Don and Willie gingerly toed some debris aside to seat themselves.

"Want to tell us what that was about? And all this mess?" Luke asked.

"There's an app on my phone, probably on all of yours too, transmitting to some guy who says he's in the FBI," Father Paul began.

"Miller?" Luke guessed.

"What? Tell me he's not really an agent!" Father Paul exclaimed, disbelief plainly written on his face.

A little smile was all Luke gave away. "You'll probably never meet his partner, Stiefellecker. They did all this?" Luke asked.

"Yes, they were looking for the hotel swipe card," Father Paul answered.

Luke processed that. Looked at his own powered-down phone. Gave Father Paul one nod. "Miller's just incompetent, not crooked, we think. We haven't been working with him, because he isn't smart enough to protect against a leak in his department, if he were smart enough to consider he might have one. Since the case involves underage trafficking, the case will eventually go to him. But solving the case is going to have to be someone else's job," Luke explained. "When did this happen?" Luke asked.

Father Paul waited for Josh to return before giving a play-by-play of last night's encounter.

"But you would have known there was someone inside," Luke interjected almost immediately.

Father Paul froze, feeling very exposed. Luke encouraged him, "We're all friends here, Father. Go on and tell everything."

Father Paul looked around, took a deep breath, and struggled through an explanation of his gift. Don and Willie wore frustrated expressions, struggling to understand. Josh was doing an over-the-top job of acting natural. When Father Paul reached out with his radar, he perceived that Josh was mainly preoccupied with not offending Father Paul, because he considered Father Paul a friend. Similarly, he felt nothing but respect and curiosity from Don and Willie.

"Thank you, my friends," he said. "I've never been able to talk about this before. Don't think it means that I always know what to do with the information I have—."

"That's what we're here for," Josh said. He had taken a seat at the kitchen table, allowing Luke to take over brewing a pot of coffee. Father Paul realized that single sentence had been the kindest one he'd heard in a long time. Willie and Don both shrugged and nodded, and Luke poured the coffee. Father Paul's chest swelled.

He told the whole story about Agent Miller.

"Miller does have an authoritative tone," Don defended Father Paul at one point, "until you realize he doesn't know what he's talking about. You got it eventually," Don consoled a bewildered Father Paul.

Luke had found an empty cardboard box, and Josh was dumping swept-up, broken glass into it. Meanwhile, Luke busied himself stacking unbroken things back into the cupboards roughly where they had been. Both men had coffee mugs within an arm's reach and took liberal breaks. Don and Willie were exempt on account of old age. But Father Paul began to feel like a turkey. Embarrassed, he filled the sink with soapy water and picked up all the silverware from the floor. Don requested a towel, as did Willie in suit. The kitchen was somewhat functional by the time they left for the eleven o'clock Mass.

Father Paul had been dreading the eleven o'clock Mass without realizing it. All four Knights were ushers counting the Mass attendance and taking up the collection. No wonder they had been able to attend Mass together and keep an eye on things. Brad sat with Lisa halfway back and on Father Paul's left side. Renee and her family sat three-quarters of the way back and on the right side, apparently oblivious to Brad's connection to Renee's abuse. Bonnie, he realized, was actually paying attention to Mass, and that snapped him back into reality.

In seminary, he'd been taught to pray each Mass as if

it were his last one. Mustering his reverence, Father Paul brought himself back into the moment. Still, it was very difficult offering The Body of Christ to certain members of the congregation. And then there was Lisa. He mentally reached out and found her numb on the surface but strong underneath, someplace deep down that she hadn't let herself go in a while. He inclined his head toward her, not sure what his little bow was supposed to convey. Uncertainly, Lisa responded in kind, holding up the line for a few extra seconds.

A spike of emotion caught Father Paul's attention. It was Josh, watching from where he ushered people into the center aisle for Communion, a little more than halfway back. Josh's concern yielded as soon as Lisa looked where she was walking and acted normal. Josh didn't want Lisa calling attention to herself, Father Paul understood.

Brad felt dead to Father Paul, like a walking void leading the way ahead of Lisa. Father Paul couldn't believe he had once thought of that vacuum as a restful, easy presence.

When Renee and her parents climbed out of their pew, Josh gave them each a respectful nod. Renee liked Josh, Father Paul realized. She had a little teenage crush on him, which wasn't altogether unhealthy. Good for her, choosing a respectful man and retaining interest in men at all, he thought. She was one tough cookie. His prayers had not been in vain, and she was surrounded by support from so many sources. Father Paul praised God for His work in her life.

When Renee approached her pastor for the Blessed Sacrament and responded, "Amen," he was so proud of the way Renee was growing up. In no time at all, she wouldn't even need him anymore. She would continue to grow up without serious intervention after just a little more time, he thought, and he didn't feel God disagree. Renee didn't need him much longer.

He fearfully realized that he was running out of a mission. When would he ever feel so useful again? He turned to God mentally with this question and got little more than a shrug in response.

So, God wasn't talking today.

Then there was no need to change today's plan either.

He and the Knights would depart as soon as the money was counted and deposited. All the Knights, Father Paul, Detective Dzielski, and some other unknown backup man from the city police would be there along with the undercover man on the inside. No bad guys would get away. It would be quick. And, according to Luke, Brad spent his weekend afternoons and evenings working at Gilded Swan. He would be arrested. Brad would not be attending Mass with Lisa again. Not during Father Paul's tenure anyway.

Father Paul had to baptize a new baby in the parish, but he had scheduled that to follow Mass immediately. All he had to do was call Dolores about rescheduling this evening's appointment. He didn't want to try flying back for that. He made the call as quickly as possible.

"Is everything alright, sweetheart?" Dolores asked. Father Paul had never been the cause of a cancellation, he realized, and for all the times Dolores had called the girls sweetheart, this was the first time she had placed him in that category. He decided not to make a big deal of it. It reminded him of his mother in a soothing way.

"Yeah, it's fine. The rectory sprang a leak," he didn't lie outright but deceptively used a figure of speech, "and it's going to take some time to fix it and clean things up. I'm going to be tied up with that today, and then as long as we don't wander back into the kitchen, it should be fine to meet Monday night at the rectory again." Dolores would handle the reschedule and text him the new appointment time.

Father Paul baptized that baby in less than thirty minutes. When Father Paul's phone bubbled a cheerful little tune due to an incoming call, Father Paul didn't hear it because he was out in the sanctuary, and the Knights didn't look at the screen. Father Jeremy was forced to leave a voicemail.

Hey, Paul! You'll never guess what I found in Tom's homily notebook. Remember how you and I used to think it was funny to write messages using Greek characters to spell out English words phonetically? We are NOT the first people to do that. Tom was passing coded notes to somebody. I don't know who. You have GOT to call me back, man. Can you imagine Tom spelling out the word 'hitman' in Greek characters? A hitman named The Administrator. You HAVE to call me back. I'm dying here. CALL ME!

If Father Paul had heard the message, which he hadn't, he would have interpreted that silence before Father Jeremy hit the 'end' button as a time when Father Jeremy wondered whether The Administrator had plugged up his flue.

But in fact, Father Paul decided that since his phone was being used as a listening device, it could also easily be used to give up his GPS coordinates. His phone would need to be turned off for the whole day, and with that in mind, there was little point in bringing it along on this adventure. What would really be funny, he smiled to himself, would be leaving all the phones on, his and the Knights', and piled up right there on the sacristy counting table. Agent Miller might have no idea where the group was, and they would get a chance to succeed at Gilded Swan without his primitive interference. Father Paul mentally patted himself on the back and left the phone there to tell the Knights his great change of plan.

Chapter Fifteen

"I don't feel right about sending you in there without radios or cell phones," Don said.

"Me either," Willie chimed in. "We're going to be your backup, and we're going to have no idea when you need us to back you up. We'll just sit in this car outside and wait to see whether you ever come out. I guess we'll know to call 9-1-1 when we see you crawling out and bleeding, but you'll have to make it to the front doors that way." He was smiling broadly at the end of that speech, as if he thought he'd told the winning joke. Scowls were the response all around.

Father Paul was content to drive the car and ignore them. He reasoned that both men were deliberately being grumpy for lack of a better occupation. Right here in this car, he didn't have a better job to offer them. Unless they wanted to be quiet.

Luke, in the front passenger seat, sighed and responded via the rearview mirror. "If we had radios or cell phones, they'd be taken away. In fact, I think we'd be shot for carrying radios. Neither of you were in military intelligence, were you?" he added pointedly. "Let's just see what Dzielski has to say."

Josh spoke up from the meager middle seat of Father Paul's suddenly very compact sedan. Josh's knees were the most visible part of him since they were in front of his face. The engine nearly drowned out his calming, mellifluous voice, so Father Paul worked hard to make out the words. Playing it back in his head a few times, Father Paul eventually understood Josh to have said, "We can't all go in the pub. It's too noticeable."

"We can all go in," Luke corrected Josh after his own pause, "but only one of us will sit at the bar and talk to Dzielski," Luke said, looking to Father Paul for a response.

"I'll do it," he volunteered eagerly. The priest figured that it was the most dangerous job, and he didn't want to risk anyone else.

Luke gave him a knowing look of annoyance, but he kept his comments about the value of Father Paul's life to himself this time. "Fine, let's do it," was all Luke said. Father Paul assumed that meant the meeting was safe enough not to be worth fighting about. That was good news for everyone, even if he was irrationally disappointed.

It felt strange to Father Paul to meet with someone and not carry his cell phone in case of last-minute changes of plan. Earlier, before piling into Father Paul's clown car, all the men had left their cell phones turned on in the sacristy by the money counting table, right where Agent Miller would expect them to be at this time, since that had been the plan until an hour ago. Luke and Father Paul voice-acted a conversation in which they changed their minds about visiting Gilded Swan today, pretending that

Father Paul hadn't located the swipe card yet. There was no need to rush counting the collection, they pretended. They hoped they sounded dejected enough to explain why they wouldn't be speaking at all while counting this week.

Appropriate shuffling, calculating, and coin clinking noises were provided by the Ladies Auxiliary of the Knights. Mostly that was Bonnie and a few widows of late Knights. Before the ladies entered the sacristy, Luke had explained that there was a ban on talking during counting, since that caused people to lose count. Bonnie had nodded seriously and made eye contact with the widows, as though she intended to enforce that rule. All the women agreed not to talk. Then they entered the sacristy. Agent Miller would think they were a taciturn crew, but he would have no idea the Knights weren't there. Hopefully. Of course, if Agent Miller did discover the lie, he'd know exactly where to come looking for them.

Then the men had visited the sanctuary and prayed. Something about being in the presence of the Blessed Sacrament strengthened their resolve. Today, all of this would end one way or another. By silent agreement, before anyone had begun to fidget, they all knew when it was time to go. First stop, Mad Hatter. Second stop, Gilded Swan.

"Should we stay in the car?" Willie asked.

"No!" Luke barked sharply. "I'm sorry, Willie. It's just that the three of you in the backseat are far more conspicuous than you will be in the pub. Let's do this."

Willie mumbled a bit about not quite understanding

that line of reasoning, and Luke pretended not to hear it.

Father Paul forged ahead without them, not slowing down until he was seated inside. He sat two bar stools away from the detective and ignored him at first. He ordered a beer. Casually, he and Dzielski greeted one another as though they hadn't met before, and in plain sight, covered by the foot-stomping beat of "Devil's Dance Floor," they exchanged the vital information.

Father Paul confirmed that he had the all-important swipe card. Then he winced, narrowly suppressing the urge to slap his forehead, because he'd just remembered to hit the ATM before arriving at the hotel. Unhappily, Father Paul added one more stop to his itinerary.

"Okay, that's good. Now I'm going to tell you what I don't want to hear today, Father. Gunfire. I do *not* wanna hear gunfire. So, you're gonna play this the way I say." The cop waited pointedly.

Father Paul didn't care, as long as he got to be inside. He nodded his agreement.

"You're staying out."

Well, wasn't that the deal breaker? "What?"

"Electronics get confiscated. They wave a metal detector wand over you before they let you past the office, that first room on your right. You'll probably even lose your belt and shoes and get them back when you're done," the detective explained.

That made sense in a nauseating way. Besides, TSA already treated everyone this way, so who would complain? Father Paul figured the hallway in that hotel corridor might be dirtier than an airport corridor, but it wouldn't be the kind of dirt to stain his black socks.

"We've got no way of radioing for backup, and that's not how we do things. You understand? No one goes in without a way to contact backup. Ever. Which is where you come in." The detective smiled expectantly, but Father Paul only widened his eyes in response. "You can tell when the good guys need help, right? Luke told me all about it."

"Why on earth does everyone believe this? It's the most ridiculous story," Father Paul gaped.

"Sure explains a lot though," Dzielski answered.

Irritated, Father Paul swirled the beer in his bottle, as if he were studying it for fly bodies. Dzielski waited expectantly. And Father Paul really had nothing to say to this, so … he gave in.

"Fine, I still have to be inside the hotel. My range isn't that great, I don't think, and there's a lot of interference, since it's such a crowded space. Even then, you have to understand I've never tried this before." He feared his lack of experience might get one of his new friends killed today. Since he was supposed to be sitting in a safe zone, it was doubtful that he would be the one in danger, no matter how vastly he would have preferred that over the present circumstances.

Dzielski sighed deeply, obviously at war with himself. "Your gift is the only reason you're involved. There wouldn't be civilians in on this operation otherwise, Father. I can't believe I'm encouraging you, but … you can do it, Father," he said gruffly. "You have to be able to, because we're out of time again. We lose our undercover in a few days. Time keeps running away from us. I don't have to tell you how tragic it is for the victims. We've lost so much time already. And I'm sick of interviewing victims. It's time."

Father Paul was startled to feel anything other than cynicism and calculated bravery from the detective, but there it was. Using cynicism to protect an emotional injury wasn't the surprise—lots of people did that. But Dzielski had suddenly opened it up, and underneath, there was a raw pain that felt fresh but aged at the same time. Saddened, Father Paul added another item—helping Dzielski heal from whatever that was—to his mental list. Weighed down by the evil in the world, he realized this one would have to wait until tomorrow.

Dzielski must have taken Father Paul's silence for agreement. He went on, "Luke said you can even tell where they are. Just keep your emo-eye on Luke, and don't lose track of where he is. When it's time, you'll signal me visually to lead the charge. Between me and the man inside, we'll have a jump on the other two bad guys, because I'll have the swipe card," Dzielski said, making it all sound so simple.

The best plans often are simple, but they're usually rehearsed in some fashion, too. There was no additional backup, since they had to protect themselves first from a mole. Consequently, they only had numbers to match the number of the expected traffickers, and their only edge was surprise. It went without saying that the traffickers were armed while Luke was not. One unexpected extra henchman, and somebody innocent would almost definitely get hurt. That unexpected henchman could come in the form of a customer who knew where to retrieve his gun. There were so many unknowns and such a lack of communication lines.

Father Paul grimaced, realizing that he was the line of communication, and nodded. This was what they had to work with, and they had to make a move now. Otherwise, it was young women and girls who would continue to be hurt instead, and it might never end.

Detective Dzielski was avoiding moles in his department by involving civilians who had been tested and were now friends. Dzielski was a smart man for getting himself publicly kicked off the case and for telling as few other cops about his business as possible. Most likely, he would lose his job for involving civilians, but at least this scenario had a chance of working. Father Paul wondered what Dzielski would do in his next career.

"When things change, you give me the nod. Got it?" the cop asked.

Father Paul had it. He nodded grimly.

He only wished that he was risking his own life, rather than so many others. Luke. The girls working tonight. Unsuspecting civilians on the other sides of walls that bullets might come ripping through. Realizing that there was nothing he could do about it, if he wanted this to end, Father Paul pushed it out of mind and into God's hands.

God's will be done. Lord, we've done all that we could to minimize risk. I lay the rest on your shoulders.

"Let me describe the setup Luke will be walking through. This will help you understand his emotions and visualize where he is. Luke can't solicit, and he can't accept sex in exchange for money. He does that, Agent Miller *is* stupid enough to press charges, because it will be on the recordings the bad guys are kindly making for us. Luke will be tense and focused trying to get the bad guys to say everything without putting himself on the wrong side of the law. Wait for some … some other emotion. You know. Do your thing," Dzielski fumbled.

Some other kind of emotion. Would Luke be afraid? Angry? Relieved? What if he didn't feel different at all? How would Father Paul know they had enough evidence recorded on the traffickers' monitoring system?

"Wait a minute. I thought there was just video footage." Father Paul had only known about silent videos texted to the girls. He assumed the security system consisted of cameras, with a visual feed only, and very large thugs.

"My guy tells me that they're recording audio and visual from the main office on back, that whole area," Dzielski confirmed. "They even record what happens in the watch office. The boss's way of keeping an eye on his employees maybe, or a way to record all the screens in sync."

Father Paul said a quick prayer of thanks that he and Luke hadn't made it into a room yesterday. They would have spoken honestly with the girls, and they would have been caught and killed for certain. *Thank you, Jesus.*

"Where are you going to be?" Father Paul asked.

"Wearing a ballcap and plain-clothes, avoiding the cameras in the lobby, same as you. I'll be loitering just between cameras and about fifty feet from the hallway we want. I'll have the swipe card, but don't reach for it now," he said urgently, and Father Paul retracted his arm from near his wallet. "Wait until we pay for the drinks." He flagged the server for his check, and Father Paul gestured that he was ready, too. With a sigh, Father Paul reached for his wallet again, certain that he was conspicuous. And horrible at spy games.

"Where am I going to be?" Father Paul asked sheepishly, hoping he hadn't missed that information already.

"I'll show you the couch and get you there without camera exposure. This is familiar territory for me," he snickered.

Father Paul felt like a toad. He would be sitting safely on a couch.

Still early in the afternoon, the men arrived at the hotel and took their places, both Father Paul and Detective Dzielski wearing ballcaps. As though sitting gingerly would keep him from being noticed, Father Paul gradually lowered himself onto the brown leather couch pointed out to him by the detective's gaze. Father Paul obeyed and stretched out his radar, getting a general feel for the space.

He didn't need to turn around to know that Luke had just walked in through the revolving door. He knew his friend's emotional signature like a familiar face. He imagined himself clapping a hand on Luke's shoulder and walking with him, accompanying Luke through "emodar" with absolute focus. Luke strode straight down the long gray corridor that led to danger. By agreement, all he had on him was cash and car keys. The swipe card was on the detective, who studiously ignored Luke as he strode by. Father Paul experienced a moment of jealousy when Luke and Dzielski became aware of one another. Mutual respect and trust washed over Father Paul's radar. He'd never had that kind of friendship with anyone. No wonder Detective Dzielski was willing to involve civilians. He had worked more closely with them than with police on this case for several months, and he'd forged a deep bond with Luke.

The feeling passed quickly. Luke felt more and more like a machine, preparing himself for the mission. Father Paul was sensitive to every nuance in Luke's emotions. He noticed a spike in openness and affability, which Luke shoved to the surface over top of disgust. He was striking up a conversation with the main guard, Father Paul understood. Without losing his hold on Luke, Father Paul felt tentatively around him and easily found the same guard they had encountered last night. That man was wary of everyone, but he maintained a mask of solicitous hospitality to camouflage his vigilance and his readiness to torment a person if he deemed it expedient to his goals. Emotions detached from principles: Father Paul thought the man felt unhinged, as if he had no conscience at all. The priest couldn't focus on that man, though.

As Father Paul witnessed it remotely, Luke was feeling

increasing disgust. Luke and the bad guys were arranging something, the priest guessed. A frustrating resolution and impatient waiting came shortly thereafter. Father Paul was supposed to send in Dzielski as soon as there was enough evidence recorded to implicate Brad, but Father Paul couldn't be sure Brad's name had come up already. Luke was waiting, not going back to one of the rooms, so more talking was bound to happen. Father Paul hesitated.

Father Jeremy had been working at it for the last three hours. That is, he'd been working on it since he'd given up expecting his friend to call him back. Paul had to be immersed in something, because he was normally very responsive. Jeremy was going through Tom's journal by himself to see whether he could find anything useful. If he did, he would try contacting his friend again.

Tom's journal was hand-written in Greek characters intended to be sounded out. It took time, but it was plain English when you said it aloud. The main troubles were the older priest's penmanship; shifting tenses, perspectives, and subjects, probably due to the carbon monoxide poisoning; and, for the same reason, the real possibility that Tom had simply hallucinated all or parts of it.

Still, this wasn't the kind of thing you ignored or dragged your feet about when your friend was in the middle of it. Paul had told Jeremy about the watch the Knights kept up, because that was context for seeking out marriage advice on Don's behalf. Now, it seemed likely enough that there *was* a hitman and that the Knights knew about him, whether or not Tom had actually discovered the man. And what if he had? Didn't that explain the older priest's death? There was enough evidence in the flue alone to suggest that this journal was right and that there was an assassin named The Administrator.

The part Father Jeremy struggled to ignore the most was the Knights' behavior. Why would they keep watch on Paul's street, when Jeremy was almost sure none of the girls lived on that street? Of course, it was chilling to consider that The Administrator had nearly caused Jeremy's death as well, when he let the thought settle in. He liked to pretend he was just solving a puzzle.

When he was a child, Jeremy's devious extended family had exchanged most-complicated-ever Christmas jigsaw puzzles with his family every year. Scenes of nothing but peppermint sticks or landscapes of snow piles to assemble were the common fare. Some of his best childhood memories were of sipping hot chocolate, eating Christmas pies with ice cream, and piecing together ridiculous pictures that should not have been. When they were done, his parents would take a time-stamped photo as proof, racing to beat his cousins' family. The next time the families met for dinner, they often had to compare the printed dates on the photos to know who had won. Only once had they held their breaths and checked the time as well before half the table cheered jubilantly and the other half groaned.

This journal was another puzzle, just like that. He felt perfectly safe as he sounded out scribbled Greek characters in his head. It was fun and interesting, that was all.

Father Tom alleged from the grave that he had followed the hitman around for a day. This was toward the end of his journal entries. Two days before his death.

Jeremy wondered where he had been while all this had been going on. Jeremy had already decided the old priest was crazy and given him a wide berth. Tom had eagerly accepted when Jeremy offered to give the older priest a day of rest, meaning that Jeremy had picked up all the pastoral duties. No one expected much from Father Tom at this point, and no one asked what he did with his days. Jeremy had assumed that Tom loafed about the rectory all day. In truth, Jeremy had been avoiding the rectory for that reason, visiting it just long enough to pick up messages and new tasks.

Guilt assailed Father Jeremy. If only he had been a decent human being and cared more about Father Tom. If only he had asked what Tom was doing with his days. Maybe Tom would have told him. Maybe they'd both be dead now, he realized. If he had known how bad things were, would he have stayed here instead of celebrating his sister's wedding? Would he have taken Tom with him? Maybe nothing would have gone differently.

From this journal, Jeremy had the name of the man he was looking for, a license plate number, and a car description. He was officially going to Google and otherwise hunt down … a hitman with the code name "The Administrator." Father Tom's killer. Father Jeremy shook his head in disbelief as he slid his laptop toward him on the desk.

The grounds around Saint Agnes Church included outdoor Stations of the Cross and a popular Marian statue frequently visited by the public because of some phone app the priest didn't want to learn. Even though it was chilly outside, Father Jeremy was still traumatized and keeping the nearest window open for now. The priest wasn't startled when he heard a stranger's cell phone pipe out the "Mission Impossible" theme song from the parking lot. The choice was appropriate to his own task, and he took it as a sign that God approved.

When the owner of the phone tried unsuccessfully to answer *sotto voce*, Father Jeremy chuckled and looked out the window. A black sedan with tinted windows sat in the back parking lot, and a tall, bald man stood close to it, wearing his best imitation of a spy outfit. Another crazy person at a church. Again, not a new experience for Father Jeremy.

"What do you mean they're at the *Gilded Swan*?" Those words punched through Father Jeremy. For a moment, he understood what it meant to feel out of one's body. He shook his head to clear it and get himself back together.

Who could this man be? Father Jeremy wondered. And why would he be right outside the rectory? He wasn't there for religious reasons.

Like puzzle pieces snapping together, Father Jeremy understood. Black sedan, tinted windows. He couldn't see the license plate from here, and the man hadn't said his name yet. But Father Jeremy would bet his best black shoes that this was The Administrator.

When the man dashed to his car, Father Jeremy didn't make a decision. He did think, though, as he gathered his wallet, keys, and phone. He thought about the fact that this was how Father Tom had died. And he realized that he had no idea what he would do at the end of this trip. Should he call the police? Would they have any reason to arrest the hitman? If they just searched his car, they'd find guns they weren't supposed to, right? Maybe a dead body in the trunk. Maybe nothing… He really did have to follow this through until he saw something himself.

Once again, Father Jeremy tried to call Father Paul, and it forwarded to voicemail. There was no need to wonder why his friend wasn't picking up anymore. Even if Father Jeremy stayed too far back and lost the black sedan, he knew where it was headed as soon as it merged with highway traffic. He was headed for Gilded Swan, where Father Paul probably was and the Knights, too. That was where this trip ended. And somehow Father Jeremy was going to stop The Administrator from killing his friend.

Chapter Sixteen

Everything would go according to plan, Luke soothed himself, so long as he kept control of his emotions. That was proving very difficult as he waited his turn for a time slot. The chief Knuckle Dragger hadn't named a price and a deal yet, so there was no evidence of trafficking recorded either. After a chin bob greeting, all the sasquatch had said was that the next available slot would be forty-five minutes, and would Luke like to wait at the bar? No, because Brad was here today, and Luke was afraid he'd be seen too early.

Brad had more than an inkling that the Knights had been keeping an eye out for the girls. Luke was certain that Brad knew the Knights were onto him. If he saw Luke at the hotel, much less waiting in line for a turn, he would know well enough to toss Luke out on his ear, and that would be the end of that. No, Luke did not want to be seen by Brad.

Although now Luke wished that Father Paul and Detective Dzielski could see him, so they would be certain not to storm in before he had any evidence. This method of communication had admittedly seemed limited from the start.

The bulky thug took a photo of Luke to open his "account" with them, but Luke was suspicious enough to think the man had actually texted it to Brad. Luke figured the thug would wonder why Father Paul wasn't with him this time, but the hulking figure wasn't asking or inviting conversation. It felt too defensive and chatty to offer the information unasked. Luke decided he would just play it cool and wait.

So, Luke made himself wait in the brown leather club chair out in the hallway with his back to the watch office, no shoes and no belt. He leaned his head back against the wall and pretended to sleep. If nothing else, it would help him stay calm and keep Father Paul from sending in Dzielski.

BONNIE'S HEART might have skipped a couple of beats. She wasn't sure. As soon as the words were out, they hung in the air.

Rose had just announced that it was silly they were all being so quiet. "The men aren't here anymore, gone on their little mission, and women can multitask," she smirked, apparently awaiting equally sexist rejoinders.

Of all the things the old lady could have said just then, that was undoubtedly the quickest way to put Luke in danger. Bonnie's husband was now exposed, but she had no way of getting in touch with him to tell him so. Not unless she got in the car and floored it all the way to the hotel.

Her schoolgirls were also exposed. Anyone listening would know, no matter how carefully the men had chosen their route out of town, that the girls had no protection and were home from Mass now. While the Knights counted the collection, the families would have met up after Mass for brunch someplace public, a support group of sorts that happened to make it difficult for Brad or his lackeys to orchestrate accidental-looking deaths. But that brunch would be breaking up soon. The girls would be at home doing their schoolwork within the hour.

Bonnie could either drive to the city and try to warn her husband, probably arriving too late no matter how many traffic laws she broke, or she could gather the girls and find a way to guard them herself. She couldn't protect both, because Luke's phone was here. She couldn't just call him. Squeezing her eyes shut, she focused on prioritizing one problem to solve.

The information Dzielski had suggested that The Administrator always wanted a face-to-face with Brad when hired to kill. The assassin knew too well how phones could be hacked, and he didn't trust his own. They had been so sure the hitman would visit Brad's house first, then tie up the "loose ends" around town. The neighborhood watch had been keeping eyes on Brad's house for just that reason. Today, if he followed his pattern, he would have to go to the hotel first to get the order and then come back. Luke and the men would be the first to be in danger, she reasoned. Maybe she had time to beat him there and back again before any harm came to the girls.

Then again, when things got critical like this, perhaps The Administrator and Brad had some kind of code for phone conversations. Brad had to call anyway just to set up face-to-face meetings. If they had a code for rainy days, maybe the killer would come after the girls without visiting the hotel first. In any case, the girls were more vulnerable because they didn't expect the threat. Her husband knew he was in danger, just not the degree or certainty of it.

In her mind, Bonnie tested out the idea of arriving to defend Luke at the hotel. Even if she arrived before the killer, she would only distract her husband and probably make things worse. That plan was still tempting but stupid. She understood that she needed to let it go.

Luke had resources unlike anyone else Bonnie had ever met, and the girls were completely defenseless. Heart torn, Bonnie went where she might do some good, and she left the rest up to God.

Decision made, Bonnie abandoned the pile of phones to the Ladies Auxiliary, righted her own chair which had fallen when she had gotten up too hastily, and she used her cell phone to gather the girls. Luckily, the families were still at the restaurant. Bonnie asked to be put on speaker phone, so that everyone would feel the full force of her commanding tone of voice. Uncertain but obedient, they were all happy enough to spend more time together. One phone call for all the families, one phone call to Dolores, and it was done. Bonnie and Dolores were throwing an emergency bowling party for the girls and their families.

Bonnie knew the owner of the local bowling alley—he was a permanent local fixture—and everyone knew he kept a shotgun in the back. Bonnie would make sure it was under the counter within arms' reach today. Just because he was paranoid didn't mean there was no one to shoot in self-defense. She would tell him everything. Any stranger bowling by himself today was going to be very conspicuous. Bonnie would personally keep an eye out for them. She could do this.

She used the growing to-do list to push aside thoughts of what could happen to her husband. Bonnie tossed her cell phone on the passenger seat of the car and quickly belted herself in. She struggled to remember how to drive, how to turn on the car. Her hands remembered how, even though her brain wasn't working well. Panic was setting in. If Luke had been there, what would he tell her to do?

She chuffed a calming laugh. He would stretch out in the passenger seat as though he had all the time in the world and tell her that she had to trust her husband to take care of himself. There was nothing she could do about it anyway. And try to have fun bowling, he would say. A peck on her cheek and the mirage was gone. He'd done his job, though, as always holding her together when things got tough. It had been this way since high school. A renegade thought asked her how she would survive if she lost him. She shoved it back and reminded herself to have fun bowling. When she pulled away from the curb, she was smiling.

"I'M TELLING you, he's cool as a cucumber," Father Paul protested. "It's not time to go in yet."

"Luke is always cool. That doesn't mean he doesn't have a gun pointed at his head," Dzielski stage whispered from behind a newspaper.

No one reads newspapers anymore. Doesn't he realize how cliche that is? Father Paul wondered. "This is not the time. You'd be making a mistake," Father Paul said in a voice that brooked no argument.

The detective looked like he was about to say something else, then changed his whole train of thought. "What are *they* doing?" Dzielski growled.

Father Paul tried to turn in such a way that he wouldn't attract too much attention, and he followed Dzielski's gaze from the top edge of his newspaper to the far side of the lobby. Don, Willie, and Josh were sauntering in. Father Paul was sure the trio had spotted him and the cop, but they weren't obvious about it. They slipped into the bar and took stools. Only Josh, the guy with the strongest back, turned around and leaned against the bar to keep an eye on the lobby. Don and Willie sat on either side of him keeping up an easy banter. They actually weren't so conspicuous. Father Paul forced himself to turn back around. Dzielski was already "reading" his newspaper again.

"You're still on Luke?" Dzielski muttered.

"It's the same. He's waiting for something, but I can promise you, he's not waiting for us. He's not in immediate danger either. He feels half-asleep," Father Paul shrugged. At least, Father Paul thought, Luke doesn't *think* he's in any danger. He had a creeping feeling that something threatening was coming close, but he couldn't pinpoint it to a specific location. He had no idea what that meant, and it was enough to justify an entire bottle of antacids when this was over.

"Is he drugged?" Dzielski worried like a mother hen.

"No." Father Paul was getting irritable. He hoped for any kind of change. Soon.

Something caught Dzielski's eye. An expletive harshly ground out of the cop's mouth.

Father Paul turned, following Dzielski's gaze again.

Was that Agent Miller striding by? Yes, that most certainly was the guy who had tossed the rectory in search of the swipe card.

And that. That was Father Jeremy. Sneaking. Right on the heels of the FBI agent. What on earth was going on? Father Paul's mind raced.

Miller made a beeline for the offices behind the front desk. No one questioned his presence, as if his charging in were an expected thing. The attendants recognized him and let him pass, immediately turning back to their screens. *Wow*, Father Paul thought, *You know your search will turn up nothing when no one demands a warrant or a badge.* One attendant looked up and met Father Paul's eye across the lobby. The priest smiled and then broke contact, pretending he was looking for someone else around the lobby but didn't turn away. Fat chance he would miss this show!

Miller reappeared from the office area, asked a few clipped questions of the front desk attendants, then strode toward the unholy hallway. Father Jeremy had taken out his white collar and unbuttoned the top button of his clerics, but he still looked very much like a priest. Father Paul thought it was amazing that Agent Miller didn't spot him as he strode by.

Father Jeremy followed Agent Miller. Father Paul and Detective Dzielski followed them, despite Dzielski's vehement whispered objection. "That's my friend," Father Paul shot back. End of whispered conversation. And behind them, the Knights from the bar followed. It was a parade.

RUFUS, THE smarter of Lisa's personal bodyguards—or jail keepers, depending on your perspective—had a clipped conversation that had to be—she was sure of it—some kind of code. Something was definitely up, she thought, and hoped it had nothing to do with Josh. He was the very best friend she'd ever had, finding ways to spend time with her and keep her sane. He told her, "This too shall pass," because it was what his grandmother had taught him. With that, he had pulled her out of alcoholism—she quit cold turkey—and had given her hope. Brad wouldn't be able to hold onto her forever. Someday, she would do more than survive.

Gabe looked jealous enough to kill, Lisa realized, but Rufus merely shrugged at him. "You're lucky the boss didn't kill you after the bird in the flue," Rufus said, but Lisa had no idea what he meant. She misheard and hoped that "the bird that flew" was a girl who had escaped. *Good girl*, Lisa thought. Still, she wished Rufus wouldn't stir up Gabe before leaving her with the idiot.

Predictably, Gabe leered at her as soon as they were alone. Lisa steeled herself for his inappropriate attentions, a problem that intensified each time he was left alone with her. The problem had been developing gradually as Gabe grew confident Lisa wouldn't complain about him to Brad. Gabe made her skin crawl, but her options weren't good.

If she told Brad that Gabe was making advances toward her, Brad might or might not believe her, and his mercurial moods were impossible to predict. If Brad believed her, Gabe would die instantly, and he would be replaced by someone either better or worse. Also risky. But if Brad didn't believe her, she would be beaten until she couldn't speak again for weeks. Since she was known as the mentally ill wife with live-in nurses, Brad had a ready-made excuse why she wouldn't be making appearances around town. What would Josh do then?

Lisa didn't want most of these outcomes. Nor could she think of an alternative. So, she hadn't even told Josh. The one time he thought he'd seen something, she had stonewalled the conversation, not wanting Josh to do something rash.

Her plan was to stave off the advances tactfully, an approach that had the barely perceptible effect of slowing things down. She just needed to buy time for Josh and his friends to play out their angle. She would not be held hostage by her crazy husband forever.

"Brad wouldn't like this..." she smiled sheepishly to take the threat out of her words.

He coiled a strand of her brown hair around his pointer finger, and her scalp tingled, instinctively preparing itself. That hair was going to get yanked. She bumped up against the kitchen counter, not far from the knife block. His whole body soon held her in place, and his other hand roamed freely. She knew better than to pull away. She angled her face toward the hand that now held a fistful of hair. Her whole body relaxed, ready to let her mind leave it behind and go wherever she needed to be mentally. She could go somewhere to feel safe. Josh didn't judge her for this, but they had talked about it. What had he said? What had it even been about?

She struggled back into her body, fully gripping her mind. What had he said?

Hit a soft spot, he'd said. And he showed her where they were. If she ever had to, she promised that she would. Her eyelids dragged open, unused to being put into service like this. Her eyes bounced a little blurrily between possible targets: Throat, upwards toward the sternum, and just below the belt. Gabe was only a couple of inches taller than her, and he had parked his legs wide around hers. He was a little close, but she thought she could get a good swing with her thigh.

She focused like she was lining up to score a goal in the upper corner of the net, where the goalie would inevitably soar too late to deflect it. Once upon a time, she'd been her soccer team's top scorer. She was long out of practice, but this would have to do. Lisa grunted with the effort she put behind that leg, and she was satisfied with the sound of Gabe wheezing out, injured past the ability to scream.

Gabe's knees hit the floor in the next second, but Lisa wasn't going to wait for him to catch his breath. *If you've got to do it, hit his throat as hard as you can, but use your palm. That way you don't break your hand if you miss,* Josh had said with an apologetic smile and a shrug. He was right to worry. Her days of athletic practice were years past, her target was moving, and she was shaking with adrenaline.

His face contorted in pain, Gabe craned his neck to turn an unfocused gaze toward her. When her palm connected with Gabe's throat, his sounds of choking cut off completely. He was not breathing for the moment, but that would change soon.

How to tie him up? She thought fast. What she had was a lot of appliances with cords that would be more useful for tying a man up if they were not attached to appliances. She also had an unnecessarily strong pair of scissors. She decided that she hated, absolutely and irrevocably, the cappuccino machine. She'd had her first cappuccino with Brad when they were dating, and she'd never had one since they married. *Snip.*

Gabe wasn't breathing normally yet, but he had one foot underneath him again and a dangerous glint in his eye. Lisa squatted to get a good shot at the final soft spot under the sternum. Using her leg muscles for momentum and holding down his shoulders with her hands, she drove the ball of her foot up beneath his sternum with all her might. Then she cried out in pain. She had definitely pulled her quadriceps, and that pain might be distracting her from something worse in her smashed toes. She was not as fit as she used to be. Lisa hated Brad for taking the best years from her.

No, she decided as she threw Gabe face-first into the floor, the past would not be her best years. Gabe didn't even groan when his head rebounded off the tile. He was finally, mercifully unconscious. Lisa decided she would exercise, finish college, get a job, and, if Josh wasn't "the one," she'd find someone else, get married, and have kids. This was the beginning of her new life! And despite the pulled muscle, it was exhilarating! She hadn't felt this good since winning the state championships with her team.

She had nothing against the toaster, so she left that cord attached as she tied up his feet. There was a particularly long dish towel that served as a gag. She slipped it in just in time, just as he managed a few strong coughs and his eyes flickered back to full awareness. When she was done, she stepped off his back and inspected her work. Gabe was struggling, but the effort wasn't getting him anywhere. He was toast.

If she survived this, Lisa was going to inform Josh that he was the sweetest, bravest, most handsome man in the world. She just hoped he felt similarly about her. She could never tell if what they had was more of a big brother, little sister thing to him. But he was all the hope she had in this moment. Without him, she'd had a lot of good intentions but no energy to fight. This was for him, because Josh believed in her. And she was pretty sure he needed her help urgently. Rufus's clipped conversation worried her.

Josh had given her a lot of information from Luke in case something like this ever happened. It was too risky before, but now if Brad came home, she'd die anyway. Nothing to lose, therefore, she was going after his black books. They were accounting ledgers naming his hired muscle and exactly how much they had earned including their special jobs, cataloguing the girls he had used, time-stamping the customers and their purchases, and enumerating all the kills Brad had ordered. It was listed chronologically, one year per book. So, if the FBI did nothing else, they could arrest him for tax evasion. And a lot of other stuff.

Brad had suspected this day was coming. He had forbidden Lisa from seeing the combination to his safe. However, because she was allowed to put on makeup whenever and wherever she felt like it, Gabe hadn't objected whenever she'd opened her makeup compact. Makeup was "for" Brad. Makeup compacts also had mirrors on them. An obvious move had Rufus been there that evening, but to Gabe? Well, Gabe wasn't too bright. He hadn't thought anything of it, and she'd only had to see it once to remember the combination.

Lisa had rehearsed the combination and Josh's phone number until she fell asleep most nights. Not that she'd ever really believed she'd be using them. They were just a comfort. No child really believes their security blanket will defend them, but they like holding their blankets anyway. Lisa had her adult version of a safety blanket in these numbers.

Click. Lisa swung open the door to the safe. Fortunately, there were duffel bags nearby. She picked a black leather one and emptied the safe into it. As she hunched over her work, she necessarily favored her injured leg, but she still managed to work fast.

As much as her leg allowed, she sprinted across the street to the church and straight back to the sacristy, breathing a deep sigh of relief when she heard an adding machine punching out a sum, paper shuffling, and coins clinking. Her relief evaporated when she saw old women rather than the Knights. No Josh.

Her face telegraphed her confusion. One of the older ladies explained, "We lost count and started over. That's why it's taking so long."

"Bonnie was talking." Another quibbled.

"Rose is the one who started it," another accused.

All eyes on Rose. She turned the color of her name.

"Where are the Knights?" Lisa asked.

The ladies exchanged inquisitive looks. "Bonnie went bowling," Rose offered inadequately.

"Bowling?" Lisa found herself asking. The Knights weren't counting, and Bonnie was bowling.

"Yes," Rose said, happy that Lisa was interested. "I'm sure I heard her talking to Dolores and arranging a bowling party for the families of the girls… who… you know." She smiled sheepishly.

"Got it. Thanks!" Bowling still didn't make sense, but she didn't want to hear any more about it. Lisa looked around and found an ancient rotary phone mounted on the sacristy wall. Bingo! She literally dialed Josh's number. A cell phone jingled behind her.

"They left those here, honey," the accusatory old lady told her a little aggressively. She indicated a pile of cell phones. A cold feeling settled into Lisa's stomach. Bowling with the victims, missing Knights, abandoned cell phones. Where had Rufus gone? This was serious. This was very bad.

"Okay, thanks," Lisa said. She was going to find Bonnie. The bowling alley was a hike from here, and she'd be doing it with a limp. "Can anyone give me a ride to the bowling alley?" Everyone offered. No one wanted to count anymore.

Bonnie would know where the guys were and how to get a hold of them. Lisa had to tell one or both of them Rufus was coming.

No one was armed except Miller and Dzielski in this parade, but Father Paul thought it was lucky Agent Miller had stopped being a moron long enough to figure out it was time to storm the castle. The ladies must have let something slip through the cell phones, and Miller must have quickly gotten a warrant. It didn't appear that he had any backup besides Jeremy. When had they started working together? Father Paul spent a petty moment or two wondering why he'd been left out, until he realized he had similarly left out Jeremy from working with the city police.

Father Paul's long stride easily pulled him ahead of Dzielski and in stride with Jeremy as they crossed the lobby.

Father Jeremy was confused and then relieved. "He's the assassin. He killed Father Tom!" Jeremy stage-whispered pointing at Miller.

Father Paul concentrated very hard, but he couldn't make sense of what Jeremy was saying. "No, he's an FBI Agent."

"Then he's a bad one!" Jeremy answered.

"Yes, he's a very bad FBI agent. But he can't be the assassin," Father Paul said, rejecting the information.

"Paul," Jeremy sighed. "Is his name Christian Miller?"

Father Paul raised an eyebrow. Nodded.

"Tom named him in a journal he kept about his personal investigation. Tom found out Miller's code name for his illegal jobs, followed Miller for a day, and then Tom died two days later," Jeremy told him. "That," he indicated Miller, "is The Administrator. That's his assassin code name!"

Miller didn't notice he had a tail until the great big Knuckle Dragger from last night popped open the door and gestured with a quick lift of his nose that Miller should turn around. Spinning on his heels, the agent's eyes bugged, he hesitated, and then he spun again and launched himself through the open doorway. Knuckle Dragger took a calming breath and let it out, obviously disapproving of Miller's brilliant plan to run away and hide. He continued to hold the door open and leveled his gaze at Father Paul first, then Father Jeremy, then Detective Dzielski and the rest of the circus. It was an assessing gaze, the kind a mean little boy gives an insect when he's deciding on the most fun way to torment it.

They couldn't leave Luke now that they'd been spotted. The two clerics and a cop followed Miller at a dignified pace, and the Knights weren't far behind them.

Luke's eyes popped open with the door to the lobby. There hadn't been a knock or an electronic beep this time. The thug emerged from the watch room and opened up seemingly without reason. Luke tried to mask his surprise when Agent Miller landed inside in a manner reminiscent of a child playing leapfrog. Luke was briefly concerned for his socked toes in the narrow corridor, since he didn't have his shoes anymore. As Miller straightened his suit jacket and seemed to mentally gather himself, he studiously ignored Luke, or so it seemed to the Knight. Miller only bothered to give a disdainful glance because Luke was pointedly staring. Upon gaining the man's attention, Luke raised both eyebrows at him, then gave him a long, disbelieving once-over, shiny bald head to shiny shoes and back again. The combination of seeing Luke there, compounded with Luke's very apparent contempt for Miller, made the agent shift from foot to foot uncertainly. Luke was satisfied.

Father Paul and another man, probably a priest missing his white collar, strode in. The door *whooshed* shut behind them. Luke was sure he heard Dzielski shout "Hey!" only a few feet from the entrance, but Muscle Man planted his boot behind the closed door until there was a tiny electronic *beep* and the *snick* of a bolt slamming home. He and Agent Miller pulled out their guns. Things happened quickly after that.

Father Paul shut his eyes, probably praying. The other man in black was eyeing Muscle Man's gun, as if he were about to defend himself somehow.

Two men launched out of the office at Luke's back, guns drawn. One of them, the more compact of the two, crossed in front of Luke, taking up a position farther down the hall and away from the action. The other man, taller and bulkier, kept a position both closer to the horrible action and to the lobby. When the bulky man turned his back on the compact man, Mr. Compact disarmed Mr. Bulky and took control of his huge body, using it as a shield. The two of them effectively shielded Luke as well. He appreciated them, but he wasn't sure whose side Mr. Compact was on.

Another electronic beep, and Dzielski joined the scene. *It took him long enough to find the swipe card*, Luke thought. The cop charged in behind the door hard enough to knock Muscle Man forward several feet.

Josh, Willie, and Don joined the fray, launching themselves at Agent Miller. Luke shook his head to wake himself, then jumped forward to help them, but he couldn't get close enough in the narrow hallway. The military retirees quickly disarmed the agent, and Luke threw an elbow hard enough that Miller's head rebounded off the wall behind him.

Muscle Man had disarmed Dzielski. The detective and soon both priests hung on the man's tree-like arms, trying to keep him from pointing the gun at anyone left standing. It was Josh who, when he finally got an opening, reached in and simply cranked down on the pressure point between Muscle Man's thumb and forefinger. Luke was proud. It had been Luke's idea that Willie and Don teach some basic self-defense moves to the guys when this whole saga had begun, and he remembered the day they had learned pressure points. Leave it to the mechanic to remember that and to execute it so beautifully.

Muscle Man spewed some nasty expletives, but he wasn't down yet. Every man piled on him punching and kicking, and down he went, nearly pinned by Don. When it happened, Luke winced mostly because it had been an accident. Muscle Man rolled into Josh, and Josh, staggering for balance in his thick-tread work boots, accidentally stomped on Muscle Man's head, rendering him unconscious. Both Josh and Father Paul bug-eyed. It was red-faced Don, still lying on top of the thug from his wrestling position, who assessed the sleeping giant and, short of breath, puffed out, "He's fine."

Then, all was quiet. A big smile spread across Luke's face as he nodded appreciation to the now-obvious undercover man, Mr. Compact, who had crossed in front of him, probably on purpose to block any bullets coming Luke's way. Even with a bullet proof vest on, that was a brave, gutsy move. The cop dipped his chin once in acknowledgment. The other gunman from the watch office was tied up by his own boot laces, prone at Mr. Compact's feet. Mr. Compact had been busy, while Muscle Man went down.

A furtive face peeked around the corner leading down the hallway that could only lead to girls' rooms. To Luke's horror, the face was followed by a full body, gun in hand, taking careful aim at Mr. Compact, who was stooping to retrieve his gun. Dzielski was still checking his facial injuries, not reaching for a gun yet, so Luke understood why the shooter would aim at Mr. Compact. He could also tell it was going to be a tough shot, since Mr. Compact was moving too fast, and Luke *knew* before it happened. He knew.

The bullet ripped through Father Paul's rib cage, a punch that sent him flying back from the undercover man and into the lobby door behind him. As Father Paul slid down the wall, the front of his shirt grew shiny with thick pulses of dark blood.

The undercover knelt and carefully took aim, firing at the head of the newcomer, while Don and Willie dove for Father Paul. To Luke, things were happening in slow motion, but he still didn't have time to react. It occurred to Luke to wonder why a cop was firing at anything but the torso. The bulk of the shooter's tactical vest wasn't visible to him until the man's body slumped to the floor, a single trickle of blood flowing from the center of his forehead to the bridge of his nose before veering across a cheek.

Luke, Josh, and the undercover sprinted for a view

down the hallway. Brad was the first customer to storm out of a room toward the office. Angry and prowling at first, while setting his clothes to rights, Brad took in the dead body and the scene around it, suddenly going immobile and pale.

Paying customers, more tentative, cracked their doors open to take peeks. Some panicked and dashed toward the back exit. Luke and Josh ran to tackle Brad first, leveling him. The undercover cop saw they were making a fine citizen's arrest and hurdled over them to block the rear exit with fire power.

Dzielski didn't check to see whether the rear exit was covered. He jogged into the office full of screens, phoning 9-1-1 from the landline.

Don and Willie had stanched the flow from Father Paul's front and checked that there wasn't a corresponding hole in his back. That second priest Luke didn't know had taken off his black shirt and belt. He helped them lift Father Paul, so they could secure the wadded-up shirt over the wound with the belt around Father Paul's torso. Father Paul wasn't groaning or struggling, but blood was pulsing out with every heartbeat. The second priest, wearing just his white undershirt now, said he was going to his car to get his Sick Call Kit. As the trio set Father Paul back down on the floor, Father Paul's face, gray and sweaty, came to rest with unfocused eyes looking vaguely in Luke's direction, who stood in his socks at the hallway corner, having left Josh securely atop Brad.

"Father?" Luke called out.

Nothing.

Chapter Seventeen

The girls and their families came over to the bowling alley after brunch. Bonnie came directly from church, and unfortunately, she hadn't dressed casually. She ended up wearing bowling shoes with a skirt suit and panty hose, no socks. She would destroy her legwear in the process, but she was going to play. You can't lead people from the cheap seats, she reminded herself as she tied up the laces, distracting herself from more distant worries.

Ollie, the long-time owner of Ollie's Alley, was missing a few of his yellowed teeth, but he was so friendly, Bonnie couldn't help but smile back at him broadly. He had tucked away Bonnie's sensible heeled shoes in a numbered cubby, all the while perched like a sage cowboy on his wooden stool behind the counter. He wore his usual gray t-shirt, which might have been white once, and jeans which had seen bluer days. His skin was as worn as a smoker's, but his spirit was childlike. Bonnie had hosted plenty of fundraiser nights at this place, and she considered Ollie a town fixture.

Bonnie clunked about as gracefully as she could manage in her bowling shoes. She greeted the families as they checked in, standing by Ollie's counter with the credit card to cover them all and to make sure they didn't try to pay. This was the least Sacred Heart could provide after what had happened to them. Ollie was his usual outrageous, charming self, and Bonnie was pleased to witness how comfortable the girls were with his compliments.

"You make my bowling alley look like a real classy place dressing up like this. You especially, pretty little lady," he told Renee, giving her a toothy, if gappy, smile and a wink.

Renee returned the smile brightly and only said, "Thank you." Not so long ago, the man's comments might have met with a cold reception. Or a boiling angry one. Father Paul had worked wonders to bring the girls so far.

Bonnie spared a moment to worry over Luke and Father Paul and the whole crew, but she could only spare a moment. She had to keep surveying the bowling alley for danger. It certainly was loud, she realized, so sight was all she had.

Dolores had selected a ball for herself and was setting up the scoreboards, greeting families as she entered names on the two lanes closest to Ollie's counter. Altogether, there were fourteen of them playing, because two of the girls had younger brothers, an eight-year-old and a twelve-year-old. The point wasn't to play quickly but to have fun and stay together. Bonnie realized that playing and keeping an eye out for trouble would be no easy task.

Bonnie regretted putting Ollie in this position, but she knew the man would gladly help. As she quickly laid out the facts and fears of her situation, Ollie's face scrunched in concentration as if he were mentally sketching the face of an assassin. Then he motioned for her to lean over the counter, and he patted his shotgun. "Old Sally's right here, if anything happens. Don't you worry," he assured her.

Bonnie experienced a moment of doubt then, but, she reminded herself, she certainly wasn't going to call the three local police officers and ask them to stand by with bullets in their shirt pockets, as per protocol. This was as good as it was going to get with the Knights and Father Paul out of town, not to mention 'outed' by the Ladies' Auxiliary. She could only pray that they would be safe, too.

ONE OF the medics taped down a square bandage on only three sides over the bloody hole in Father Paul. The priest didn't even moan.

"What is that?" Josh asked.

The medic hesitated. Luke figured the medic couldn't decide whether Josh wanted the wound or the bandage identified. "That's an occlusive bandage. I taped it on three sides, so that air can escape but not get inside the chest cavity. It will help your friend breathe. Your friend has lost a lot of blood, so we're going to get fluids in him next. We're doing everything possible to take care of him," the medic answered with professional detachment. A few more medics trooped in, weighed down with more equipment. "I need a blood pressure right now. Get a line started," the focused medic said, staying in charge.

Firefighters had been standing by. Two of the three

now exited the narrow hallway in favor of setting up the gurney out in the lobby area. Why there were firefighters was beyond Luke. Clearly there was no fire, but the medic in charge had arrived with the fire crew just a minute or two after the swarm of police officers, who were working down the hall, closer to the girls' rooms. He had heard the police officers instructing girls to stay in their rooms and out of the narrow hallway. The johns had already been handcuffed, and Luke thought some or all of them had already been taken out the back exit, avoiding the bottle-neck on this end of the hallway.

One firefighter attached a machine with a blood pressure cuff, while the two new medics worked together to start an IV on the opposite arm, and the first medic studied his bandaging job on Father Paul. Luke didn't know what was in the IV bag, but the guy holding it squeezed like he couldn't get the fluids into Father Paul fast enough. Father Paul was lying in a pool of blood, but the machine read fast, faint heartbeats. He was still alive. For now.

The firefighters in the lobby got the gurney down to floor level and as close to the door as possible without tripping anyone. Everyone in uniform either grabbed a piece of equipment or helped to haul Father Paul to the lobby. They loaded him and some of the equipment onto the cot, belted his gangly body in, and then two men co-ordinated efforts to raise the cot to full height and roll him away with his feet hanging over the end. A crowd of first responders Luke hadn't known were standing in the lobby either rushed ahead to hold automatic doors or followed along behind. Police had been preventing the merely curious public in the lobby from loitering, and now they cleared a path.

Father Jeremy, as Luke had now learned his name, moved to stay with Father Paul, but a police officer held up a hand and shook his head. "We still have questions for you here, and you're not a direct relative of the patient," he explained. Father Jeremy's face cleared with the serenity of a prayerful man, although his eyes drifted back to the door through which Father Paul had been taken, then to the floor still covered with his blood. Father Paul was in God's hands, not theirs.

Dzielski had paused his work preserving the recorded evidence to watch Father Paul roll away. "Whether or not he dies, your career is over, Dzielski," a hard-nosed city police officer informed the man. Reading his name badge, Luke consoled himself that it was not the city's chief of police, who had yet to arrive. Few in the city police, if any besides the chief, would have known about the undercover operation or the mole. Luke hoped that Dzielski's career wouldn't end because a civilian had gotten caught in the crossfire.

Dzielski didn't carry himself with Father Jeremy's serenity, but he did seem to accept his colleague's dour dictum as stated. Luke realized that Dzielski had been prepared all along to lose his career or his life to see this takedown happen. He suddenly wondered why it was so personal for the man. Now that it was over, Luke might never find out. This might be the last time Luke ever saw his friend.

As various law enforcement officers watched over his shoulder, Dzielski made copies of the recording for the FBI, state police, and county police courtesy of the city police. The FBI was the only agency yet to arrive, unless you counted Miller, who was in custody, so the interrogations had yet to begin in earnest.

Josh refused to get checked out in the hospital, but someone was irrigating and bandaging cuts on his forearms. Dzielski still hadn't cleaned all the blood off his face, and it had dried. When the medics moved toward him, he was still busy, so he swatted the air irritably in their general direction. Some more medics trooped towards the girls' rooms after making sure no one else here wanted anything.

When the FBI finally arrived, instead of asking anything related to the case, they asked whether anyone had seen an Agent Stiefellecker. Luke didn't know who they were talking about until they showed him a picture. It was Agent Miller's partner, although the two often split up. Luke hadn't even known the man's name until now. He'd never even seen the partners interact, only drive together. It was hard to know what Stiefellecker suspected or knew.

ROSE PULLED—laboriously, as though she were driving a tank—around the corner to the bowling alley, when Lisa spotted Rufus' car in the parking lot. It was a huge lot that included other stores and a movie theater. Rufus' car wasn't parked particularly close to the bowling alley, though.

"Drive by the bowling alley," Lisa ordered Rose.

Rose wasn't listening. The car began to slow—nearly to a stop—as if to turn into the parking lot.

"No!" Lisa shouted. "Keep driving." And she waved frantically to indicate the direction Rose should steer them.

"I'm sorry," Rose said primly. "I thought you wanted to go to the bowling alley."

It was insane, and part of Lisa knew that at the time, but she was paralyzed in terror when Rose acted offended. She briefly imagined Rose stomping on the gas pedal, wrecking the car, and killing both of them. Lisa took a discrete look at Rose. Most people weren't capable of the violence Lisa had been forced to live with for so long. In fact, Rose appeared to be a shining example of non-violence. The woman was driving comically slowly, and it appeared that her petulant response was the end of her reaction. She was nothing like Brad or his goons.

Your Father in heaven wants to forgive you, Father Paul had preached a few Sundays ago. *He wants you to come to Confession, so that He can speak the words of forgiveness and grant you peace.* That homily combined with many, many hours of talking with Josh, when he sneaked through a window to see her, helped Lisa believe she could have a life after Brad. There was a lot more love than hate in the world. She took a deep breath.

"I'm sorry, Rose. Could you circle around the block once? I see someone's car parked here, and I wasn't expecting him. I need a minute to think about what to do."

What she needed was a minute to think about what Rufus could be doing here. All there was besides the bowling alley was a bargain store in which most items sold for a dollar; a liquor store; a movie theater; and a couple of cheap chain stores for toys and other things that couldn't be of interest to Rufus. It wasn't as if he could come here to stock up on bullets.

Lisa was almost sure Rufus had been called out for some kind of job, but the only job here could be the bowling alley with Bonnie and the girls. That seemed to imply that the guys at the hotel were already … taken care of, and Rufus had been told to take care of loose ends here finally. Lisa's heart clenched in pain. She didn't know anything for sure, she reminded herself. But she was afraid for Josh and the others.

It took a ridiculously long time to get around the block in the huge red Buick. But timing was on their side. Lisa spotted Rufus carrying some shopping bags behind the bowling alley. The bags were bulky but looked as though they didn't weigh much. She couldn't make out what was in the bags, but she did see that he was headed behind the bowling alley.

"Should I pull in this time?" Rose asked ceremoniously. She actually tilted her head so that her nose went up in the air.

"Sure. Thank you, Rose."

When Lisa hopped out with her black duffel bag, she knew she'd gain unwanted attention from anyone who considered her to be mentally unstable. She hid the duffel bag for safekeeping behind some bushes along the wall. Then, she waited until Rose had driven out of the parking lot before following Rufus's tracks. Lisa knew that people thought she was crazy, and they would likely call the police or Brad to come and take care of her if they saw her out here alone. It was a small town, after all. She was grateful for Rose's neglect on that score, and she hoped no one spotted her as she purposefully strode behind the bowling alley.

Lisa entered the back of the bowling alley and took a few steps down into relative darkness before her eyes adjusted. It was nearly impossible to hear anything over the noise of machines and thundering bowling balls and thumping music. The owner had the radio playing the best of the 80's, 90's and maybe close to today. At the moment, "Macarena" was playing, a song Lisa hadn't heard since grade school. It was encouraging, as though she were an invincible kid again. But she really wished she could hear or see the present better.

Searching for signs of Rufus, Lisa tiptoed, crossing underneath the lanes and their ball returns, and the rest of their machinery. She had never seen how a bowling alley worked from below. There was a sweeper for pins that got knocked over, and a pin machine that gripped pins by the neck and reloaded another machine that set them up to get knocked over again.

Lisa was normally a pragmatic woman, but something about finally escaping captivity and possibly losing her best friend, Josh, had her feeling a bit emotional. Her eyes filled with tears as she imagined seeing the faces of Josh and the other Knights on those pins, thrown away like the girls at Brad's hotels. Lisa hadn't even known about the girls Brad was using and throwing away, not until Josh had told her. Lisa wasn't allowed to read the newspaper some days. Now she knew why. She wasn't the only person her husband kept caged until their usefulness had run out.

Jesus, save me! All she wanted to do was find Rufus, see what he was doing, and report it to the police. The bowling alley would have a phone upstairs. She would just have to convince one more person that she wasn't crazy today. Then she needed to find out how Josh was, and she needed to see him again. Josh just couldn't be hurt. She needed him.

She didn't find Rufus until she reached the last two lanes. At that point, she had basically given up and stopped tiptoeing. She thought he must have entered some other building. Shocked to finally see him, she gasped and tripped over a heavy electric cord. He was squatting and hunched over, concentrating on something in his hands and didn't notice her, giving her time to scurry for cover. There had been no chance he would hear her over the din.

A wicked looking military knife was on the floor beside him with hunks of sponge material scattered around it. Rufus had a block of what looked like wax, wires, and little round pieces about the size of poker chips but thicker, and he was stuffing that mess in the toy ball where the sponge material had been. He tapped away at his phone until finally the messy block and wires blinked their lights once, as if he had set something. Then he was taping the thin skin of the toy ball shut with electrical tape. He was situated near a ball return.

Lisa angled her head in an effort to see up the ball return and make out faces of the players in the first lane. Her suspicions were confirmed as soon as she saw Dolores, the school counselor, next to a beautiful girl with long, curly dark hair. The Sacred Heart girls Brad had victimized must be here, and Bonnie was probably nearby. Rufus had put together two bombs, one for each ball return. It sure looked to Lisa as if he could detonate them remotely with his phone.

Rufus had already taped one ball shut while Lisa had been hiding, and he was finishing his second one now. Good thing she hadn't waited for the police to arrive.

It seemed so hopeless. Anyone her husband wanted dead would have little chance of survival. She wouldn't be safe from Brad, not until he was arrested. Even then, she wasn't sure. Lisa's heart squeezed painfully at the thought that Josh might be gone, that he might have suffered, and that she might never see him again. There was nothing she could do about that now, though. For the girls here today, Lisa could stop Rufus, but she was only buying the girls a day at best.

Lisa decided it was worth it to give them that day. She would certainly die when Brad found out about everything she had done in the past hour, whether or not she helped the girls. Besides, with Josh very likely gone, Lisa was out of hope. She didn't want to live like this anymore, and the only way to end it was by being brave and maybe doing some good along the way. For all she knew, maybe the black books would fall into the right hands and this would all end soon.

Lisa did not have to look hard to find something heavy. She did have to scrounge for something she could lift. She spied some extra sheets of flooring material leaned up against the wall. One was light enough but too awkward to use. She dismissed that as a possible weapon. On the wall above that, her brain registered the importance of the fuse box.

She raced to it, flung it open, and pulled down the big red switch. When the whole place went dead silent, including the games and music upstairs, Lisa screeched "BOMB! BOMB! Get out, there's a booooomb!"

Silence stretched for another second or two. Then feet pounded the floor upstairs, and staccato conversations punctuated the dull roar. There were sobs when someone fell, squeaks of shoes making tight turns, crying for no reason at all it sounded to Lisa. But Lisa could not hear what was happening right in front of her. And she couldn't see anything.

BONNIE SAID controlled, motivational things like, "We're going to go outside now, and everything will be alright," automatically, while she searched the area for that man in the brown suit. Of course, he was nowhere in sight now that someone was screaming about a bomb. Either he had made the bomb, or he was here to protect the girls. Bonnie didn't know for sure. He had been creepily watching them for thirty minutes, and Ollie had been hairy-eyeballing the man right back. Not that the man in the suit had noticed. Bonnie estimated that his IQ was nearly equivalent to his height in inches. Then the man disappeared. That was not quite fifteen minutes ago.

Only the exit signs and the safety lights offered any illumination. Ollie pulled the fire alarm, now openly carrying his shotgun, and he heavily shuffled toward a "Staff Only" door behind his counter. Bonnie imagined that it led to the basement, and she wondered whether the man in the brown suit had somehow slipped past Ollie and gone that way. Since Ollie was headed closer to a bomb, possibly in proximity to another man with a gun, Bonnie ran in her clunky bowling shoes to catch up to him before he got too far below.

Father Paul's mind drifted foggily, sleepily. He imagined that he was riding in the passenger seat of a fast car, jarred painfully with every pothole, and a baby was wailing. But nothing captured his focus for very long, and gradually, he could tell that everything was getting dimmer, would eventually fade to an inky black pool of nothing. He felt like maybe he was drowning a little, or not. Maybe it was just a little hard to breathe, or maybe he was picking up that feeling from someone else. The bumpy ride and the wailing seemed farther away. He wasn't concerned about any of it. Even the pain was fading. It was very peaceful, easy.

In the darkness, Lisa's scared face appeared. Someone was hunting for her with a Ka-Bar knife. All Father Paul could see was the blade and her face right next to a fuse box.

A voice he instinctively identified with God asked Father Paul, "Will you give your life for her?" The voice was asking which life would be sacrificed. In order to make so much evil right again, something had to be offered up to balance the scales of justice. Nothing less than justice would allow for true peace, but something more lay at the core of this question. Father Paul hadn't committed the evil, and he didn't think Lisa had either. If Father Paul or Lisa gave away their life, it would be an act of charity, something more than justice, and it could bear even greater fruit. He saw Lisa's face through God's eyes and made the choice that God already knew he would.

"Me." He would do it. And he hoped that whatever Josh had going on with Lisa would make them both very happy. He was pretty sure he had picked up on something during Communion this morning. He hoped he had. He felt a rush of God's paternal pride in him, and Father Paul was filled with joy.

There was a terrible weight on his chest, a gripping sensation. His heart had stopped. There just wasn't enough blood or oxygen to keep it moving anymore. *For You, God.* And he realized that it was true. Father Paul loved Lisa because he couldn't help loving what God loved, protecting whom God wanted to protect.

The light that had been illuminating Lisa's face suddenly moved just as her expression changed from terror to surprise. He wanted to know what would happen next, though he was absolutely certain that she would live. He just couldn't stay awake to watch what God would do.

RUFUS'S CELL phone lit like a headlight, and Lisa was the deer that couldn't run away. She couldn't even get her legs to respond. It wasn't as though her legs knew where to run anyway. The fire alarm was doing its best to get her moving, but all Lisa could see besides his cell phone was that same, wicked military knife Rufus had been using to cut open the sponge-filled balls. She was going to end up like one of those balls, stuffing spewed all over the floor.

If enough of the girls and school officials came to her funeral, maybe Rufus could use her body to hide a bomb just like the ball, she thought absently. She really didn't want anyone to come. Her husband would have to come in order to keep up appearances. That irritated her. Josh, she was afraid, might not be alive anymore. That thought troubled her more than anything else. He should get a chance to meet some new woman, a thought that hurt less than the alternative. Lisa wondered whether they could have been something more. Since there was no harm in it now, she wished for it, too.

Then Rufus turned his cell phone away from her toward something very close on Lisa's right. It was the owner of the bowling alley, and he pointed the long barrel of a gun at Rufus. Bonnie sneaked a peak around the wall. Lisa hadn't noticed the staircase there until now.

She'd been looking for Rufus, looking for a weapon... She could have been safe now, if only she had looked for an escape route before switching off the power.

"Drop that knife now, son. Lisa, could you put the lights back on so we can see?" the owner projected over the fire alarm. It was impressive how distinct his words were over the cacophony. And even more impressive that he had recognized Lisa in the dark.

Rufus assessed the old man, considering his odds.

Lisa flipped the main switch in the fuse box back up, and from her left, back the way she had come, a man in a brown suit spotted them and picked up his pace. "FBI! Drop your weapons!" Since he spoke in the plural, Lisa assumed he meant Ollie's gun and Rufus's knife. The agent in the brown suit had only a handgun, which—Lisa happened to know from overheard conversations at home—was only accurate at close range. Since the agent was still a hundred feet away, he had a trip to make before he'd be useful.

The owner of the bowling alley held onto his gun.

Rufus lunged at Lisa with his knife. She wondered, *Why would he do that right in front of the FBI?* Then she realized he had just created two bombs, so he'd be going to prison for a while anyway. Maybe he was just mad at her.

He didn't make it very far. The owner of the bowling alley blasted Rufus in the torso, throwing him back, away from Lisa. Rufus did drop the knife.

"Ollie!" Bonnie shouted, worry clear on her face as she watched a now angry FBI agent come into close range.

Ollie kept his gun pointed in the direction of Rufus, not the agent. "I want to see a badge before I put this down, you understand." He wasn't even straining to shout. Ollie's voice boomed over that fire alarm. The man was a bullhorn.

The agent kept his handgun and a scowl trained on Ollie as he fished his inside coat pocket for the badge. When he produced the item, Ollie nodded him closer. Then Ollie set his long barrel to lean against the wall. Ollie held the badge with suspicion at first, then read aloud, "Agent Scott Stiefellecker," he stumbled over the last name. "FBI alright." He nodded to punctuate the finality of his judgment.

Bonnie came the rest of the way down the stairs, placing herself close to the long barrel, eyeing the agent as if she weren't sure what to make of him yet. When Agent Stiefellecker checked Rufus for a pulse, then dialed 9-1-1, Bonnie relaxed a bit, but she stayed close to that gun.

Lisa didn't know what Bonnie's reaction was about, but Ollie was asking Lisa how she was doing. The agent barked for both of them to get away from the fuse box. "Go sit by the stairs," he ordered. "You too," when he remembered Bonnie.

"Actually," Bonnie responded, "I have some questions for you first." And in the manner of school principals, she asked Agent Stiefellecker how he managed to be ignorant of his partner's crimes. As Lisa watched, the man in the brown suit actually shrank in height due to the verbal hammering.

THE FIRE alarm had long since been turned off. The girls and their families were being questioned, and Bonnie wasn't allowed to check in with her own people to put them at ease. She hated how this was being handled.

Then something boomed in the distance and shook the floor she was standing on. She had plenty of time to worry about that before radios dispatched the news. The Coppini house had blown up, and it was a total loss.

"Anybody hurt?" one agent asked.

A voice over the radio said that it wasn't safe to check inside yet.

The first agent ordered, "No matter what else you see in there, secure the safe. Keep eyes on it. Do you hear me?"

"Affirmative," responded the dispassionate voice over the radio.

"Are you looking for Brad's black books?" Lisa asked. She was watching from the seating area at a bowling lane she occupied with Ollie. Neither of them had been questioned yet. Ollie was patting her arm to comfort her about the loss of her house.

Both agents narrowed their eyes at her, but they didn't speak.

"I put them in a black leather duffel bag. They're hidden behind some bushes out back, just before the entrance to the basement," Lisa said. The agents exchanged amazed expressions. Ollie patted Lisa on the hand affectionately. It was the sort of gesture a proud grandparent might bestow on his favorite grandchild, though in this case he couldn't have known what was happening. The astonished agents' faces were his only clue. Bonnie had suspicions about what might be in some black books in a safe that Brad would want blown up.

The first agent texted someone, and minutes later, a man who actually wore sunglasses indoors and an FBI windbreaker jogged in with the duffel bag Lisa had described. Suddenly, all the agents were interested in who Lisa was. This time Bonnie cut them some slack—this was a confusing situation, and they hadn't gotten to question Lisa yet. To the agents, Lisa was just some woman who spotted a bomber and nearly got stabbed for it. You'd think her last name would have registered earlier, but Bonnie couldn't remember when they had cut the alarm. Perhaps they hadn't heard her clearly.

When they realized Lisa's house had just blown up and that she was married to Brad, the reaction was hesitant and mixed. "I'm sorry about your house, ma'am," the agent in the windbreaker offered. "Was anyone inside?" he asked.

Lisa had to explain about Gabe, and that was complicated, since he was tied up with the cords of appliances. The agents informed her that the fire department would look for his body in the kitchen, once it was safe to do so. They also told Lisa that since Gabe had held her hostage and assaulted her, she should file a report in the event that his body was missing. They would keep her informed.

"And thank you for retrieving the black books... for

us? How did you know about them? Did you know the house was set to detonate?" the first agent asked, sounding lost at sea.

The questions went on and on and on. And no one was offering information about Luke or what happened at the hotel. Bonnie was too proud to cry, but she suspected these were the type of men who couldn't stand to see a woman shedding tears. The ploy would get her some basic information. The idea tempted her.

It was Lisa who thought to make a dignified deal.

"I tell you what," Lisa said. "I'll keep answering your questions, if you answer mine." That earned her some raised eyebrows. "Is there something happening at Gilded Swan Hotel right now?" The men exchanged telling looks among themselves. "I'll take that as a 'yes'," Lisa told them. "Those guys taking down my husband at his hotel, those are our friends. Luke is Bonnie's husband, and Father Paul is our pastor. And Josh is very important to me." Lisa's eyes quickly flooded, and she couldn't say any more.

As Bonnie had suspected, the men had to look away from the crying woman. Bonnie wanted to stand up and clap.

The first agent told Lisa, in what was probably his best soothing voice, "Everybody is safe, Josh and all the rest of those guys, except for Father Paul. He's at the hospital. He's critical, and they're working on him."

Bonnie thought it was pitifully inadequate as soothing voices went. But she rejoiced that Luke was safe. "What happened to Father Paul?" Bonnie spoke up.

"I can't say. All I can say is that they took him to the hospital, and they're working on him."

The news weighed heavily on Bonnie.

With a thick voice, Lisa asked, "What about Rufus?" He had been taken away on a gurney thirty minutes ago.

"I'll check," the agent answered. He texted something and received a phone call immediately.

When he was finished, he poked the 'end' button as aggressively as possible and announced, "Well, that solves the mystery of how the house blew up. Agent Stiefellecker was dumb enough to give Rufus his cell phone back once he was conscious. Fortunately, he blew up the house before he tried to blow us up, but according to Stiefellecker, we were a near miss." The group of agents standing around the bowling lanes called Stiefellecker and Rufus some foul but creative names. It was as though they had all the time in the world.

"Stiefellecker is losing his job, this time," an agent commented sagely. All the junior agents who wanted to appear in-the-know agreed with him.

Bonnie thought they were probably right, but inside, she was fuming over how much time this was taking.

"Could we please hurry up?" Bonnie asked politely. "I need to visit Father Paul as soon as possible."

Chapter Eighteen

Cheap metal folding chairs, exactly the kind Brad had replaced at Sacred Heart Church for exactly this reason, were bruising his backside. At least the feds had cuffed his hands in front of him for the interrogation, and he had the best lawyer money could buy.

Still, Brad's gut was churning, probably because of something they served in the godforsaken cafeteria, and his head pounded. He knew why he had a headache, too. He could never fall asleep in his cell. There was always some new shuffle, snuffle, or snore to jar him back awake. He had to get out of this place.

How had everything fallen apart so fast just because of some stupid priest and some small-town losers? None of them had anything. They were just out to get him, and he was going to have to be smarter. And he was going to have to spend a lot of money. His lawyer was going to have to be smarter. The lawyer cost enough that he should be able to out-smart God, Brad thought, cutting a glance at the man. Since Brad was guilty, though, he wasn't sure he or his lawyer would be smart enough. And his lawyer would still get paid.

Brad locked down his emotions and focused. It didn't come easily on so little sleep, but he managed.

"Sir." The interrogating agent, the meathead, wasn't sure he had Brad's attention.

Brad answered very politely, "Yes, sir," all business now.

"I asked whether you recognize these ledgers from your safe." The agent's face was blank, giving away nothing.

"You didn't have a warrant to get those," the lawyer asserted defiantly.

"We didn't need a warrant. They were in the Coppinis' joint residence, when Mrs. Coppini retrieved them. She offered them to law enforcement officers in the context of two—no, three—simultaneous emergency situations." The agent looked bored. Facing Brad again, he asked, "Did you know these ledgers were in your safe?"

"She didn't have a right to get into that safe. It was mine," Brad tried. It seemed flimsy even to him.

The agent's features sparked with something too briefly to identify it. He resumed his bored expression. "Did your wife live in an apartment within the residence, sir?"

"What? Of course not," Brad said, getting angry.

"How was her living space defined?" the officer stayed doggedly fixated on the subject, but impassive.

"What do you mean?" Brad was tired of these interrogations. He'd been through so many, and he'd heard so many meager excuses in his defense. His mouth was watering, and he struggled to swallow the excess.

"Was Mrs. Coppini's living space restricted within the house somehow? The entire residence is listed as her legal residence, so I'm asking whether that is correct." The officers' voice carried the same cadence as one of the snores that had kept Brad awake last night. He gave away nothing, but Brad was sure Lisa had told the police she was some kind of captive. The officer was asking about her right to give away joint possessions, but what he wanted was to nail Brad for imprisoning his wife.

Suddenly, Brad felt very sick. Before he could warn anyone, before he could even turn, he disgorged right over his handcuffs. He just couldn't get them out of the way as wave after wave of nausea clenched and tossed out orange fluid again and again.

His wife. It was all her fault. He wanted to kill his wife. She should have been chained in the basement, when he didn't need her. He calmed himself by imagining the ways he could make her pay, all of them as slow and painful as possible.

For the rest of the interrogations and as much of the trial as possible, Brad let his lawyer speak for him. Brad couldn't even listen any longer, it was all so stupid. He was above this kind of thing.

Rose followed the investigations and court trials in the newspapers for the next two years. When the conviction came through and Brad was moved to a new prison, he was killed within days. The attack seemed to the prison authorities to be racially motivated, but it seemed equally likely to Rose that Brad was actually the worst offender in prison, and he was probably judged by the other inmates on the grounds of his character. Rose liked to think that even prisoners had that kind of enlightened thinking.

The whole story, of course, made going to the hair salon much more interesting for everyone, since Rose had so much first-hand knowledge of the "takedown". She had been Lisa's "wheelwoman," she told her stylist and everyone else who would listen. Hardly anyone could avoid hearing about it. Rose started frequenting the salon to have her hair permed in addition to her usual dye job once there was so much to talk about.

Former customers and hired muscle at Gilded Swan and the other hotels Brad owned were documented in the black books and prosecuted to the fullest extent of the law, which wouldn't have been the case had Lisa shown up at the bowling alley just a little later. Rose had given Lisa a ride, and that enabled Lisa to deal with those C-4 bombs that Rufus had planned to dispatch up the ball returns and, well, everything.

What if Rose hadn't realized Lisa was sane? What if Rose's car hadn't been in such good repair? What if Rose and Lisa hadn't been communicating so well that day? They had fit together like the ends of a wet noodle. Those girls and their families, Bonnie, and Dolores all owed Rose their lives. She might have reminded them a time or two over the years, but they mostly remembered to be grateful on their own. Rose was content.

Law enforcement saw no need to offer bargains in exchange for one criminal testifying against another, thanks to Lisa. She had gotten the real story in those little black books. Unfortunately for the newspapers, that meant that there had never been any dramatic confession from Brad like you get in the movies. Rose regretted that.

Still, Rose thought it was pretty dramatic when they pulled down the statue of Midas in the town center. In its place, the Knights had built a gazebo where people could sit down and eat or just talk. There were too many bugs out there for Rose, but it sure looked a sight different from that golden statue.

As Rose drove past it, she saw the DJ arriving with his equipment for a wedding reception, as evidenced by the white bows decorating the gazebo today. Rose smiled knowingly and continued past it toward the church she was supposed to help decorate.

LISA HAD been living with Luke and Bonnie since her own house had blown up (and indeed, Gabe with it). She didn't miss the old place. It hadn't ever been a home for her, a place where she had felt safe. Rather, it had been a prison. She had intended to stay with Luke and Bonnie for only a few weeks or months, until she got on her feet. When it became obvious to everyone that she would be marrying Josh, it only made sense for her to get a job waitressing, to start paying rent and helping out around the house, and not to bother getting a place of her own. Josh already had one. Josh helped her pick out a good used car, and he changed her oil for her, too.

Lisa tried to imagine Brad changing the oil. She failed, snorting. Josh was just so sweet and couldn't be more different from Brad.

"Everything okay?" Bonnie asked her. Bonnie was putting flowers in Lisa's hair, which Lisa had wanted instead of a veil. Now, a veil seemed like the simpler option. It certainly would have taken less time to arrange.

"Perfect," Lisa smiled into the mirror.

As annulment cases go, Lisa's had been just as heartbreaking as any of them, but it had been mercifully quick on the grounds of fraud and willful exclusion of marital fidelity, both of which became obvious when the FBI obtained a warrant for Brad's phone and laptop. The public records from the federal trial were submitted to the tribunal. Brad refused to be interviewed for the annulment process, too, which helped to speed things along. Arguing that Lisa had been unaware of Brad's criminal activity, which began prior to their relationship, and that Brad had never intended to be faithful to her, two dioceses rendered decisions without even an attempted defense in favor of the bond. The marriage had, in the eyes of God, never happened.

It was terrifying and freeing and confusing. And it hurt, even though a part of her had known all along. Josh had been there to hold Lisa through each of the worst moments. Having someone hold her, finally, had made all the difference.

> "And why did you need those two employees at your residence, Mr. Coppini?"
>
> "My wife is mentally ill, and she needed around-the-clock support."

"Is that also why you kept tranquilizers in the house?"

"Yes. That was for her."

"What was she diagnosed with?"

"What do you mean?"

"What was her mental illness? You must have tried to get her psychiatric help at some point. Surely, she attended regular therapy sessions, or she had been declared incurable by at least one professional before you gave up on her."

"Her illness was clear to anyone who knew her."

"So, your wife never received a mental evaluation or diagnosis?"

"There was no need."

"And was there ever a prescription for the tranquilizers?"

"No, there was no need—," Brad was cut off by the prosecuting attorney.

"Your Honor, I submit the written testimony of three independent psychiatrists who have evaluated Ms. Lisa Coppini, who was held against her will…"

Lisa was a free woman for the first time since dropping out of her sophomore year of college. She needed to finish her degree, and while her choice of majors was influenced by her life with Brad, he hadn't made this decision for her.

In the fall, she would begin studying Journalism and Mass Communication with an eye toward investigative reporting. She found she had a taste for getting the real scoop.

She'd thought about studying Criminal Justice. That was probably just an emotional reaction to having been figuratively caged and held powerless for so many years, combined with the influence of Luke's friend, the former Detective Dzielski.

Dzielski had smoothly transitioned into the FBI rather than being fired or forced to resign from the city police force. When the agent visited his elderly parents, he usually swung by Luke's place and met up with the rest of the Knights. He had always been very kind to Lisa in his own gruff way. She liked him. But law enforcement just wasn't "her."

When she was being really honest with herself, Lisa realized that her choice of majors probably had more to do with Father Paul than anyone else. He had gotten the story right, and that was all that had been needed. He had changed her life. And in Lisa's own way, she was following in the footsteps of a man who really was like a father to her.

Lisa shook her head at the silliness and waste of all Brad had taken away from so many people. And yet, that was all part of her story, hers and Josh's. Bonnie huffed and took out a flower she seemed to think ill-placed and tried again, careful not to dislodge the up-do secured by an elastic band under a blue ribbon. Meanwhile, Lisa worked to repeat the makeup job she'd practiced yesterday. They were in the guest bedroom of Luke's and Bonnie's house, which had been Lisa's bedroom these past two years. Starting tonight, she would be living with Josh. She wondered at why it meant so much more this time around. The wedding, marriage, making a family. It was both more meaningful and more certain this time. Lisa might still have nightmares, but Josh would never become one of them. He would be there to wake her from them instead.

Against all the rules, Josh had run over to Luke's house this morning, knocked at the back-porch door beaming, and handed her the blue hair ribbon. "It used to be my mom's, so it's old and blue. Oh, and you're only borrowing it! The ring will be new. You're good?"

She realized he was shaking, and it seemed that she was too. They were both so excited. He was excited to be with her! Deliberately pushing out of mind unhappy memories of Brad's arrogance, she had thrown herself at Josh, bubbling with laughter, and kissed him. "Get out of here!" and she playfully swatted the air after him.

He took a flying leap off the porch like a boy, stopped when Luke called his name to invite him in for coffee. Josh obviously didn't need coffee and said so. "I'm good! Thanks!" He waved and ran off to get ready.

Josh burst into the back of the church, breaking off the slow and steady progress of the decorating committee. Every woman in the place raised her head to see what the ruckus was about. Rose pursed her lips and narrowed her eyes in irritation at the interruption. When Josh merely stood in the doorway blinking back at the ladies, Father Paul decided to break up the awkwardness.

"Josh, could you give me a hand back here?" Father Paul was nearly done saying a rosary anyway.

Josh willingly strode to Father Paul, slowing down only when he reached the taller man. Father Paul was still moving slower than he had before getting shot two years ago. Lucky to have survived, he had taken more than a year to recover to this degree. One of the doctors along the way had informed him that his height had been a huge help in isolating the injury. The bullet had only taken away about half the volume of one of his lungs, thanks to the length of those organs.

He'd started out with a walker that had a seat feature on the back and gradually worked himself up to playing kickball again. He'd been having trouble sidestepping or doing anything crazy, but kickball fixed that. His physical therapist approved, even as she'd warned him not to overdo it. Now, he could pick things up off the floor and do almost anything. He just noticed that he had less energy for it. His body probably had finished healing at this point. He was never going to be the same.

Father Paul was aware of keeping his stride shallower due to the injury, but he still kept up with shorter people easily. Josh slowed his pace for Father Paul's sake, though.

"Is it time to get you in your priest clothes?" Josh asked.

Father Paul thought that was a great name for vestments. "Yes, but I might need another sit-down when we get to the sacristy." He didn't get short of breath much anymore, but it was too early to vest. He actually thought Josh needed to sit down for a while. Josh nodded seriously and followed him. As they sat at the money counting table, it occurred to Father Paul to ask, "You know, I never heard just how you and Lisa met in the first place. By the time you would have moved to town, Lisa was already a virtual prisoner. What happened?"

The question seemed to pull Josh up short. "Oh. You know I used to do night watches on your block."

Father Paul thought about it. "That's why you were here when the bat got stuck in the belfry! I haven't thought about that in forever!" It was a relief to laugh without pain, and Father Paul thought he would never forget to be grateful for that reality now that it was his again. "So, you would have been watching that house from outside. How did you connect with Lisa?"

Josh appeared to be struggling, putting together an answer. He studied the table, hands in his lap, eyes concentrating. "She was in the living room, and she pulled out a laptop. I could see she was watching a video, and I guess I was just bored. No, I had seen her through the window often, and I felt bad for how Brad treated her. It was stupid to do it, but I think I was too tired to think right then. I just wanted to know what she was watching. I checked to make sure the coast was clear and then walked right up through the bushes in the dark. She was watching *Firefly*." He said it with a tone of awe, as if that explained the connection completely.

Actually, Father Paul had loved that briefly lived series show, too. "So… you just tapped on the window, or what?" Father Paul asked.

"Not right away, no. But that's when I started to like her instead of just feeling sorry for her. I guess I didn't talk to her until a while after that, when I was sure she wasn't crazy, and that Brad was abusing her. She needed a friend, and I could do that. That's what the Knights are about, right? So, I picked a moment when Brad had both those other guys in his office, and Lisa was alone with the window open. I scared her, but I explained that I was a Knight and that we look out for widows and orphans and people who need help. I told her that I would help her get away from Brad someday. Oh, and I told her that I liked *Firefly*, too. We had a lot to talk about after that." Josh's smiling face glowed with nostalgia.

"When it was time for me to go, she started to cry. I couldn't reach her, and I knew no one else was going to hold her. That was the worst thing, not being able to hold her when she cried," Josh said. He appeared to stop himself from saying more, not wanting to show too much emotion.

"But it was so important that she'd found someone she could trust. I bet that meant a lot to her," Father Paul observed as he reached across the table and gripped Josh's shoulder. "I'm sorry." He didn't let go until Josh met his eye and nodded back. "She hid a lot from everyone except for you, huh?"

"Yeah, but that's how she's going to be a great reporter.

She's so good at hiding things, she'll be able to tell when other people are hiding things, too. She'll always get the real story," Josh beamed with pride.

Father Paul thought Josh had probably heard that from Luke first, and they both just might be right about Lisa. He hoped anyway.

LUKE WALKED Lisa down the aisle and made Josh promise to take care of her before handing her over. Luke winked, but that didn't mean he was entirely kidding. He slid into line as the Best Man just ahead of Don and Willie. Bonnie, the Matron of Honor, fluffed and fussed with Lisa's train before stepping back and exchanging conspiratorial smiles with Luke. They were probably remembering something from their own wedding day. Dolores and Renee completed the wedding party.

Renee and her friends had bonded with Lisa during the trial. Father Paul hadn't been there—he'd been convalescing in the hospital—so he wasn't sure how it had happened. One day, they had all visited his room in the rehabilitation center together, accompanied by Dolores and asked for a group session. He'd been surprised when they showed up and even more surprised when it appeared they already knew one another. That session had proven fruitful, so they reprised the event weekly for some time afterward. He had admitted it only to Jeremy, but those visits had helped more than anything else to keep him sane and purposeful during his recovery.

Renee was wearing a pastel pink dress that Father Paul found very becoming on her. She had given up the extremes of wearing flashy clothes or baggy clothes. She looked confident and comfortable, as did her friends in the back pews. They too had graduated and gone off to other schools now, but they had returned for this wedding. The entire parish had shown up, in fact. This was a special weekend.

The choir included two male voices today. It turned out that Agent Dzielski was a mellow tenor. Father Paul had mistakenly pegged him as a baritone, if not a bass. Josh's younger brother was the bass, his excuse from joining the wedding party. It wouldn't matter much in the pictures, since there was no color scheme, no matching dresses. It mattered for the music a great deal, though, Father Paul noticed happily.

Lisa was the first to blush, as Josh stared at her. When she recovered and met his eyes again, she studied his face with the same devotion she saw in his. Josh was the second to blush.

The couple chose to sit in chairs placed just before the Communion railing, front and center so that everyone could watch them during the Liturgy of the Word. Judging by the whispers and tittering, Josh and Lisa weren't the only ones having trouble paying attention to the readings they'd chosen.

Father Paul had grown strong enough to stand for an entire homily without tiring more than a year ago, though this day was beginning to wear on him like a marathon. When he presented Josh and Lisa to the congregation as a newly married couple, the prolonged applause forced Father Paul to grip Josh's shoulder in order to keep from sinking. He wasn't sure those people were ever going to stop cheering, clapping, whistling, and even stomping. He briefly worried about the kneelers, always easily damaged no matter the design. Lisa and Josh kissed, laughed, and then went in for yet another kiss, taking their cue from the congregation.

Then, Father Paul decided, "Why not?" He tucked the clunky book under his arm and clapped for a while, too. When he was quite finished, everyone else quieted down with him. Actually, one rowdy old man needed to be elbowed into silence. His bony wife took care of things sharply. Finally.

The Mass proceeded normally from there, excepting the markedly more beautiful music and the thrill of the crowd. When Father Paul elevated the consecrated host, it was as though he lifted up every sleepless night, every pain, every sacrifice that had been necessary to end the tragedies and to heal those freed.

He still wondered sometimes why God hadn't actually taken his life. Perhaps Father Paul's decision alone had sufficed for a sacrifice. Perhaps living was more of a martyrdom, since his heart had been set on giving the ultimate gift. Living was certainly more painful and less glorious. Looking around today, he didn't wonder why he was alive, though. Gazing at the Eucharist, Father Paul simply gave thanks.

Not everyone had been invited to the small church for the wedding, but the reception was open to the whole town, including many families with young children. The DJ at the gazebo played all the predictable romantic pop tunes and some country songs, too. The Knights grilled steaks under their cooking canopy. There were tents for drinks and desserts, and there was a long tent for the main buffet line.

Father Paul's now famous chocolate cake made an appearance in the dessert line. This time, he dressed it up with chocolate flakes and strawberry slices. But there was no white cake, a fact that Rose clucked her tongue about. "What is Lisa supposed to eat without risking that beautiful dress?" she wondered aloud to anyone who would listen and countless others who didn't. Rose found some comfort in the compliments the flowers received, and she took full credit each time before remembering that others had done most of the work before she'd arrived.

White wooden folding chairs and tables covered in red-and-white checkered plastic welcomed guests to sit down for a family meal. Field flowers in Mason jars decorated the center of each table with bursts of yellow, white, and tiny blue blossoms. Another area was clearly staged for dancing. Some people waited for the buffet lines to diminish by dancing in the interim. The place was a swirl of familiar music, dancing feet, and happy voices.

> "Someone, tie up that dog before he gets into the food or burns himself on the grill."
>
> "How are you feeling, Father? Can I get you something to drink?"

> "Oh, who made this *cake*? Can I get the recipe?"
>
> "I'm just, um, visiting my brother, that's Josh. I don't live here. Well, at least I don't right now."
>
> "I love you."
>
> "I love you, too."
>
> "Hey thanks, I made the dress myself! I want to design clothes that make women feel and look their best. That's what I'm going to school for!"
>
> "Who's ready to play kickball?"
>
> "Does it look like the girls are still doing okay?"
>
> "Of course, they are. Quit worrying. Dance with me, woman."
>
> "We got plenty of beer and wine coolers, but if it looks like we're runnin' low, text me."
>
> "I was the wheelwoman!"
>
> "Where's a body supposed to use the bathroom out here?"
>
> "Look. Coming out of the gazebo roof. Is that a bat?"

Luke broke up the dancing to offer a toast. Standing in the white gazebo with the microphone the DJ handed him, he took a moment to collect his thoughts or to clear his throat. When he looked up from his shoes, his eyes were tearing up, but he pressed on resolutely.

"Josh, I met you five years ago when you first moved to town, and I knew right away that you would make an excellent Knight of Columbus. You jumped at the opportunity to be of service for your community, and you became a loyal, trustworthy friend. It's only fitting that you met your beautiful bride in the course of your service. Because of you, Bonnie and I got to know Lisa like she's our own daughter. You're both like the children we never had." Luke wiped at his eyes, unashamed of the tears that astonished his neighbors, who viewed him as the composed, detached grocer and helpful neighbor.

"Count on us whenever you run into trouble," he continued. "Marriage isn't easy. It takes courage and strength, loyalty, and selflessness. You both have that in spades. For all I know, marriage *will* be easy for you two!" Scattered laughter gave way to applause.

"God bless and keep you both. Father Paul will be proud of me—I'm about to quote Scripture here." Luke pulled a piece of paper out of his shirt pocket under his suit jacket. He read, "*Give us joy to balance our affliction.* That's from Psalm Ninety. I pray that God will give you both many years of much deserved joy."

An exuberant round of applause broke out. Woops and whistling, glasses clinking to indicate the crowd's wish to see a kiss. Josh and Lisa obliged, both of them blushing self-consciously.

"And now," Luke announced, "we need Father to say Grace, so we can get on with dinner!"

A few sheepish people put their forks down. Everyone applauded Luke, who handed over the microphone to his pastor. "Bow your heads," Father Paul began. "Heavenly Father, you have blessed us with friendship, love, beautiful weather, and the chance to celebrate the lives of these two young people. Bless them and this celebration of their union. Bless the food and bless the cooks!" Father Paul made the Sign of the Cross over the whole assembly.

A resounding "Amen," boomed back to him, followed by another applause. The DJ started up the music again, this time a slow country tune.

"I don't feel much like eating yet," Lisa whispered to Josh. She turned longing eyes toward the dance floor.

"May I have this dance?" There was a light in Josh's eyes.

"Always," Lisa answered. Luke cut in for the next dance. With alcohol on his breath, he wept and repeated his sentiment to Lisa that she was like a daughter to him, and Josh was like a son. Lisa hadn't known that a few drinks would bring out a weeping Luke, but without his usual inhibitions, his gentle heart was plain to view.

Father Paul pulled up a chair to supervise Willie and Don at the grills. Don's wife talked with another woman from the parish nearby enough that she could be heard calling her husband a hero. Don had long since moved back into his own house, and happily most people didn't realize he'd ever been kicked out. Willie and Don were cooking the last steaks from the ice coolers, just so all the meat would be cooked and less likely to spoil. They reacted coolly when Father Bob popped in for one of his supervisory visits, diverting him with a tender and juicy steak for his inspection. He belched out approval and drank enough that Father Paul discerned it would be best for him to stay the night at the rectory. It was just as well when the man fell into a light doze on a lawn chair and missed the main event.

It happened when the sun was setting, and the clouds broke up the light in a way that reminded Father Paul of the rays of Divine Mercy flowing from the side of Jesus. The Knights were moving to plug in the strings of clear lights decorating the tents, hanging about the gazebo, and strung like a luminous crisscross ceiling over the dance floor. Father Paul was still seated near the grill, and perhaps the bird that winged his way had been attracted by the smell of delicious food. Still, it landed on Father Paul's arm, which rested on the arm of the folding chair. He had a soda in the other hand, and he didn't want to risk scaring the bird by moving. He gazed at the perfect white dove, taking in the jet black eyes, the round little body, and the twig in its beak.

It dropped the twig in Father Paul's lap and flew off. Father Paul lost sight of the bird around the peak of the gazebo almost immediately, and he never saw it again.

Father Paul took that leafy twig as a promise that all the damage from this evil had been washed away, and something beautiful and new was beginning. Of course, there would be other troubles for him and his people. But God would carry them through it all.

THE END

Made in the USA
Monee, IL
02 September 2023